LAL SALAAM

Smriti Zubin Irani is a seasoned politician, former TV actress and producer. She represents the constituency of Amethi in the Lok Sabha, to which she was elected in 2019. Earlier, she was a member of the Rajya Sabha, representing the state of Gujarat, between 2011 and 2019. She is currently the Union Minister for Women and Child Development. She has also served as the Union Minister for Human Resource Development, Minister for Information and Broadcasting and Minister for Textiles.

This is her first novel.

SMRITI ZUBIN IRANI

LAL SALAAM

A NOVEL

First published by Westland Publications Private Limited in 2021

1st Floor, A Block, East Wing, Plot No. 40, SP Infocity, Dr MGR Salai, Perungudi, Kandanchavadi, Chennai 600096

Westland and the Westland logo are the trademarks of Westland Publications Private Limited, or its affiliates.

ISBN: 9789391234638

10 9 8 7 6 5 4 3 2 1

This is a work of fiction. Names, characters, organisations, places, events, and incidents are either products of the author's imagination or are used fictitiously. Any resemblance to actual persons, living or dead, or actual events is purely coincidental.

Typeset by SÜRYA, New Delhi

Printed at Thomson Press (India) Ltd

For Shanelle

'An eye for an eye will only make the whole world blind.'

– Mahatma Gandhi

CHAPTER ONE

Darshan Kumar stifled a yawn and shifted his position in the navigator's seat of the armoured vehicle. It had been a long, hard patrol and the deputy commandant of the Central Reserve Police Force battalion posted in the Maoist hotbed of Ambuja had walked alongside his men for most of it, only getting into the vehicle for the final stretch back to camp.

Shifting around to get comfortable, he grunted as the jeep hit a bump. It wasn't a proper road, more of a dirt track that had been hacked out through the forest, barely wide enough for two vehicles. If you stepped off the road into the jungle, the path vanished completely as if swallowed by the dense vegetation—mostly sal trees along with a thick undergrowth of shrubs, bushes and grass.

The forest was a treasure trove of plants used by the locals for medicinal purposes. Darshan had often thought of documenting the plants and the remedies they were used for, but work and exhaustion had got in the way.

Another twenty minutes or so to go, he told himself, thinking longingly of the bed that awaited him. Have to phone the wife and kid too. Maybe after I've had a nice nap and a quick shower and shave, he thought.

He stretched his back and shoulders and heard a click.

Then all hell broke loose.

The ground beneath the jeep erupted in a shower of dirt even as the shockwave from the bomb slammed into the vehicle. The explosion threw Darshan well clear of the vehicle, very close to the dense trees that surrounded the path. He landed on the ground near the trees with a sickening thud, the breath knocked out of him, and blacked out.

It was a scene straight out of a horrific nightmare. His co-passengers weren't as lucky. They sprawled grotesquely, limbs contorted at impossible angles. Mangled body parts, many fused with bits of steel from the vehicle, were strewn across the forest floor.

The majority of the patrol party had been on foot. Those walking close to the vehicle were killed instantly. The others, wounded by shrapnel from the explosion, were still struggling to make sense of it when the attackers emerged from their hiding spots and opened fire. The patrol party was now trapped with hardly any cover available.

Some ran towards the trees. Others crouched behind the mangled remains of the jeep, to use whatever pitiful protection it provided as they desperately attempted to fight back.

Darshan woke up with a start, his ears ringing, his brain sluggish, as though a fog had engulfed it. He shook his head, trying to clear it. Dimly, he saw that some figures had emerged from the forest surrounding the path. They were converging on the blast site, firing their automatic weapons indiscriminately, yelling with the reckless abandon that is triggered when bloodlust runs amok.

Ambush, he thought frantically. He moved his limbs, checking to see how badly injured he was. He ached all over, as though he had been battered for hours. He was bleeding from multiple cuts, but there seemed to be no major injuries or wounds. He looked around, assessing the situation.

Amidst the noise from all the firing, Darshan made out the distinctive rat-a-tat-tat of a light machine gun. He looked around, trying to pinpoint its source. There! It came from a hillock slightly to the left of the road and had a clear line of fire towards the ambush site.

At 11 o'clock from here. Maybe 500 metres down the road as the crow flies, he estimated. There was no way he could mount a frontal assault without being gunned down. But if I get into the forest and go straight for about a kilometre, I'll get past the attackers. Then I can turn right, come up behind the hillock and attack them from behind. If I can get my hands on the gun, I can turn it on the Maoists. We might still have a chance, Darshan concluded.

The plan was fraught with risk, involving rapid movement through dense vegetation and past several attackers. Darshan refused to think of the obstacles—he couldn't afford to. Slowly, surreptitiously, he inched forward, trying not to make any movement that might attract attention, his back rigid, expecting a bullet to slam into him at any moment.

He heaved a sigh of relief as he made it to the treeline safely, then sprang to his feet and drew his revolver. He had lost his assault rifle in the blast, and his only other weapon was the jungle knife that hung at his hip.

As he ran through the forest, he thought of how well executed the ambush—set up a mere hour since the CRPF's last patrol—had been.

Engrossed in his thoughts, he didn't notice the thin, almost invisible wire strung up between two trees at a little above ankle height. He tripped on it and went sprawling into a clearing. It was a small open space, the vegetation hacked away to carve out a camp site. A few plastic sheets served as bedding and there was some camping equipment lying around. It was deserted—except for an old man whose attention was on the battle raging on the dirt track, his back to Darshan. He had presumably been left on guard duty as he was not in prime fighting condition, and was armed with only a shotgun.

The old man whirled around as Darshan came to his feet. As the two stared at each other, Darshan felt a chill go down his spine. He was looking at the cold, vacant stare of a seasoned killer.

Don't be fooled by his appearance. This man will slaughter you without a second thought, he reminded himself. In the time that it took Darshan to process the thought, the old man raised his weapon. Darshan snatched up his revolver and pressed the trigger. There was a loud click—and nothing else.

'Shit, it's jammed,' he cursed, hurling his revolver at his adversary, charging at him even as the other man fired. Darshan felt a burst of agony in his left arm, but kept going. He grabbed the man's wrist and twisted it, forcing the barrel of the shotgun towards the sky. The two struggled, each trying to overpower the other. Then Darshan slammed his head into the man's face, at the same time kicking his foot out from under him. The old man fell to the ground, stunned. As he tried to get back on his feet, Darshan smashed his elbow into the man's forehead. The old man slumped back, knocked out cold by the blow.

Darshan waited to see if the man would get up again. But he remained unconscious. As the adrenalin slowly receded, Darshan sank to his knees, the pain hitting him with full force. He felt a wave of giddiness and nausea sweep over him and peered at his upper arm. The bullet had made a clean exit but left the limb a bleeding mess. Well, I'm not going to get any fighting done with that, thought Darshan. He cut a long strip of clothing from his unconscious foe's body, then tied it around his arm as tightly as he could, awkwardly using his right hand and mouth to fasten a makeshift tourniquet.

As Darshan wiped the sweat streaming down his face, he heard a branch snapping behind him. He froze for a moment, then turned slowly, careful not to make any sudden movement.

A young boy, who seemed to be still in his teens, had an AK-47 pointed at him. His face was innocent, almost angelic. He had a thin wisp of a moustache, and a few strands of curly hair marked his attempts to grow a beard. He's just a kid, thought Darshan disbelievingly.

The boy's finger tightened on the trigger, but before he could press it, he began to shake. 'Wait!' said Darshan, raising his hand. 'Don't shoot!'

The boy eased off on the trigger. Maybe I can talk my way out of this, thought Darshan. He spoke out loud. 'You don't have to do this.'

The boy replied in a breathless, high-pitched voice. He spoke rapidly, in the local dialect. Darshan could only make out a few random words. '... have to ... no choice ... they'll kill me ...'

Darshan's heart was racing, but he forced himself to speak slowly and calmly, trying to soothe the boy. 'Turn around.' He made a circular motion with his hand. 'Walk away.' He wiggled his index and middle finger, miming walking. 'You go your way, I'll go mine. Nobody needs to know.'

The boy stared at Darshan for a long moment, then nodded. He lowered his gun and started to turn away. Darshan felt his body sag with relief. Then, suddenly, he heard loud, excited voices ring out nearby. The boy heard them too. He whipped around, brought the gun up and opened fire, his mouth stretched wide in a prolonged, savage yell.

Darshan's body jerked gracelessly like a marionette on a string as the bullets poured into him. He hit the ground with a thump, every inch of him screaming in agony. As darkness began to settle over his eyes, he saw a group of men approaching. One of them was casually twirling a machete, whistling a jaunty tune as he loomed over Darshan.

CHAPTER TWO

Darshan's son weeps as he clings to me. He barely reaches my knees, and his tears are soaking into my trousers. I bend down, desperate to pick him up and hold him close, but he hugs my legs even more tightly. I settle for stroking his curly hair, my heart breaking into a million pieces.

Seema, Darshan's wife—I can't bear to use the word 'widow' for her—has a sad, faraway look in her eyes. 'Remember the last time you were at our place, Vikram? I'd begged you to tell him to get another posting. And you'd said, "Arrey, where will a lion go if not to the forest?" How the two of you laughed! And now ... now just look at him.' She turns to the body on the floor, which lay covered with a white shroud ....

'Sir? The DGP will see you now.'

I snap back into the present. I'm sitting in the reception area outside the office of the state police chief, Satyadev Chandrakar. His staff officer, a bright young man who would have been handpicked for the post, respectfully knocks on the door. There's a muffled 'come in' from inside. The staff officer opens the door, then closes it behind me. I walk up to Chandrakar's desk and salute.

'SP Vikram Pratap Singh reporting, sir!'

Chandrakar nods at me. 'Take a seat, Vikram. I'm sure you must have already guessed why I've called you. You're the best investigator on the force, you have a track record of cracking supposedly impossible cases, and you have an outstanding reputation for integrity and impartiality. All of which are needed to track down Darshan's killers. So, even though he was a friend of yours, I want you to handle this case.'

I sit down, my heart pounding with excitement. This is exactly what I'd been hoping for. But I'm careful not to let my emotions show on my face.

'How's his wife, by the way? I went to meet her after the funeral, but was told that she was in no condition to receive visitors.'

I nod, my mouth a thin, bitter line. 'She was hysterical and had to be heavily sedated. The amount of medicine they pumped into her, I'll be surprised if she wakes up before a couple of days at the very least.'

'I'm not surprised. The condition in which they found Darshan's body ….' Chandrakar trails off, as though reminded again of the photos he'd seen of the head smashed with a rock, the nose and ears chopped off and placed next to the head, the fingers that had been cut off.

Rage and grief churn inside me, but my voice is steady. 'That kind of elaborate mutilation would suggest that it wasn't a random killing. They planned his death and deliberately made a spectacle of it to send out a message.'

A part of me marvels at how calm I sound. But then, I'm very good at using a stoic exterior as my shield against the world. I've been doing it for years.

Chandrakar takes off his spectacles for a moment to wearily rub his eyes, then looks at me. 'The very fact that you can analyse this so dispassionately tells me that you're the right person for the job.' He pauses. 'Darshan had a small boy, didn't he? Who's taking care of him?'

'Seema's parents,' I say. 'They're thinking of asking her to shift with them to their home in Noida. They don't want her to be alone here, in Raipur.'

'That would probably be for the best,' says Chandrakar. 'Well, to work then. I wish I could have given you a little more time to grieve for your friend. But I'm afraid I don't have that luxury.'

He waves a hand at the newspapers scattered all over his desk. 'Local papers, national papers, even the international media is going to town, talking about the complete breakdown of law and order in the region. And the news channels, don't even get me started. They seem to think solving problems is like snapping your fingers. Snap! Naxalism over. Snap! No more terrorism. Snap! Crimes against women eradicated. If only it were that simple.'

He picks up a glass of water from the table and drinks from it. On the wall to my right, a TV shows people marching and chanting slogans, holding up protest banners. Then the image changes to the leader of the opposition in the state animatedly addressing a rally while making expansive gestures with his hands. Since the TV is on mute, I can't hear what he's saying, but it's obvious that he's making a fiery speech of some sort. His supporters raise their hands and roar their approval.

Chandrakar follows my gaze. 'The opposition is demanding the chief minister's resignation, saying that he has no moral right to continue if things in the state are so bad that even the guardians of the law are not safe and can be slaughtered with impunity. The CM is calling me night and day. He wants results, and he wants them fast. I need to send someone I can trust, someone who's clean and who doesn't mind whose toes he treads on as long as he gets the job done.'

I look at the map on the wall behind him, and my gaze zeroes in on the place we're talking about. Ambuja. The most infamous district in the state. A hellhole where demons are born and dreams go to die. A place where the long shadow of the past eclipses any feeble, flickering hopes for the future. They say that a person's destiny may be shaped by God, but even God can't help those unlucky enough to be born in Ambuja. It comes last in the state rankings on every major quality-of-life parameter. Poverty, crime, illiteracy and unemployment are rampant here.

For police officers, Ambuja is the worst sort of punishment posting. People pull as many strings as possible to wriggle out of an assignment here. And this is where I need to go to find the people responsible for the deaths of Darshan and sixty-nine other CRPF personnel.

Chandrakar peers at me. 'I know you have at least a year more to go in your current assignment, but I'm afraid desperate times call for desperate measures. Your transfer letter is ready. I can assure you that you will have my full support, as well as the department's.'

A grim smile flits across my face. He's trying to motivate me for this assignment, when the truth is I would have pleaded for the opportunity. I rise to my feet, pull on my cap and salute. 'Yes, sir. Thank you.'

'Arrey yaar, what did you say to Chandu that he's packed you off to Ambuja? Teri toh lag gayi, bhai.'

'It's not just the back of beyond. It's the smelly armpit of the back of beyond. Poor you!'

'Mrs Garware is heartbroken. She was eyeing Vikram for her daughter, but that's ruled out now that he's going into the lion's den.'

'Oh, stop demoralising the poor guy. And can we please change this crap music? Let's play some stuff that we can dance to. Come on, Vikram, you need to enjoy your last night in civilisation.'

I glare with disgust at my colleagues, who are too drunk and too busy laughing raucously to notice. A fine bunch of investigators they'd make. They're completely clueless about how close Darshan and I were, about how important this case is to me. This excruciating farewell dinner feels like it's been dragging on for hours. Finally, to my relief, it comes to an end and I make my escape.

All my stuff is already packed and ready to move. A folding cot, my bed linen and a side table that I'll carry with me in my car. A long time ago, I'd promised myself that I'd never accumulate more than I could pack up and move on a single day's notice. So far, I've stuck to that resolve.

There's a single framed photograph on the side table. I pick it up. It shows a couple in their wedding finery. The man is tall and wiry; has close-cropped hair and a rakish moustache. The woman is slender, pretty, and her eyes are filled with laughter, mischief and pure joy.

My parents. Neither of them is in this world any longer, but this is how they are preserved in my memory. My father went first, killed while leading a counter-terrorism operation in Kashmir. The news of his death snuffed the laughter out of my mother's eyes. But she soldiered on with her teaching job in the day, her tuition classes till late at night, ensuring that I got the best possible education.

Her students adored her. On the rare occasion when she and I went out to attend a wedding or some social function, there would always be some local dignitary—a businessman, a bureaucrat, a hotshot young entrepreneur, even a politician or two—who would rush to her and touch her feet. The conversations inevitably began with, 'Ma'am, do you remember me? I used to be your student.'

I felt proud of my mother, but unfairly, I also resented the fact that she seemed to have so much time for her students and so little for me. As a young boy desperate for the attention of his sole surviving parent, I couldn't understand the struggle she was going through to try and secure my future. Instead, I sulked at what I perceived as her neglect. Having grown up in cantonments, which always bustled with children and lots of activities, being suddenly plunged into a small town with hardly any facilities added to my sense of dislocation.

One evening, I stormed out of the house while she held her tuition classes and sat in the park, seething. I missed my father desperately. I was bitter about my loneliness, angry with my mother, and guilty about being angry with her. I clutched at my head, feeling as if it would explode, in fact, wishing that it would—anything to put me out of my misery. And just then, a football rolled up and hit my leg.

Irritated, I snatched it up. I had half a mind to puncture it. Then I heard a cheerful voice. 'Arrey yaar, ball toh pass kar de.'

I glared at the source. A tall, thin boy, with a mop of curly hair and a friendly smile, exuding the effortless charm that is the preserve of only those blessed enough to be completely at ease with themselves.

At that moment, though, the charm was wasted on me. I kicked that ball with all my pent-up fury, not caring where it landed. It soared high into the sky before hitting the other end of the ground. I glared at the boy, hoping he'd start a fight. I was more than ready, spoiling for it, in fact. Instead, he burst out laughing.

'Well, you've got a powerful kick. Why don't you come join our game? Hamari bechari team ka bhi bhala ho jayega,' he said.

That was how I met Darshan.

In the years that followed, I pretty much grew up in his home. I'd go there right after school, spend the evening hanging out with him, and go home only to sleep. We studied together, played together, and went through the joys and heartbreaks of adolescence together. His parents treated me like a second son. They handed out boxes of sweets in the neighbourhood after I cleared the UPSC exam and got into the IPS, and they comforted me when my mother, who had silently battled cancer for years, finally gave herself permission to die, secure in the knowledge that I would be able to take care of myself.

As I carefully put away the photograph, I think of everything that I owe Darshan and his parents, and then I remember them at his funeral, numb with grief, suddenly aged and stooped, as if they had lost all reason to live. My mother had looked like that when she heard about my father. I remember Darshan's son clinging to me at his funeral, and I'm reminded of myself as a small boy, trying to cope with the fact that my father had been brutally taken away from me forever. As I fill up with rage and grief, I promise myself I will bring the men responsible for Darshan's death to justice, come what may.

CHAPTER THREE

It's been a long, tiring drive to Ambuja, but most of it is done now. I'm just a few minutes away from my destination. My home for the duration of my stay in what is starting to feel like the back of beyond.

The town itself is shabby and depressing, with narrow, potholed roads. It's dusk, but already darkness seems to be settling over the place. For all the horror and outrage that the massacre in the vicinity had generated, the town itself seems to have simply absorbed it and returned to a somnolent state.

There's a sudden screeching of tyres behind me as a vehicle slams to a halt, followed by loud honking. I turn around and see an open jeep, modified to give it a sporty look, music blaring loudly, with three young men sitting in it. They angrily gesture at me to move. I lock eyes with the driver, then jerk a thumb towards the traffic light.

The driver says something to his friends, gets out of the jeep and starts walking towards me. I open my door and step out.

'Kya baat hai be?' he begins. 'Why did you stop the car?' He has shoulder-length hair and is wearing skintight jeans and a shirt that is open almost to the waist. His face is bright red and he's giving off a faint whiff of liquor.

'The light is red,' I say mildly.

'Toh? Are you new in town? Harishchandra ki aulaad!' he

responds, spraying spittle in his fury. 'I am telling you ... drive! What're you parked bang in the middle of the road for? Baap ki sadak hai kya?'

'Why go to my parents, boss?' I say.

'Teri toh! Are you teaching me manners now?' He swings at me.

I step to one side so that his fist brushes past me, then grab his wrist with my right hand. I step behind him, stick out my leg, reach under his armpit with my left hand and grab his shoulder so that his arm is neatly trapped, and pull him towards me. He trips on my leg and goes sprawling to the ground, the breath knocked out of him.

His two friends come rushing up. The first tries to punch me. I block with my left wrist, then push hard at his chest with an open right palm. Gravity does the rest.

The other man tries a change of tactics. Instead of punching, he comes up from behind me and wraps his arms around me. I calmly kick his ankle. He gasps and instinctively loosens his grip. I flip him over my hip and he joins his two friends on the ground.

The whole fight must have taken about a minute. None of them is seriously injured, but they all look dazed. I'm not even breathing hard. Not for the first time, I'm glad that the lessons we got at the Police Academy had turned me into a passionate martial arts enthusiast.

'Oye, what's going on here?'

A policeman on a motorcycle pulls up. It's so like the Bollywood cliché of the police arriving when everything is over that I can't help smiling.

'What's so funny, eh?' he demands. 'And what the hell happened here?'

'Arrey, Ghanshyam, thank God you're here. This fellow was sitting daydreaming in the middle of the road. When we politely asked him to move, he started abusing us. We told him there was no need to get abusive. Then he started beating us,' says the jeep driver in an abject tone.

'Really?' I ask. 'One person starts beating up three?'

The cop leans in for a whispered exchange, then he turns to me. 'You're in serious trouble. Apologise to these boys and give them Rs 5,000 as compensation and we'll settle the matter here and now.'

'And if not?' I ask.

'I'll take you to the lock-up and hammer some sense into your thick skull,' he blusters. 'See this laathi here? I'll put it to good use.'

For a moment, I'm tempted to give him a piece of my mind, but then I decide to play along and see how it goes. 'So you want to take me to the lock-up? On what charges?'

'On what charges, he asks! Chal beta, I'll teach you all the sections I can book you under while you enjoy yourself in the lock-up. Pull that junk heap of yours over to the side and give me the keys.'

'Ghanshyam, let the air out of his tyres as well,' enthuses the jeep driver.

'Beta, think before you touch my car,' I growl.

He leaps back and turns towards the policeman. 'Look at him! He's still threatening me! You need to teach him a good, hard lesson. He's not going to get it otherwise.'

The cop glares at me. 'Tujh jaise bahut achche achchon ko seedha kiya hai. Chal, gaadi ek side pe laga aur mere saath chal.'

'Is it okay to leave the car here? Wouldn't it be better to bring it to the police station?' I suggest.

'Why? Who'd want that khataara scrap of metal?' he asks, then reconsiders. 'Though that is better than leaving it here. You follow me.' He turns to the youths. 'You guys leave now.'

'Arrey, shouldn't they come too? They were also party to the fight,' I protest.

The cop looks at me, incredulity combined with fury. 'Abey, what the hell is wrong with you? First you ask me about the charges, then you tell me how to do my duty! Beta, you're going to well and truly regret this.' He waves away the three youths. 'You guys get going! I'll be in touch if needed.' Then he turns to me. 'Chal. You can be my special guest at the lock-up tonight.'

The police headquarters at Ambuja are housed in a grimy building that desperately needs a new coat of paint. The peeling paint, the extensive water stains, the dirt and exposed cement, all present a shabby visage to the world.

The constable guides me to the parking space and demands the keys. 'Chaabi laa.'

'Kyon bhai?'

'Because I said so. Waise bhi you won't need it. We're impounding that piece of scrap metal,' he says officiously.

'What's my car done though?' I ask.

'Abey, are you the policeman? Cut the questions and hand over the keys before I beat them out of you!' he snaps.

'What's the issue here?' A short, tubby man walks into the parking lot. He's accompanied by a couple of uniformed cops.

'Sir, this fellow has been creating a ruckus on the road. Abused three young boys from good families and when they protested, he started beating them.' The cop replies with a salute.

'That's not what happened ....' I begin meekly.

'Shut up. Can't you see I'm talking to sir?' the constable snarls.

The tubby man looks at me. 'He beat up three people alone?' There's a note of scepticism in his voice.

'I saw it from a distance, sir. He was using those judo-karate moves.'

'Hmm, a martial arts champion in our very own Ambuja.' The officer looks me over. 'You're new here, aren't you? I don't recall seeing you before, and I'm sure I'd remember you. What's your name?'

'Vikram Pratap Singh,' I reply, keeping my voice casual.

'What a long name! Baap re baap, naam hai ya title!' he sniggers as the others laugh appreciatively.

'Ek title bhi hai na,' I say.

'Oh, really? Do tell, maharaj, if it pleases you,' he sneers.

'Superintendent of Police, Ambuja. SP Vikram Pratap Singh,' I say.

He's still laughing as he processes my words. Then it hits him. An expression of horror appears in his eyes even as the smile stays frozen on his face. The contrast is almost comical.

'SP Vikram Pratap Singh?' he repeats, as though he didn't hear me properly the first time. I nod. His expression turns to one of pure panic. He salutes and starts talking hurriedly, mangling the words in his rush. 'Sir, so sorry ... sir, you were expected tomorrow ... why didn't you say who ....'

I hold up a palm and he stops. I look around coldly. Everybody else is frozen mid-salute, their mouths open. The constable who brought me here has turned purple, his eyes bulging in shock. He desperately averts his gaze, refusing to look me in the eye.

I turn back to the officer in front of me. 'And you are?'

'I'm DSP Keshav Rai, sir,' he says, slightly more composed. 'Sir, I'm extremely sorry about this. We were told you would be taking charge tomorrow. In fact, I was just finalising the plans for your welcome.'

'Well, I certainly got a memorable one,' I say dryly, still looking at the constable.

Keshav follows my gaze. 'Yes, sir, sometimes our men get carried away enforcing the rule of law,' he says defensively. 'They're very enthusiastic about doing their job properly.'

'Really?' I arch an eyebrow. 'How many more such enthusiastic personnel do we have here? I'd love to see their files.' I beckon the constable towards me. He shuffles forward reluctantly, his gaze fixed on the ground.

'Now, I want to see a little more of the enthusiasm that's been on such fine display today,' I tell him. 'Pick up that laathi you seem to love so much. Now, raise it over your head and do fifty laps of the building. Get going.'

The constable nods resignedly and shuffles off. I turn to Keshav. 'You're in charge here?'

'Yes, sir,' he says. 'Ideally, your predecessor should have handed over charge to you, but he has proceeded on medical leave. I've been holding interim charge. Don't worry. I've taken care of everything. Sab chakaachak hai.'

I look at him silently, and then at the building. He flushes as he gets my drift. 'Er ... yes ... the building could do with some work. But that will require heavy expenditure. I thought it would be better if you took the decision.'

'Get it started first thing tomorrow,' I respond. 'How are we going to inspire any confidence in the public if our HQ looks so dilapidated?'

'Yes, sir,' he replies, his tone carefully neutral.

I nod. 'Well, I'll go now and see you first thing tomorrow morning. We have a lot to get done.'

The ancient air-conditioner in my room groans and sputters, fighting a losing battle with the sweltering heat. The paint on the walls is peeling, the carpet is threadbare. The towel draped over the backrest of my chair was once white but has now settled into an indeterminate shade of grey. I reach for it gingerly, but Keshav snatches it up before I can touch it and hurries to the door.

'Get rid of this rag and get a new towel immediately,' he snaps.

I conceal a smile. He's learning. I settle down in the chair, which creaks in protest before accepting me. 'Okay, Keshav,' I say. 'Let's review the crime situation here.'

Keshav has a presentation ready and begins reeling off facts and figures. Of course, the case I'm really interested in is the CRPF ambush, but I'm not willing to let anyone know just how important it is to me. I let him ramble on for a while, taking notes every now and then. Then I hold up a hand, frowning.

He pauses. 'Sir?'

'Something doesn't add up, Keshav,' I say. 'I've been told that this is a crime-prone area. But the statistics you're showing me are all on the lower side, and even those have been declining over the years. Rape, murder, theft, kidnapping—there hardly seem to be any cases. What's going on?'

'Sir, ab joh hai woh hai. I'm giving you the numbers exactly as they've been recorded. Maybe people have wrong notions about Ambuja,' he says.

'Or maybe people just don't come to the police for help because they don't trust us. Or maybe they do come and are shooed away without being given a hearing,' I snap.

Keshav's mouth sets in a thin, stubborn line. 'Sir, I can't say what people think. I can only tell you what's in the paper in front of me.'

'You could try interacting with people and hear what they have to say. Anyway, there's at least one major case that indisputably happened here. So tell me, what's happening about the attack on the CRPF convoy? Have we begun our probe?'

'There's a special investigation team of three men on the job, sir,' he responds. 'It's a crack team. The very best guys we have.'

'Oh? In that case, I'd like to meet them now,' I reply.

'I'll go get them, sir,' he says, springing to his feet.

He's back a few minutes later, with three men of very different ages, shapes and sizes, who march in and salute smartly. I nod. 'At ease. I'm told you're the investigation team for the Maoist attack on the CRPF contingent. Could you introduce yourselves?'

'Sub-inspector Bhoomi, sir,' begins the first. He's short, thin to the point of being emaciated, and blinks frequently behind his oversized glasses, which give him a slightly owlish air.

'He's our tech wizard, sir,' says Keshav.

'Is that so? What's your area of expertise, Bhoomi?' I ask.

'I can use Microsoft Word. I also know how to operate email, PowerPoint and spreadsheets,' he responds, slightly smug about his accomplishments.

I stare at him incredulously. 'What about digital forensics?' I ask.

'Yes sir, that's in PowerPoint, no,' he says with complete confidence.

I look at Keshav quizzically. He beams back, bursting with pride at Bhoomi's skills. I supress a sigh and turn back to our so-called tech wizard. 'Bhoomi. You have an unusual name for a man.'

'My parents were villagers. They believed the earth was the most precious entity. They named me accordingly, sir,' he explains.

Oh dear God. Cocky and preachy. Then I notice he's holding something. 'Is that the evidence log?'

'Yes, sir. I thought you might like to see it,' he says, handing it over.

I leaf through it. Spent cartridge shells, slippers, the odd piece of torn clothing. There are pages and pages of the stuff, and the entries span several days, but nothing that looks particularly promising.

'Have we sent this stuff to the FSL?' I ask.

'FSL, sir?' asks the second person quizzically.

As I glare at him, he snaps to attention. 'Relax,' I say. 'You don't have to come to attention every time I look your way. You are ...?'

'Gayaram, sir,' he says. 'Hawaldar Gayaram.'

He's tall and has the fleshy look of someone who used to be well-built in his prime but has let his exercise regimen slide and doesn't worry too much about his diet. There's more than a sprinkling of grey in his hair. Early to mid-fifties, I guess.

'How long have you been with the force, Gayaramji?' I always make it a point to ask for a few personal details about the men serving with me. Doesn't take more than a couple of minutes, and it makes for a better working relationship.

'More than thirty years, sir,' he responds, a touch of pride in his voice.

I nod. 'Family?'

'Wife and two children. Both settled in good jobs and married, by the grace of God. Neither of them is in the police,' he replies.

'You sound quite proud about that,' I say.

The sarcasm is wasted on him. 'Ab dekhiye na, sir, I didn't even get to know when they grew up. My wife keeps scolding me for not having spent any time with my children. The job kept me so busy that they grew up before I even realised how time had flown. But I hope to remedy that with the next generation. The children have their own houses in big cities now, so we'll go visit them from time to time. But of course, we'll stay in our own house here. Home is home, after all.'

'Even if it's in a place like Ambuja?' I can't help asking.

'Sir, which place doesn't have problems? Do you think there's no crime in Delhi or Mumbai? At least people here know their neighbours.'

I'm not sure if he loves his hometown or is just plain delusional, so I change the topic. 'You must have seen quite a lot in your long stint here?'

'Absolutely, sir. These old eyes have seen quite a bit,' he agrees. 'I used to tell some of those stories to my children. They would say, "Baba, you should write all this in a movie script. It will be a blockbuster." In any case, all of us are big film fans. We've seen *Sholay* some seventy-five times.'

'So, did you ever write that script?'

'Nahin sir, kabhi time nahin mila,' he mourns. 'Though, for the longest time, I used to keep scribbling notes, thinking someday I would organise it all nicely. Maybe I'll sit and work on my memoirs once I retire.'

'I'd love to read them whenever you do write them,' I say. 'So, tell me, you must pretty much know everybody in Ambuja?'

He laughs politely. 'I wouldn't exactly say that, but I do know a lot of people, yes.'

'Anybody who can serve as an informer for us?' I ask.

His cheerfulness evaporates. 'Last year, the Maoists pulled out one of our informers from his home and publicly beheaded him. Then they tied his body to a pole with "Police ka Kutta" painted on his chest. After that, who's going to come forward to help us?'

'What! How come I never heard about this? There should have been national outrage about this!' I say.

'Here someone dies every other day, sir. Kis kis ke liye outrage karenge? If we were to print such headlines, Ambuja would be on the front page every day.'

I'm struck by his matter-of-fact, almost resigned tone as he talks about the number of deaths in the town.

'You went to the crime scene? You saw it with your own eyes?'

'Yes, it was a bad day,' he grimaces. 'I didn't get to go home till really late, and we were supposed to go to my sister-in-law's place for dinner. My wife gave me a real earful and told me I could go to bed hungry.'

And that seems to have been the real tragedy for you, I think sourly. I bite my tongue and change the line of questioning. 'Well, did you gentlemen find anything useful at the site?'

'Not really, sir,' responds the third person, who's been silent all this while. I turn towards him. 'Hawaldar Lokesh,' he says, before I can ask. He's of medium height and has an athletic build.

'Khilaadi ho?'

He beams. 'Hoon nahin, sir, tha. I used to be a middle-distance runner. Represented our state in the inter-police championship a few times. I don't run competitively any more, but I like to get in some running whenever I can.'

I nod. 'And why did you find the site visit useless?'

'It was a complete mess, sir,' he replies. 'Our rescue teams had rushed all over the place. Then there were the medics, who were more concerned about helping the wounded than preserving any possible evidence. Quite understandably, from their point of view, I suppose. The bottomline is that the whole place was churned up and any clues were hopelessly trampled on.'

'So we basically have nothing to work with.' It's as much a conclusion as a question.

Lokesh hesitates. 'Well, sir, I did put together a file of news clippings, if you'd like to see,' he offers.

And what would it tell me that Google News can't? I sigh inwardly. Still, if the man has made the effort to put it together, there's no harm in taking a look. 'Show it to me, please.'

He hands it over with the pride of a mother displaying a newborn baby. It's quite voluminous—the Ambuja massacre had generated a lot of news reports. It'll take me several hours to read everything. I leaf through it, speed-reading headlines and the odd item, when my eyes spot something. 'Why is there a clipping about a cricket match here?'

'Eh, that's not possible,' says Lokesh. 'Show me, please.' He examines the file, then looks embarrassed. 'Sorry, sir. I must have pasted the item the wrong way around. The relevant news is possibly on the other side. I'm so sorry.'

'It's okay,' I say, taking the file back. I leaf through a few more pages, then pause. 'I keep seeing the same reporter's name, but in different newspapers. Someone called Devika Doria.'

'She's a freelance journalist, sir,' says Bhoomi. 'In fact, she's been requesting an appointment with you ever since word got out that you'd been posted here. Just a courtesy call to introduce herself.'

'It'll have to wait,' I say, flipping through the file. Then I stop. Darshan's face stares up at me from a grainy black-and-white picture. It's in a news report headlined 'Locals mourn death of popular CRPF officer'. I quickly read the report, then look at the byline. Sure enough, it's Devika Doria.

'What do we know about her?'

'Tough but fair, sir,' says Bhoomi. 'She's been harsh on us from time to time, but she's also written extensively on the brutality of the Maoists.'

'Hmm,' I say. 'Okay, gentlemen, you can get back to your seats for now. Keshav, stay back please. I'd like to talk to you.'

I wait for the men to file out before speaking. 'Is this really the best team you have, Keshav?'

He shrugs. 'They're the best available, sir. One makes do with what one has. It's not as if Ambuja gets the cream of the talent available to the police.'

If this is the team, I think, I'll have to do most of the investigative work myself. 'One of our so-called star investigators doesn't know what FSL is. How long has it been since any of them went for training?'

'Sir, people here are going weeks, sometimes months without taking a single day off. When do we send them for training?' he responds.

I shake my head. 'There's a lot that needs to be fixed here, Keshav. I want the word put out. We are to file FIRs if anyone comes to us. We have to make sure that cases get investigated on a time-bound basis and we take legally strong cases to court.'

He looks sceptical. 'Things have been this way for a long time, sir.'

'Then things are going to change,' I snap, before adding softly, 'in the meantime, you might as well brief me about the CRPF ambush case. It's a big one and I don't want it to be said that we messed it up.'

'Yes, sir,' says Keshav, the words belying his sour expression.

'Start by explaining the lay of the land,' I prompt.

He pulls out a notebook and a ballpoint pen. Then he makes a small circle. 'Let's say this is Ambuja town, where we're sitting.' He marks a dot at a slight distance from the circle. 'This is the CRPF camp. It's about five kilometres outside town.'

He draws lines that radiate out from the dot and shades the area covered by them. 'This is a sort of buffer zone between the area controlled by the state and the Naxal-dominated area. It's about twenty-five kilometres. After that, it's dense forest and ... well ....'

'You can speak with me frankly, Keshav,' I say flatly. 'Don't beat around the bush and don't try to sugarcoat unpleasant facts.'

'Yes, sir. Well, to be honest, the Naxals have complete sway over the forest. There are lots of small villages and settlements in this buffer zone, and government presence is tenuous at best. You have schools, but no locals are willing to teach there because they don't want to become Maoist targets. There are primary health centres in one or two of the bigger villages closer to town, but they are poorly stocked, and again, there are no local doctors, although the DM has brought in some teachers and paramedics from Kerala. Bas yun samajh lijiye, Kerala is fully responsible for Ambuja's health and education. As you go farther from town, even those facilities vanish. Maoists flit in and out of the villages, often picking up supplies. Some villagers cooperate out of sympathy. The majority do it out of sheer terror. But either way, they get what they want. Then this very good officer came along. Darshan Kumar.'

My ears perk up, but I carefully keep my face expressionless.

Keshav continues, oblivious. 'Darshan Kumar understood that the Maoists can't be defeated just by treating them as a law and order problem. You have to win the hearts and minds of the locals as well. Before he arrived here, there was hardly any effort by the authorities to reach out to the villagers. He changed that. He conducted aggressive patrols against the Maoists. But he also started organising medical camps even in the remotest of villages. He started classes for local children near the CRPF camp.

'Since no qualified teachers were available, he called for volunteers from among his men, as well as civilians, to conduct classes in any subject they knew. At least once a week, he'd teach himself. Children were walking in from ten, fifteen kilometres away to attend these classes. I believe there were even plans to start coaching classes for various entrance exams. As you can imagine, the Naxals weren't happy about it. It didn't fit in with their propaganda of a cruel, oppressive state. I think his growing popularity made him a marked man.'

'You think they staged an ambush and killed seventy-odd men just to get one officer? Isn't that a bit far-fetched?'

Keshav shrugs. 'Who knows how the Maoists' minds work, sir. The net result is that the poor man is dead. He was a good man, but bewakoof bhi. You should take your pay and do your job. Where was the need for all this reform? People may think of the good he did for a few days, then life will go on. He lost his life, but left behind a wife and kid. Woh bechare to uske liye rote rahenge.' He stops as he sees my face. 'I'm sorry, main kuch zyaada bol gaya.'

I compose myself, silently cursing myself for the slip. 'No, I suppose you have a point. To some, his idealism might seem foolish. Anyway, I think I should go see this school for myself. And while I'm at it, I might as well check out the ambush site too.'

CHAPTER FOUR

There's a huge crater bang in the middle of the dirt track. A few labourers are trying to fill it up. A couple of others are chopping away at some overgrown vegetation. It's only been a few days since the attack, but the jungle is already trying to reclaim the path that was torn out of it by human hands.

The labourers are surrounded by CRPF personnel who scan the surroundings intently. Every once in a while, they glance at me as I walk around while Lokesh recounts the events of that tragic morning.

'The clearing where they found the body is a few hundred metres into the forest. Would you like to see it?' he asks.

Bhoomi and Gayaram look distinctly nervous. 'Sir, with all due respect, are you sure that's a good idea?' asks Gayaram.

'It's broad daylight, Gayaramji,' I respond. 'And there's a CRPF contingent right here. The Maoists are hardly likely to be lurking around right now.'

They still look uncertain but I end the discussion by turning to Lokesh and saying firmly, 'Let's go.'

As Lokesh and I set off, they exchange glances and then reluctantly follow.

The moment we enter the wooded area, it gets perceptibly cooler and darker. Gayaram coughs hesistantly. 'Chaliye na, sir.

Everything's already been filed. You can read it in office. Why come here?'

I ignore him and continue walking. We enter a small clearing and Lokesh gestures with his hand. 'This is the place.'

I walk around the entire clearing, scanning every inch with my eyes. It's such a quiet, peaceful place that my mind struggles to reconcile the horror that was perpetrated here in these idyllic surroundings. I look around, and suddenly the entire area seems to turn red, soaked in blood. I stare at it, horrified.

It's not possible, I tell myself. I shut my eyes for a moment, then open them again. Everything is back to normal.

Lokesh looks at me. 'There was a lot of blood, sir.' His words are so eerily similar to my thoughts that I can't help starting. 'When we found him, that is. Also, the grass was trampled quite badly. It seems there was a hand-to-hand fight.'

I nod, composing myself. 'Were any samples collected?'

'Yes, sir. They were taken to Raipur for analysis. We haven't heard back yet,' says Lokesh.

'Hmm,' I grunt, still looking around.

'We went over the area very carefully, sir,' says Lokesh. 'You won't find any clue lying around here after all these days.'

At some level, I'd always known that it was very unlikely that I'd miraculously spot a clue after all this time. Still, it's irritating to have Lokesh rub it in. I finally admit defeat and look at the three men. 'Tell me, gentlemen, did the location of the ambush strike you as odd?'

The three exchange glances. 'Odd, sir?' asks Gayaram tentatively.

'Odd matlab ....' I begin.

'Convenient,' interjects Bhoomi. As I turn to him, he says, 'It was very close to the CRPF camp. The patrol passed that spot on its way towards the forest around sunrise on Thursday. It returned barely twenty-four hours later. In that time, the Maoists were able to set up an ambush with heavy-duty weaponry. That means they must have kept all the men and material nearby for a while, ready to move at short notice.'

'Which means that somebody must have informed them about the patrol's movements,' I say. 'And the Maoists must have been staying close by, waiting for the tip-off to come. Any villages nearby?'

'There are a couple, sir,' says Bhoomi. 'We went and spoke to them soon after the ambush. They flatly denied that any Maoists were ever there.'

'They would say that, wouldn't they? Let's go visit them again,' I say.

The three exchange glances. It's Bhoomi who speaks. 'Sir, with all due respect, we've been operating here for years. Please don't go there without a sizeable escort party.'

'I'd like to strike a friendly note. We can't achieve that if we march in with a big contingent,' I say.

'Respectfully, sir, the Maoists may not share your sentiments. And they can be pretty brutal if they get their hands on cops, particularly a senior officer,' says Bhoomi. His tone is still mild, but there's a slight edge.

I look at Lokesh and Gayaram. 'He's right, sir,' says Gayaram politely. 'Panga lene ka point nahin hai. Don't go looking for trouble. We can always return later.'

Lokesh simply nods in assent.

They're probably right, I realise, feeling like an idiot. I have a lot to learn.

'Fine,' I say, grumpily. 'Let's go to the CRPF camp.'

'Let's leave that for tomorow, sir,' says Gayaram immediately.

'Why tomorrow? Let's go now,' I say. 'I want to retrace the route the CRPF convoy took that day, all the way to their camp.'

We return to the police vehicle, where the driver is waiting patiently. I gesture to him that he should move to the shotgun seat. He looks horrified.

'Humour me,' I tell him. 'I like driving.' It's true. Driving calms me down, and right now I could really do with some soothing.

He scuttles over. I hop behind the wheel and start the vehicle. Lokesh and Bhoomi take turns giving me directions, keeping up a running commentary. After some time, the dirt track develops into a road of sorts, even though it's bumpy and potholed like the rest of Ambuja.

The CRPF campsite is visible from a long way off. It's on flat ground, with a clear line of view on all sides. Any surrounding vegetation has long since been chopped down to make sure no one can sneak up on the camp without warning. There are high walls, with barbed wire on top. There's a single gate, which is manned by two alert sentries, and a barrier in front of it. I stop the vehicle and a sentry walks up, an inquiring look in his eyes.

I take out my I-card and show it to him. 'SP Vikram Singh. I'd like to meet the camp commandant for five minutes, if possible.'

The sentry goes back to an outhouse behind the gate and makes a call. About two hundred metres away, there's a small building, which seems to be made of some sort of wood. At some distance from it, there's a small shack with earthen walls, a thatched roof and an ancient stove. A few cots are arranged outside it, but there are no customers there right now.

'What's that building?' I ask, pointing at the wooden structure.

'That's where the classes were held, sir. A porta cabin, really. A lot of schools in these areas have similar structures. Usually made of imported prefabricated material like bamboo and ply. Waterproof, fireproof and easy to build. The locals call them pota cabins because the schools give free midday meals and pota means food in the local language,' explains Bhoomi.

'Interesting location,' I muse.

'I think they located it within viewing distance of the camp so that they could keep an eye on it, but civilians wouldn't be walking in and out of the camp,' says Bhoomi.

Meanwhile, the sentry returns to his post. The barrier is raised and the gate is opened. As we enter, he points to a red building at the end of the driveway. 'Commandant sahab is in his office,' he says.

Unlike the squalor of the police building, the CRPF camp is neat and tidy. But an air of despondency hangs over it, as if its inhabitants are still trying to come to terms with the horror that befell their comrades.

'Commandant sahab' turns out to be Darshan's old boss, Samuel Chandy, whom he'd mentioned on a few occasions. Technically, Darshan was his second-in-command, but Samuel was happy to delegate most of the operational responsibilities to him, while keeping a paternal eye on the unit from a distance. It was an arrangement that had suited them both well.

'Come in, come in, have a seat,' he says as I enter his office. He's a stocky man with a thin, greying moustache that is trimmed to millimetric precision. His uniform is immaculate, his thinning hair is neatly combed, but there are deep shadows under his eyes. As I settle into a chair, he looks around. 'I was told there were more of you?'

'I've asked the others to wait in the reception, sir,' I respond. 'Just wanted to have a quiet word with you.'

'Yes, of course.' He rings a bell lying on his desk and a constable appears. 'Take care of the men outside, will you? Make sure they get some water and tea.' He turns to me. 'Can I offer you some tea or coffee, young man?'

'I'd love some black coffee, sir,' I reply. 'Without any sugar.'

He makes a face. 'Don't know how you can imbibe that poison.

Anyway, you're the one who has to drink it.' He turns to the constable. 'Send a cup of black coffee, please. And some tea for me, the way I like it.'

The constable salutes and leaves.

Samuel turns to me. 'You're here about the ambush, I take it. Terrible business. Horrible what they did to that poor boy.'

We make polite conversation for a few minutes, till a young man who looks barely out of his teens walks in, bearing a tray. He sets down a cup of coffee for me, then places the tray in front of Chandy. The CO pours so much milk into his cup that he seems to be having milk with tea rather than the other way around. Then he takes a spoon of honey and adds it to the cup, stirring vigorously. I almost gag as I look at the concoction that he's created.

'Great for immunity,' says Chandy, taking an experimental sip. He shuts his eyes, savouring the taste. 'Perfect,' he intones. Then he gestures to the attendant. 'Clear this, will you? There's a good fellow.'

I wait for the attendant to leave, then ask, 'Sir, do you mind if I speak frankly?'

'Go right ahead.'

'Sir, have you considered the possibility that there might have been a mole in the camp?'

He stares at me for a long moment. 'All these boys are like my sons. I know each one personally.'

I spread my hands in a placatory gesture. 'Sir, I admire your loyalty to your men. I know that it's not easy to consider that you might have a traitor in your ranks ....'

He raises his hand. 'Stop right there. I appreciate that you're eager to find his killers. But let me tell you, there is already an internal inquiry going on. And we're quite capable of conducting our own investigations, thank you very much.'

'Sir, I don't mean any offence. It would be improper of me to pull jurisdiction, but I am at the investigation stage and any help I can get will be most welcome. I'm sure you're as invested in finding the truth as I am.' I keep my tone as respectful as possible.

He's not mollified. 'Let me tell you, I find it hard to believe that any of my boys would betray their comrades,' he says, his voice still edgy.

'We're not just talking about your men, sir. There could also be locals working in the camp. Are you absolutely certain that each one of them is above suspicion? The boy who just served us tea, he's not in the force, is he? Can you guarantee that no one in the support staff had access to papers about movements?' I ask. 'We're both trying to reach the same goal, which is the truth. Let's work towards it together.'

He glares at me for a long time, but finally nods. 'Okay, we'll share any information you need. Any specific questions?'

'Were there any suspicious activities in the days before the patrol? Did anyone who was supposed to be on the patrol not go, for whatever reason? Is there anybody here who spends a lot of time mingling with the locals?'

He shakes his head. 'Not that I know of. But just to be sure, I'll check with my officers and get back to you. Is there anything else you'd like to know?'

Before I can answer, there's a discreet knock. Chandy's assistant enters. 'Sir, there's a lady waiting to see you. She says she has an appointment.'

'Oh yes, of course. I'd forgotten about that,' says Chandy with a grimace. He picks up his cup, drains it and sets it down, then turns to me. 'Maybe we can talk on the phone, if you need to ask anything else?' he says, brusquely dismissing me.

I take the hint and set down my cup. 'Just one more request, sir. I'd like to see the place where Darshan held his classes.'

Chandy nods. 'Okay. In any case, we'll probably be shutting

that place down, now that he isn't around. Anyway, I'll get one of my men to show it to you.'

I salute and leave the room. As I step out, I hear a female voice snigger, 'Here comes the angry young man,' followed by a giggle.

Bhoomi frantically makes shushing sounds, but it's a bit too late for that. I've already heard the remark.

I look at the person who had spoken. She's young and dusky, with curly hair that's been pulled back into a ponytail. Even in the kurta and jeans she's wearing, one can tell that she's quite petite. Not conventionally good-looking, but she would definitely get a second look, especially because of her eyes, which sparkle with intelligence, and the rather attractive, infectious smile on her face. If she's abashed at my having overheard her, she doesn't show it.

Smile still firmly in place, she walks up to me confidently and introduces herself. 'Devika Doria.'

Why is that name familiar? I peer at her, trying to place her. Then the penny drops. It's Devika Doria, the journalist. 'Naam suna hai,' I tell her.

'You know about me? Waah! I must be famous,' she says cheekily. 'But not as famous as you are. You've made quite the splash. Beat up three young men, taught a lesson or two to your junior officers. Sab aap hi ki charcha kar rahe hain!'

What? That's not what happened at all! But I keep my face expressionless.

If she's disappointed by my lack of reaction, she doesn't show it. 'I've already made inquiries, and I know that's not true. But sir, news—true or false—spreads quickly here. This place is full of activists ready to go to town about police atrocities.' She fishes out a card and hands it over. 'If you ever need to get in touch with me to share your version of the truth, please feel free to call.'

I examine both sides of the card. The front simply lists her as 'Devika Doria, freelance journalist' and mentions a couple of phone numbers and email IDs. The other side lists all the publications that she is a contributor to. It's a long list and includes several national and international dailies.

'She's very good, sir,' says Bhoomi. 'And she's absolutely authentic. We can trust her.'

'Oh? If she's so good, then why isn't she working full-time with someone?' I ask, slightly irritated at Bhoomi for leaping into the conversation.

Devika throws back her head and laughs. 'Arrey Bhoomi, your sir doesn't know, does he? Newspapers don't like to have full-time employees in these remote places. It's costly to hire people, you know. You have to pay them a fixed salary, provident fund, gratuity, etc. No, they'd rather spend money paying people located in big cities who cover exciting subjects like Bollywood stars. Actually, I'm the idiot for staying put in this small town. But what to do, I'm an emotional fool. This place may be hell, but it's home. I like to believe that the stories happening here need to be told, whether people are interested or not.'

Before I can respond, we hear the bell ringing in Chandy's office. His attendant goes rushing to answer. We hear Chandy's voice bellow, 'Where's the person who had come to meet me?'

'Oops, that's me. I'd better go see the old Grumpus,' she says, shaking my hand. 'Nice talking to you, SP Vikram Singh.'

She dashes off, leaving behind a trail of an understated but rather nice perfume. A CRPF man walks up to me. 'You wanted to see the cabin, sir?'

I nod and gesture to the team to follow. We get into our vehicle and drive to the structure. The man opens it. It has a musty smell, as if it's been closed for a few days. There's a board on an easel, a desk with some chalk boxes and a pointer lying on it, a few tables and chairs, and some rugs scattered around. In one corner, there's a desert cooler.

It's dark and dingy. Bhoomi switches the lights on. I nod at him gratefully, and then notice that some pictures are stuck on the walls with tape. I walk across and peer at them. They are mostly group photos with Darshan smiling and laughing with some young people.

'Would you know who they are?' I ask.

'The students and volunteer teachers,' responds the CRPF man.

'Mind if I take these?' I ask, taking down the pictures without waiting for permission.

The man shrugs. 'I don't think we'll need them. I've been told all this will be demolished in a few days.'

'What'll happen to all the stuff here?' I ask.

'I don't know, sir. Garbage, most likely,' he answers.

I feel a wave of sadness wash over me, followed by anger at Darshan. You idiot. You stayed away from your family. You never went home for holidays. You practically threw away your life. And all of that for what? For this little dump? Nobody gives a damn about the work you were so passionate about. For them, it's only worth a garbage bin.

The escort is still speaking. '... the students will miss the classes. They used to love them, especially the sessions Darshan sir taught. Afterwards, he always treated them to chai and pakodas from Mangtu's. Sometimes here, and at other times, they would walk down there.'

'The shack down the road?' I query. 'How long has he been around, this Mangtu?'

'Probably as old as the hills,' he responds. 'He's been there since any of us can remember.'

I walk around the cabin leisurely, but don't find anything else of interest. 'Thank you. You've been most helpful,' I say. We exit the cabin and he locks up the place. As he walks away, I turn to my team. 'Feel like having some pakodas?'

They exchange glances. Finally, Gayaram says cautiously, 'Begging your pardon, sir. You don't seem to be someone who'd go for pakodas, sir.'

I gesture towards the shack. 'You have the pakodas. I'll have some conversation.'

As we near the shack, a grey-haired man wearing a three-day stubble, a vest and pyjamas greets us and gestures towards a plastic table with some chairs. There are several colourful menus lying on the table. The stains on them seem to indicate that they have been frequently handled by greasy fingers. I turn towards Gayaram. 'Any suggestions?'

'Maybe a plate of mixed pakodas, sir,' he responds. 'If we like them, we can get a repeat.'

I turn to the man. 'Mixed pakodas, one plate.' As he starts to walk away, I follow him. 'Kab se ho yahaan pe?'

'I've spent my whole life here, now counting down the last few years.' As he speaks, he lights the stove and starts making the pakodas. For all his talk of old age, his hands are steady and his movements are quick and certain. He's in fairly good shape too.

'You don't look that old,' I probe.

He shrugs. 'Only God knows my age. My parents didn't keep track for sure.'

'Did you ever go to school?' I ask.

'What would I do with that stuff? Pakodas are what I was meant for, so I kept on at them.'

'So you never went to school, but you send pakodas for school children,' I observe.

He shakes his head. 'Who'd go so far to deliver pakodas? Not me!'

I keep my face expressionless, not wanting him to realise that I've just caught him lying. 'Didn't you deliver pakodas to Darshan's school?'

Again, the shake of the head. 'Darshan?'

'The CRPF officer. He held classes in that cabin,' I say, watching his face closely.

'Oh. They're high and mighty officers. What have they to do with me?' He avoids eye contact, as he's done throughout our conversation. My instincts are screaming by now, telling me there's something not quite right with this guy.

I change tack. 'You work here alone?'

'My wife helps me. But she's not well, so she's resting,' he says.

'Oh! What happened?' I ask.

'Old age. Happens to all of us. These days we take to bed more often than we're able to work,' he says.

Again, that projection of himself as weak and ailing when he seems perfectly hale and hearty.

'So, who comes for your pakodas here?' I ask.

The pakodas are coming along nicely by now. He wipes his face before answering. 'Some jawans from the camp. Sometimes a few trucks stop.'

'Where do the trucks go?' I ask.

'There's a village in there,' he says, angling his chin towards the jungle. 'They buy stuff from them and sell them elsewhere,' he adds, still concentrating on stirring and flipping the pakodas.

'Aren't they scared of the Maoists?' I ask.

It's almost as if a veil drops over his face. 'I wouldn't know, I don't talk much.'

'Yet, you seem quite happy to talk to me,' I point out.

'You're the one doing the talking. I'm merely responding,' he says tartly.

'Talk to the truckwalas from time to time. Help the police,' I say.

A lovely aroma fills the air. He empties the steaming contents of the kadhai on to a plate. 'Pakode,' he says, handing it over unceremoniously.

The plate is sizzling hot. I almost drop it.

Lokesh comes rushing up and takes it from me, holding it with a handkerchief. 'Please, sir, let me take that.'

'It's okay, Lokesh. Thank you,' I say, resisting the impulse to put my fingers into my mouth to soothe them. 'Why don't you guys get started? I'll join you.'

Lokesh gives Mangtu another glare. 'Chutney?' he asks.

'Table par hai,' says Mangtu sourly.

Lokesh returns to the table, holding the plate. I clear my throat, ready to resume our conversation. 'You must've heard of the tragedy that happened with the CRPF the other day.'

Mangtu nods.

'Did you see the patrol leaving camp that day?' I ask.

'Nahin, I was resting at home. It's right here, behind the shop,' he responds.

Before I can ask another question, a small boy emerges from behind the shack. 'Is there anything I can do?' he asks.

I stare hard at Mangtu. He continues to avoid eye contact and focuses on the boy instead. 'How's she?'

'Asleep,' says the boy.

'Wash the plates once these guys are done,' says Mangtu.

I butt in. 'Who's that? Didn't you say it was just you and your wife?'

If he's abashed at being caught lying, he conceals it well. 'That's my wife's relative. He's here to help around and learn the trade. It's only been a few days, so I forgot.'

'I wonder what else has slipped your mind?'

He keeps quiet. So do I, though I continue to look at his face intently. Sometimes, people get so flustered by an awkward silence that they end up babbling something just to break the tension. It doesn't work with Mangtu. He keeps his gaze averted and starts fiddling with his utensils.

The silence is broken by Gayaram calling out, 'Sir, we're almost done with the pakodas. Don't accuse us later of not leaving any for you.'

'Leave the last one for me,' I call out without taking my eyes off Mangtu. Then I address him again. 'Give me your number.'

He shakes his head. 'Hai hi nahin, sahab. If I did, wouldn't the school have called me to deliver the pakodas?'

'No phone? Even today, when you can get very affordable ones?'

'Arrey sir, what use are phones here?' Gayaram interjects, walking up to me with the plate, a solitary pakoda on it. 'Who's heard of home delivery in villages?'

'That works well for you, Gayaramji, doesn't it? Or your wife would've got to know each time you tucked into a plate of pakodas,' calls out Lokesh. He and Bhoomi laugh uproariously. Gayaram joins in, the three united by the easy camaraderie of men who have worked together for a while.

I pop the last pakoda into my mouth. It's oily and spicy. Delicious!

'Dil khush ho gaya na, sir?' says Gayaram cheerily. 'Health food-shealth food is all fine, but nothing beats desi snacks.'

Their good humour lasts till we get into the jeep. Then I say, 'Keep him under watch.'

'Why?' asks Gayaram, incredulity in his voice.

I look at him. 'Open your eyes, Gayaramji. Look at the location of his stall. Nobody can move in or out of the camp without him knowing. When I was talking to him, he had his eyes on the road throughout. And he says he doesn't even have a five hundred rupee phone? That's impossible. Get his phone number.'

'But sir, what'll you do with his number? We'll need permission to track it,' reminds Bhoomi.

'Leave that to me,' I say, turning to look at Bhoomi, who is sitting in the back. He begins to say something, then stops. 'Yes? You want to say something?'

Bhoomi takes a deep breath before replying. 'Begging your pardon, sir, but Mangtu has been there for a long time and he's never been in any trouble. If you don't mind my saying so, this seems like a bit of a long shot.'

'I know,' I reply. 'But given the sorry state of our investigation, right now, a long shot is all we have.'

CHAPTER FIVE

I shut down my computer, then yawn and stretch. It's been a long day, and I'm finally ready to head home. Just then, there's a knock on the door and Keshav steps in.

'Excuse me, sir, aren't you coming for the party tonight?'

I look at him, mystified. 'What party?'

He points at a fancy envelope lying unopened on my desk. 'This had come in for you in the morning, sir. It's an anniversary dinner being hosted by Mr Purshottam Sethi at the Ambuja Club. He's called a couple of times to confirm that you're going. Apparently, he's keen to welcome you.'

I raise an eyebrow. 'Who's Mr Purshottam Sethi?'

'Local businessman, sir. Does lots of charity work too.' Keshav's voice drops. 'He's very well connected. The MLA here is his brother-in-law.'

I roll my eyes. 'Oh God, please make some excuse for me, will you?'

Keshav hesitates. 'Sir, your place is barely five minutes from here, and the club is another five minutes from there ....'

'Everything seems to be within five minutes of each other in this town,' I interrupt.

He laughs politely. 'Quite right, sir. It's not exactly a sprawling metropolis. Well, my suggestion would be that you could go home, freshen up, and then go the club. No one will mind if you show up late.' He pauses, then goes on, 'Sir, two minutes ke liye hello bol dijiye na. He does a lot of charity work. Who knows, his CSR might help give our building a facelift.'

'I'll see,' I say dismissively. Corporate Social Responsibilty or not, I've already made up my mind that I won't be going. 'Chalo, I'll see you tomorrow.'

'Tomorrow? Er ... it's Saturday, sir,' says Keshav.

'So? Criminals don't take the weekend off, no?'

Keshav looks worried. 'Well, no, sir. Er, umm, uh ... do you want me to come in as well?'

I look at him without saying a word. 'Yes, sir, of course, sir,' he says hurriedly. He salutes and leaves, a frown on his face. It's still there the next morning.

'Arrey waah, you're at work all bright and early,' I observe.

'Aap ne hi kaha tha, sir, criminals don't take the day off,' he shoots back. 'There are a couple of visitors on their way to see you.'

'This early?' I ask.

'Yes,' says a brisk voice behind me. 'We didn't want to be told you were too busy to meet us.'

I turn around and see Devika Doria.

'Oh, hello,' I say, surprised.

'Good morning,' she says. 'I didn't see you at the party last night. I heard you're quite a serious guy, but there's a difference between serious and khadoos.'

I ignore the barb. 'Aapko kuch kaam tha?'

'Yes, I'd like you to meet this young lady if you can spare a couple of minutes, please.' She gestures to a young woman who's standing a little behind her. 'This is Anjali.'

Anjali is tall and slender, with delicate features. She would be very attractive, if it weren't for an air of sadness that seems to envelope her like a cloak. As she walks up to us, she joins her hands in a namaste.

'Thank you for seeing us,' she says in a low voice.

I lead them into my office. 'Have a seat, please. How can I help you?'

Anjali looks at Devika, who nods and clears her throat. 'We're here to invite you for the foundation stone laying ceremony of a school that Anjali is starting. It's tomorrow evening. We would have done it last night, but you didn't come for the party, so ....' She hands over an invitation card.

'Wouldn't it be more appropriate to invite the DM?' I ask.

'He's already been invited and has confirmed he'll be there. But we'd like you to come too,' says Devika.

'Why do you need me there? Police waalon ka school opening mein kya kaam?'

'Sir, if there were more people in the force who thought like Darshan, there'd be more schools, and half our problems would've been solved,' says Anjali.

'Darshanji's work was a great inspiration for me. I was so saddened by his death, and I wondered what would happen to all those children. Then I had this idea of starting a school that would be free for tribals and disadvantaged children. It will be built very close to the cabin where he held classes. In fact, until the school building is ready, we'll be using his cabin. Luckily, my father has been very supportive and is fully funding the construction.' For the first time, Anjali looks a little animated.

'That's nice,' I say. 'I'm sorry, your father is ...?'

'Oh, how stupid of me, I didn't introduce the two of you properly,' says Devika. 'Anjali is the daughter of Mr Purshottam Sethi.'

My surprise must have shown on my face because Anjali hastily says, 'We were so keen to see you yesterday. Then you didn't turn up, so we decided that our best chance was to call on you in your office. So, here we are.'

I'm genuinely at a loss for words. While I try to figure out what to say, I buy some time by looking at the invitation card, which requests my gracious presence on the auspicious occasion of the foundation stone laying ceremony of the Dhruva Muriya Memorial School.

'Who's Dhruva Muriya?' I ask casually.

Anjali's face crumples. 'He ... he's my late husband. The Maoists killed him early last year.' Suddenly, tears begin streaming down her face. She pulls out a handkerchief from her handbag and furiously dabs at them.

I look at her, not sure how to react to this sudden turn of events. Devika scowls at me and then speaks to Anjali in a low, soothing tone. After a few moments, Anjali looks at me apologetically with a wan smile.

'I'm sorry. Can I please go clean my face? I must look like a total fright,' she says.

'Please step out and go down the corridor. The ladies' toilet is to the right.' As she heads for it, I fervently hope that it's been cleaned in the morning and doesn't look like a complete dump.

Anjali closes the door behind her. I turn back and find Devika still glaring at me. 'My God, you really are clueless about handling sensitive subjects, aren't you?'

'And how am I supposed to know about her husband?' I ask, nettled at her tone.

'Maybe by reading your files? And not because it involved the murder of the son-in-law of this area's biggest businessman, but because someone who was committed to helping the people here got killed,' she shoots back.

'Thanks for the advice. I'll read those files the moment you leave,' I snap.

She nods. 'Don't worry, SP sahab. I'll leave as soon as my friend gets back. And you know what, you don't have to come if you don't want to. I came here because I wanted to support a friend who's trying to get back on her feet. But it was stupid of me, I shouldn't have encouraged her. When she gets back here, just make some polite excuse. Let her live in the fantasy that every officer is a Darshan Kumar.'

Before I can reply, we hear footsteps approaching. Anjali re-enters, her face scrubbed clean.

'I'm so sorry about this,' she says. 'I haven't broken down like that in some time. I think your question took me by surprise. It's been a while since I met someone who didn't know Dhruva.'

'Please don't apologise. If anything, I should be saying sorry for upsetting you.'

'Thank you for seeing us,' Devika cuts in briskly. 'We'd love to have you over, but we do understand that you're new here and still coming to grips with everything you have to do. If you can't make it, no problem. Chalo, Anjali.' She picks up her bag decisively and rises to her feet.

Anjali looks a bit startled but recovers quickly. 'Er ... yes. Thank you so much for seeing us and sorry for getting your day off to such a dramatic start,' she says, before following Devika out of the room.

Almost as soon as they leave, Keshav walks in, a concerned expression on his face. 'All okay, sir? What did they want?'

'Who's this Dhruva Muriya?'

Keshav glances at the door, then leans forward and speaks in a low voice. 'It's a long story, sir. Anjali met him while at college in Delhi. He was a handsome boy from a poor family who was there on a scholarship. They fell in love. Her parents weren't thrilled. But they came around and agreed to the marriage, on the condition that Dhruva would live with them and work in the family business.'

'That's rather romantic,' I say.

'The funny thing is, once the old man started working with his son-in-law, he took a great liking to him. Dhruva pretty much became his right-hand man. He was almost as shattered as his daughter when Dhruva was killed. Last night was the first time the family has had any sort of celebration since his death.'

'And what exactly happened to him?'

'He'd gone into the forest to pick up some tribal handicrafts. He'd started this project where he'd buy stuff from the tribals and then sell them in the big cities. Apparently, there were also some export deals being talked about. Anyway, he set out one morning with two guards and a colleague. He was supposed to go to his native village but never reached there. A search party was sent out and found all of them in their vehicle on the road. The vehicle was riddled with bullets and so were the bodies. There were slogans like "Death to Traitors" painted all over.'

'Case ka status kya hai?'

'Open, sir. When are such cases closed so easily? If we have to investigate further, we'll have to go into the Maoist stronghold and interrogate their commanders. I don't think that will happen any time soon,' he says mildly, belying the sarcasm in his words.

'Hmm, I'd like to see the case file,' I say.

'Sure, sir, I'll get it pulled out and sent to you.'

'Dhruva Muriya was a fine young man who took pride in his heritage but also dreamt of a better future for his people. This school is a fitting tribute to him and I am sure it will transform the lives of many young and promising children.'

As the MLA finishes his speech, the audience claps enthusiastically. With the formalities over, people walk around, exchanging pleasantries. I feel a tap on my shoulder and whirl around, fist drawn.

'Whoa, easy there, Jackie Chan!' It's Devika, accompanied by Anjali.

'Sorry, you surprised me,' I say.

'No, you surprised me,' she responds. 'I must say I wasn't expecting you after our last conversation.'

I ignore her barb and turn to Anjali. 'Congratulations on getting this effort started. It was a nice ceremony. Short and very moving.'

'Thank you for being here. I'm so glad you could make it. You hadn't arrived when the function began, so I thought perhaps you might not be able to attend after all,' she answers.

'I got a little late,' I confess. 'When I got here, I saw the function had already begun, so I quietly sneaked into one of the back rows.'

'Late for a function? Tsk tsk. I had you figured for one of the die-hard punctual types,' says Devika.

'Well, I know this will sound lame, but my car actually broke down on the way and it took me a while to fix it and then get my hands and face cleaned up. I think Ambuja's roads are too hard on my old beauty's ageing parts,' I explain.

'Band baaje ke saath nahin aaye?' she asks.

'Excuse me?' I respond, puzzled.

'Arrey, didn't you come in your official car, all self-important and sirens blazing? Why did you use your own car, especially if it's getting unreliable?' asks Devika.

'I'm here on a personal visit, not an official one. Why should I use my official perks?'

She shakes her head. 'You know, you really are a walking, talking rule book. Come, let me introduce you to Purshottam uncle—he's very keen to meet you—while Anjali mingles with her guests.'

'Yes, I do need to see to them. Again, thank you so much for making the time to be here,' Anjali says to me, inclining her head.

'You go ahead and circulate, I'll take care of SP sahab,' says Devika.

I follow as Devika leads me into the thickest part of the

gathering, right up to a tall, distinguished-looking gentleman in a spotless white kurta-pyjama, who is holding forth to a group of men that are hanging on to his every word. 'Purshottam uncle, I've got a special guest for you,' she says.

The man turns towards us. His leonine mane of grey hair is brushed back, and he has a full but neatly trimmed grey beard and an aquiline nose. His sharp, penetrating eyes focus on me as if trying to assess me.

'Purshottam uncle, meet SP Vikram Pratap Singh,' Devika makes the introduction.

He continues to stare at me for a long moment. I stare right back into his eyes, unblinking. Then his face suddenly relaxes into a smile and he extends his hand.

'SP sahab,' he says. His voice is a deep, rich baritone. 'Welcome to Ambuja. What a pleasure to finally meet you.'

We shake hands and I note that he has a firm, rock-steady grip. 'Belated congratulations on your anniversary, Mr Sethi,' I say.

He smiles. 'We missed you. I'm glad to finally meet you. When I learnt that you'd agreed to grace us with your presence today, I said I must make it a point to be here. It's been a long time since I made such an effort just to meet someone in Ambuja.'

He's still smiling, but the rebuke is unmistakeable. A couple of his cronies titter. I feel my hackles rising.

'It's a better place to meet than the alternative. I usually meet people at the police station,' I reply bluntly, not bothering to couch my words in politeness.

I see a flash of anger in his eyes. Everybody around us freezes as they register my words. There's a long pause. You could cut the tension in the air with a knife. Then Sethi throws back his head and laughs.

'You have such a wonderfully dry sense of humour, SP sahab. Well, I'm doubly grateful that I'm getting to meet you here rather than at your preferred location,' he chortles. Everybody else relaxes and conversation resumes.

We make small talk for a couple of minutes, then a short, heavyset man walks up to us. 'Excuse me, sir,' he says.

'This is Prashant, my assistant,' says Sethi, introducing us. 'Yes, Prashant, what is it?'

'Sir, aapke liye urgent call hai,' he says. 'I said you were busy and asked if I could take a message. The gentleman requested that you call back immediately.'

Sethi frowns. 'Please excuse me,' he says to me and walks a few steps away, gesturing to Prashant to follow. The two men speak softly and then Sethi nods at him and walks back. 'I'm afraid I will have to take your leave. A rather urgent business matter has come up and I need to attend to it right away. It was a pleasure meeting you.'

'Likewise,' I say, and we shake hands. I gaze at his receding back as he walks away.

'Knock knock,' says Devika, interrupting my reverie. 'I've been instructed to make sure that you're taken care of, so here I am. Would you like to have something? A shikanji or a lemonade?'

'A lemonade would be good,' I say.

She gestures to a hovering waiter, picks up a glass and hands it to me. As the waiter walks away, I speak to her softly. 'I read the file, and one thing is bothering me.'

She quickly looks around, then indicates that we should move to a slightly secluded spot.

'Okay, what's bothering you?' she asks, once she's satisfied that nobody can overhear us.

'Dhruva was a high-value target. Why not just kidnap him and demand a ransom? Woh bada hath maar sakte the. Why kill him?' I ask.

She starts to answer, then looks torn.

'You know something?' I ask.

She nods slowly. 'I'll tell you, but you're not supposed to have heard this from me, okay? Apparently, the Maoists did send a ransom demand for a huge amount. Purshottam uncle was even ready to pay, but it took him a while to arrange the money. Even somebody as rich as him doesn't have that kind of cash just lying around. By the time he got it, Dhruva was dead. He thinks Dhruva may have tried to escape and got killed in the process. He never made this public because he thought it would devastate Anjali.'

'How do you know this?' I ask.

'He told me one day, when I asked him the exact same question. But he also swore me to secrecy. So, if you ever quote me, I'll deny having told you this,' she says, a fierce expression on her face.

'But why didn't he just tell the police?' I ask.

'Well, to be honest, the police didn't exactly ask too many questions when the investigations were on. And I think Purshottam uncle was probably worried about ensuring the safety of his wife and child, so he didn't want to stir up trouble. Anyway, I guess the reason for Dhruva's death will remain a mystery,' she says.

'Doesn't that bother you? You're such a dedicated journalist,' I say.

'Dedicated, yes, but I'm also pragmatic,' she retorts. 'Do you know how many such cases remain unsolved? Look at your records, you'll find a whole bunch! Speaking realistically, I don't think we'll ever get to the bottom of this mystery, though it does rankle. It's not just Angry Young Men who butt heads with problems.'

I smile at the angry young man reference. She widens her eyes in mock surprise. 'Oh my God, he actually smiles! If I'd known you'd find it amusing, I'd have called you that sooner. Maybe it's the lemonade you're drinking.'

I spread my hands. 'It's actually rather good lemonade, I must say.'

She laughs. 'Courtesy of Foodie's Paradise, the pride and joy of Ambuja. You can go there any time you feel like having some more.'

'I'm not so stupid that I'll visit a place just to have glorified nimbu paani,' I smile.

'Oh no, you can also go there for their killer Chilli Manchurian Paneer,' she chortles.

'Is it any good?'

'Well, a Chinese crew had come down to Ambuja some time back to shoot a documentary. I was working with them as a sort of local coordinator. I took them to the place and asked them to serve their best Chinese dishes. The crew said they absolutely loved the food, then asked what cuisine it was,' she says.

'Really? I have to try this place,' I say. 'While I was studying for the civil services exam, I pretty much lived on two-minute noodles and instant soup.'

'Yes, you should check it out,' she says. 'But don't assume that I'm offering to take you there. I'm busy tonight. My father is making his special mutton curry for me.'

'Oh, family night, is it?' I ask.

She nods. 'Yup, Dad only makes a few dishes, but they're quite amazing. I always tell him he should have been a chef instead of a patrakaar.'

'Oh, is your father a journalist as well?'

'Used to be. He was the bureau chief for a local regional daily. It shut down a few years ago, but he'd almost reached retirement age by then, so it didn't really hurt us financially, though, of course, Dad was very sad to see it go. My mother always joked that the paper was his true love.'

'She must be happy to have him to herself now?' I venture.

'She was, for a while. Then she had a heart attack one night, a couple of years ago, and passed on.'

'I'm sorry.'

'No, it's okay. She went peacefully in her sleep. We should all be so lucky,' says Devika. There's a faraway look in her eyes.

I try to lighten the mood. 'You mentioned that your father used to be a journalist. So you basically followed in his footsteps, huh?'

'Oh yes, it's entirely his fault. I used to be a real bundle of energy as a kid and Mum would be at her wit's end trying to keep me occupied, especially during vacations. Once, Dad saw her literally tearing her hair out in frustration and took me along with him when he went to cover an election rally. After that, whenever he could, he'd take me along. Then, one day, I submitted a piece for the special students' edition of a national daily that used to be distributed in my school and it actually got published. Dad was so proud, he cut out the clipping, framed it and hung it on our drawing-room wall. He'd brag about it to all our guests. That pretty much sealed my fate.'

'He sounds wonderful. You're lucky to have him,' I say. It's completely heartfelt.

'I know. Just don't tell him I said so, okay?' she laughs. 'Right, enough about me. What about your family?'

'Both parents long gone,' I say. 'No siblings. There's just main aur meri tanhaai.'

Her eyes soften at my words. I realise, with a start, that she has rather beautiful eyes—big, dark and very expressive. But when she speaks, her tone is brisk. 'Hmm, that explains a lot. By the way, have you retained the business card I gave you, or have you thrown it away?'

'Er ... it's lying safely somewhere. I'll just have to look for it,' I say, a little embarrassed.

'Yeah, right. Just give me your phone,' she says. I hand it over. She quickly feeds in her number, then saves and dials it. The sound of a bird chirping metallically fills the air. 'Right. So now I have your number and you have mine.'

I take my phone and glance at the clock—the time has certainly flown. 'I'd better head back.'

Early next morning, I see a couple of messages from her. I open them and pictures pop up of a richly coloured, very tempting dish. 'Just letting you know what you missed:),' it says.

'My loss entirely,' I reply, adding a sad emoji, then put away the phone and head to the bathroom. As I shave, I realise I'm smiling. And a thought hits me. For the first time since I heard about Darshan's death, I've woken up not feeling gloomy and angry with the world.

'Shame on you, Vikram Pratap Singh,' I mutter. 'Losing your edge because of a girl.'

But the good mood persists right till I walk into my office and find Bhoomi, Gayaram and Lokesh huddled there looking serious.

I raise an inquiring eyebrow at Bhoomi. 'What's the matter?'

'You were right, sir. Mangtu does have a phone,' he replies.

CHAPTER SIX

'I knew it! There was something off about that guy,' I say. 'So, tell me how you found out.'

'I went back yesterday and spoke to the boy. He's no relative of Mangtu's, by the way. He used to work as a cleaner with some truck driver who left him there one day. It was supposed to be for a few hours, but the driver never returned. Bas gaayab ho gaya, no one knows where. He's been working there ever since, in return for food and shelter.'

'Okay, and this boy gave you Mangtu's number?'

Bhoomi nods. 'There's some other information that may interest you. He delivered chai and pakodas for Darshan Kumar and some other officers in the camp the evening before the patrol left. Apparently Darshan spoke to him for a couple of minutes and tried to persuade him to start attending his classes. The boy was supposed to collect the empty glasses and return to Mangtu's. But the officers were looking at a map and one of its edges kept curling up, so Darshan used one of the glasses as a paperweight. He told the kid that he'd get it sent back later.'

'Did the boy see the map?'

'Yes, sir,' says Bhoomi. 'He says it looked like a map of the forest route, though he couldn't be sure.'

'And did he tell Mangtu?'

'Yes, he had to, because Mangtu asked him about the missing glass,' says Bhoomi.

I slap my palm on the desk. 'So this child saw the officers looking at a map. Nobody would worry about him because he's just a kid. He went and told Mangtu, who was able to put two and two together and come to the conclusion that a patrol would be going out soon.'

Lokesh speaks up. 'Shall we bring Mangtu here, sir?'

I shake my head. 'It makes sense, but it's still only a theory. We need proof. Keep him under watch 24x7.' A thought strikes me. 'Set up a small post there. We're going to say we're worried the Maoists might attack the school building that is coming up, so we're going to have someone keeping an eye on the area.'

'Sir, the CRPF camp is right there,' pipes up Gayaram. 'Why would the Maoists attack a building so close to the camp?'

'The same way they wiped out a patrol party just a few kilometres from the camp? Gayaramji, that building needs watching over. And you're just the man for it—you're so fond of Mangtu's pakodas.'

Gayaram starts to protest, thinks better of it, then opens his mouth again, only to shut it one more time. It's a very good impression of a fish out of water.

'Yes, Gayaramji, is there an issue?'

He shakes his head. 'No, sir, I'll be on my way.'

'Excellent,' I say briskly. 'Enjoy those pakodas.' Then I turn to Bhoomi. 'Get in touch with the mobile service provider. I want all the call records from Mangtu's phone, especially for the period just before and after the ambush.'

'Sir, they're not going to be released on just a request. They'll need a formal request from an SP-level officer,' says Bhoomi.

'Talk to them. Get me the relevant email IDs. Tell them the email will be on its way in the next few minutes and they should get started on digging up the information right away. Let's not get wrapped up in red tape. I want that information today.' I'm buzzing with energy, literally bouncing on my toes.

A few hours later, Bhoomi knocks on the door and peers in.

'Yes, Bhoomi?' I ask.

'Sir, did you send that email?' he inquires.

'Which email?' I ask, puzzled.

'The one to the mobile service provider, asking for the CDRs,' he reminds me.

I slap my forehead in irritation. 'Damn, I got busy doing other stuff and completely forgot. Don't tell me they've been waiting all this while?'

'Well, I'd impressed upon the person in-charge there that it was really important, so they've sent us the information, though he's requesting that we send the mail as soon as possible.'

'Of course, of course,' I say impatiently. 'Okay, so what have we found out?'

'A call went out from Mangtu's number at 4.40 a.m. It was just a few minutes after the patrol left.'

'Do we know whom he called?'

Bhoomi hesitates.

'Come on, bolo bhi. Kisko call kiya tha?' I prompt.

'Mr Purshottam Sethi's secretary.'

'What?' I sit back, stunned. 'Are they sure about this?'

'Yes, sir. The SIM card was activated a little over a year ago,' says Bhoomi.

'Well, then, let's go talk to Prashant,' I say.

'Sir, should we just tell him to come here?' asks Bhoomi. 'He'll probably be with Mr Sethi right now. Should we go barging into Mr Sethi's office?'

'If he's mixed up with the Naxals, asking him to come here will only serve to warn him that he could be in trouble,' I respond. 'Let's go talk to him.'

Sethi's office turns out to be inside a heavily fortified compound, with high walls, barbed wire and paramilitary personnel manning the gates.

'Expecting an invasion, is he?' I ask dourly.

'He has always had security cover, and after his son-in-law got killed, it was stepped up even further,' explains Bhoomi. 'I believe he pays for it himself.'

'And he has a Maoist mole living right next to him the whole time. Isn't that ironic?' I say, as we walk into the office building.

By Ambuja's standards, it's a tall building, which means it has four storeys. The ground floor is one cavernous hall that serves as a waiting area, with a couple of glass-walled conference rooms to one side. As we make our way towards the reception desk, a lift door opens and Sethi and Prashant step out, flanked by two burly men who are clearly the former's bodyguards.

It's hard to say which of us is more surprised. We all stop and stare at each other. Sethi finally breaks the silence. 'Well, this is an unexpected pleasure,' he says. 'And I thought you only meet people at the police station.'

'Actually, I'm here to meet your assistant,' I tell him. 'I had a few questions for him.'

'Prashant? What's he done?' asks Sethi. He turns and looks at the man, who shakes his head and turns his palms upwards in a universal gesture of puzzlement.

'You needn't concern yourself with it right now, Mr Sethi. We'll let you know soon enough,' I tell him grimly.

'On the contrary. Prashant has been with me for years. I will most definitely concern myself with it,' he responds. Then he looks around and notices that people in the waiting area are starting to stare at us. 'If you don't mind, let's go to the conference room,' he says. 'We can have our discussion in some privacy.'

The conference room has a long table, a projector screen on one wall, and deep, comfortable chairs. Sethi walks to the head of the table and gestures to us to be seated. 'Please make yourselves comfortable. Would you like some tea or coffee?' he asks.

'This is not a social call, Mr Sethi. We'd just like to get started with our questions,' I snap.

'Of course,' he says. 'Please go ahead. Prashant, please cooperate fully with the police. Whatever misunderstanding they have, I'm sure we'll be able to clear it up.'

'We'll see about that,' I mutter to myself. Then I turn to Prashant. 'Where were you at around 4.40 a.m. on 16 June?'

He looks nonplussed. 'Sleeping, I suppose. I mean, how am I supposed to remember what I was doing at 4.40 a.m. on a random date?'

'Oh, but it wasn't a random date, Prashant,' I reply. 'Did you get a call on your mobile phone?'

He shakes his head. 'No, I'm pretty certain about that. I would definitely recall getting a call at such an early hour.'

'Is there someone who can account for your movements on that day?' I ask.

'Yes, Sethi sahab can,' he replies instantly. 'I stay in an outhouse in his bungalow, and I travel to office and back with him.'

I look at Sethi, who nods. 'Yes, I start my day with an early morning walk. Prashant usually joins me then and records any ideas that strike me. I do some of my best thinking at that time. He's with me till we return from work, after which he has the evening to himself. By the way, is there some logic behind these questions? I can't say I see any so far.'

'You'll see it in a moment,' I reply. 'Can you tell me your phone number, Prashant?'

'I have two,' he says, and proceeds to rattle off the numbers.

I look at the sheet in front of me and frown. 'There's another number registered in your name,' I say. 'Would you like me to read it out?'

'That's not possible,' he says immediately.

'You've had it for a little over a year. Does that ring any bells?' I ask.

'Wait, did you say about a year?' he asks.

'Yes, are your memory cells starting to stir?' I ask sarcastically.

He ignores my jibe. 'Would you tell me the number?'

I recite it. A look of horror appears on his face.

'Yeh aapko kahaan mila?' he asks.

'Kyon, isme itna ghabraane ki kya baat hai?' I ask. I've got you now, I think.

'I picked up about ten phones in one go last year,' he says.

'Really? And why would you need so many phones?'

'It was a welfare measure by Dhruva bhaiyya. He wanted to gift phones to the children of our Adivasi employees who were doing well academically. He asked me to buy ten phones, get them activated, and give them to him so that they could be passed on, ready to use. So all the ten phones were registered in my name. The money was deducted from our CSR budget. I can even take you to the shop from where I bought the phones if you like,' he says.

'I see. And how come you remember this specific number?' I ask.

He looks up, a stricken expression on his face. 'It was a strange coincidence. The last four digits matched the date of birth of one of the boys. He mentioned this and Dhruva bhaiyya started speaking to him and really took a liking to him. He asked him to join him as his assistant. He was with Dhruva bhaiyya when they ... when they went into the forest. We found him along with Dhruva bhaiyya. That's how I remember the number, at least the last four digits.'

'So what happened to his phone?' I ask.

Prashant shakes his head. 'It never even occurred to us to look for it.'

'Could one of the people who killed them have taken away their phones?' asks Sethi. His voice is shaking and there is an ashen look on his face.

I nod grimly. 'It seems that Dhruva's killers are somehow mixed up with this ambush too.'

'Oh my God,' says Sethi, sitting down heavily. He looks at me, a pleading expression on his face. 'Could you please try to keep this quiet? My daughter's wounds have barely begun to heal. Learning this will rip them wide open all over again.'

'We'll go wherever the investigation takes us,' I say grimly. 'Well, thank you for seeing us. I'll let you get back to your work now.'

He shakes his head wanly. 'I don't think I'm going to get any work done now. I might as well go home.'

I turn to Bhoomi. 'And we need to head back to office. Lots more work to do.'

CHAPTER SEVEN

'The phone has been used very infrequently, sir. Maybe once in a few months, each time from a different location. And then it's switched off again.' Bhoomi looks up from the sheet he's reading and rubs his eyes. He looks exhausted.

I feel exhausted myself, but I refuse to let it show. 'Have you tried calling it?'

'There's no response, sir. We checked with the mobile service provider. The phone has been switched off since the day of the attack,' responds Bhoomi.

'Hmm, so whoever has it now is using a phone taken off a dead man so that we can't trace his identity, and may not switch it on any time soon. What was the last location from where it was used?' I ask.

'In the forest, sir.' Bhoomi pulls out a map of the area and points at it with a pen. 'Let's say this is the site of the ambush,' he says, making a small dot. 'And this is the village closest to the site.' Another dot. 'The phone was triangulated almost exactly in the middle of the two spots.'

'So, the person who received the call must have been camped in the forest, waiting for the signal to spring the ambush. That's the only explanation that makes sense.'

The others exchange glances, then nod. 'Haan sir, can't think what else it could be,' says Lokesh.

There's a knock on the door and Gayaram peeps in. 'May I come in, sir?' he asks.

'Aaiye Gayaramji. How were the pakodas?' I ask.

'Arrey, leave it, sir. It's the mosquitos that have had their fun with me,' he grumbles. 'Waste of time, sir. There's only a small boy who comes there daily.'

'Haan, I've already spoken to him,' says Bhoomi.

Gayaram shakes his head. 'Not him, this is another kid.'

Bhoomi throws up his hands. 'Arrey, how many kids work in that pocket-sized dhaba?'

'The kid you spoke to works there, the one that I spoke to comes from the village to attend classes daily,' explains Gayaram.

'Okay, fine. So there are two separate chottus. What did yours tell you?' I ask.

Gayaram looks disgruntled. 'It cost me five chocolates to get the bugger to open his mouth,' he says.

'Haww, you bribed him?' I can't resist the temptation to tease Gayaram.

'Arrey sir, you need to keep your informants happy, don't you,' he says.

'Hmmm. So did your informant give you anything useful?' I ask.

Gayaram sighs. 'It's strange, sir. He told me of some Rudra bhaiyya who visits them sometimes. He's given the boy some papers to pass on to Mangtu.'

I sit up, instantly alert. 'Papers? The boy is being used as a courier. Has he read what's in them?'

'That's it, sir. It's just blank sheets of paper,' says Gayaram.

'What? That makes absolutely no sense,' I say.

'Yes, sir. But they really are blank. He showed me one after I handed him the chocolates,' says Gayaram.

I frown, trying to wrap my head around this. 'Why would someone send blank notes?'

'Who knows, sir, people are strange,' says Gayaram dismissively.

'Gayaramji, that kid might've just played you for a fool,' says Bhoomi.

I shake my head. 'Doubt it. Who is this Rudra bhaiyya?'

'Don't know much, sir. He comes to stay in the village sometimes. Takes turns staying with different families. Right now, he's staying in the mukhiya's home,' says Gayaram.

'What does he look like?' I ask.

'Thin, bearded, wears spectacles, and is usually in a kurta and jeans. The jholawala type,' responds Gayaram.

'Chalo, let's meet him. There's not much else to do here anyway,' I say.

'Sir, let's put together a proper party,' says Bhoomi immediately.

I nod. 'Okay, but make it fast. Where's Keshav?'

'He'll be coming in late today, sir. He had to go to his kids' school,' says Bhoomi.

'Oh yeah, he messaged me,' I say. 'Okay, let's get going.'

A little later, the party is ready to head out.

The road disappears as we approach the village, replaced by a dirt track surrounded by thick vegetation. The village suddenly leaps into sight in the middle of the greenery. It's a small cluster of houses with mud walls and thatched roofs. There are only a handful of brick buildings. The biggest has red sloping tiles and a boundary wall around it. It sticks out in the midst of the poverty and deprivation.

Bhoomi points at the red-roofed house. 'That's the one,' he says.

The men drive up to the house and quickly take up positions around it. Several people look at us curiously. As I step out of my vehicle, I try to make eye contact with them. They look away and hastily scuttle into their homes.

The boundary wall has a gate. As I approach it, a big, burly man with a shaven head and handlebar moustache steps in front of it, blocking access.

'Aap kaun?' he demands.

'SP Vikram Pratap Singh,' I identify myself. 'Are you the village head?'

He nods, his eyebrows raised. 'It's been a while since someone of your rank visited our village. How can I help?'

'Can we talk inside?' I ask.

'Kya, is there a problem?' I get the distinct feeling he's stalling. But why?

Suddenly, there's a crash from within. The headman turns towards the sound. I unceremoniously shove him aside and charge in, yelling, 'Quick, he's trying to get away.'

Even as I race into the house, I'm confused. Why is Rudra running away? We've just come to talk.

Focus, I tell myself sternly. There will be time enough for explanations once he's caught.

A woman screams as I peer into one of the rooms. I hastily mutter an apology and start to back out. Then I notice that a window is open and the curtain is still billowing.

'Over there,' I yell. I run to the window and pull aside the curtain. A figure with a backpack is hauling himself over the boundary wall.

'He's getting away!' I yell as he straddles the wall and jumps over. I run outside, and across to the wall, pull myself up, then drop to the other side. I realise with sickening certainty that nobody from my team will manage to get to this side of the house. In a few seconds, he'll disappear into the forest.

I get on one knee, pull out my revolver, steady myself and aim at his legs.

'Rudra, stop or I'll shoot,' I yell. He keeps running. I take a deep breath and get ready to take the shot. But suddenly, a figure appears between me and the rapidly receding Rudra, blocking my line of sight.

'Lokesh, what the hell are you doing? You're blocking my shot! Get out of the way!' I yell in frustration.

Lokesh ignores me and puts on a burst of speed, closing the gap between him and Rudra. I suddenly remember my first conversation with him, when he'd claimed to have been an athlete.

'Get him, Lokesh!' I yell, rising to my feet and racing after them. Rudra gets right to the edge of the forest and I fear that we might lose him, but Lokesh hurls himself through the air, grabbing him from behind and sending them both crashing to the ground.

Rudra and Lokesh rise up together. Rudra shrugs off his backpack, then takes a wild swing at Lokesh, but misses. Lokesh grabs him by the collar and the two men grapple. Lokesh is taller and stronger and steadily starts to overpower Rudra. But Rudra suddenly changes tack. Instead of trying to break away, he leans in and butts Lokesh hard in the face. Lokesh yells in pain and lets him go.

I reach them just then. Rudra takes a swing at me. He's not a very skilled fighter, I can see the move coming from a long way off. I easily duck under it and sweep his legs out from under him. He lands hard, the breath knocked out of him.

As he struggles to rise, I point my revolver straight at his forehead. He freezes, the fight fading from his eyes.

'Get up very slowly. Keep your hands where I can see them,' I order, backing away but keeping my weapon pointed at him. He nods and rises to his feet. The two of us lock eyes, staring at each other, neither blinking.

'Rudra bhaiyya,' I say. 'What a pleasure to meet you.'

CHAPTER EIGHT

'Look at this beauty, sir,' croons Bhoomi, pulling out a laptop from Rudra's backpack.

'Kyon, garib ke paas laptop nahin ho sakta?' scowls Rudra. Now that the shock and fear have worn off, his voice is starting to take on an aggressive edge.

I give him a long, appraising stare. Rudra is young, probably in his mid-twenties. He's slim, has short hair, and a stubble that is just starting to develop into a full-fledged beard. His hair is cut short and he wears spectacles that give him a scholarly look. He looks like he belongs in a library or a classroom. But look closely, and you can see the anger in his eyes, the stubborn set to his mouth hinting that his mild appearance may be deceptive.

Bhoomi, meanwhile, has opened the laptop and is peering at it intently. He whistles softly and mutters, 'Interesting.'

'What's so interesting?' I ask.

'Yeh aisa waisa laptop nahin hai, sir. It's quite fancy. Has a fingerprint reader for biometric identification,' says Bhoomi.

'Aisa?' I turn to Rudra. 'We came to have a chat with you here, but I think we'll now have it in the thaana. Let's go.'

'Why? Just because I have a fancy laptop? I didn't know that's a crime,' sneers Rudra. I'm rapidly starting to develop a dislike for him.

'A lot of things about you don't add up, Rudra. The laptop is just one of them. Let's go,' I say. Then I turn to Bhoomi. 'Keep some of the men with you here. Do a thorough search of all his belongings and the room he was staying in. I'll take him back to the lock-up. And I think I'll pick up Mangtu along the way. We need to have another chat with him.'

But when I reach Mangtu's, I'm told by the boy that he's not around.

'Matlab? Kahaan gaya?' I ask.

The boy shrugs. 'Pataa nahin, sahab. He got a phone call, then quickly packed up and left.'

What about his wife?' I ask.

'She left with him,' he responds.

'Any idea when they'll be back?' I ask.

The boy just shakes his head.

'Damn,' I curse softly. 'Should have taken him in when I had the chance.' I pull out my phone and call Keshav.

'Sir?' he answers.

'Are you back at work?' I ask.

'Yes, sir. I got back some time ago and was told you'd gone for some investigation. I'm really sorry, sir. If I'd known I'd be needed, I wouldn't have gone to the PTA. But the teachers were very upset with my son and my wife said it was very important, so ....' He trails off apologetically.

'A lot has happened, Keshav,' I say. 'We've picked up a suspected Maoist. And Mangtu has disappeared.'

'What? Disappeared? When? How?' he asks.

'If I knew all the answers, we wouldn't have a problem,' I snap, irritated. 'Anyway, I want a search organised for Mangtu. Put the word out at all our chowkis and barricade points. Give his description. And mention that he's travelling with his wife.'

'Yes, sir. Right away, sir,' he says.

'Try to track his phone,' I say, and read out the number. 'Also, find out where that last call he received came from.'

I cut the call and return to my vehicle. Rudra greets me, a disdainful smile on his face. 'All well, sahab?'

'Shut it, unless you want to stir things up!' growls Lokesh. His face is swollen where Rudra had butted him, and he's glaring at the boy with undisguised hostility. Rudra's lip curls in a sneer, but he wisely refrains from saying anything.

As soon as we reach the station, Keshav comes rushing to meet me. 'Anything?' I ask him.

He shakes his head. 'Nothing yet, though I've got our men looking at all exit routes.'

'His phone?' I ask.

'Switched off, sir,' he replies. 'The call to him was made from a PCO. We checked with the owner. He said the caller was a man with grey hair, heavyset and bearded. He overheard him saying something like "watch out, you're about to receive some special guests."'

'In other words, get out,' I say. 'Well, keep looking. Both for Mangtu and this mysterious caller. Meanwhile, I'll go talk to our special guest.'

I walk across to the room we've locked Rudra in. I pull up a chair and sit down, facing him.

'So, my friend. Let's get started,' I tell him.

He looks around. 'Doosra nahin aa raha?' he asks.

'Doosra kaun?' I'm genuinely mystified.

'I thought, whenever questioning takes place, there are two interrogators. Good cop, bad cop,' he explains.

'You watch too many foreign shows,' I reply. 'Yahaan par main hi hoon. If you don't cooperate, I'll start off as bad cop and then move on to being worse cop.'

'Brrr, I'm terrified,' he shudders mockingly.

I ignore his sarcasm. 'Tum yahaan ke toh nahin lagte?' I begin.

'I'm a PhD student. I was staying in the village as part of

my research work on how tribals coexist with modernity,' he replies.

'A PhD student, eh? Impressive,' I reply. 'Toh hum ko dekh kar bhaage kyon?'

'I'm not going to answer any more questions. I want to see a lawyer,' he says.

'You attacked a police officer on duty. That's a serious offence. You're in big trouble. I suggest you cooperate fully,' I say.

He shakes his head stubbornly. 'Keep your advice to yourself. Why am I in trouble? For being a student? I'm not some illiterate tribal you can browbeat. I know my rights. I want to see a lawyer.' He leans back in his chair dismissively.

His arrogance triggers a wave of anger in me. I have this sudden urge to grab his head and bang it hard on the table. I fight it down, take a deep breath, rise from the table and walk away.

Back in my room, a thought strikes me. I check the photos I recovered from Darshan's cabin. They're up on my soft board. I scan them one by one, until I come to the group photo. Rudra is standing with the other volunteer teachers at the back.

Someone clears his throat behind me. I turn around and find Keshav, Bhoomi and Gayaram at the door. I wave them in.

Gayaram points at one of the students sitting in the front row. 'That's the chottu who was carrying letters to Mangtu.'

I nod. 'Looks like they'd pretty much infiltrated Darshan's classes.' I turn to Bhoomi. 'Aur kuch mila?'

Bhoomi smiles and holds up two clear plastic bags with a mobile phone in each. 'One of these phones was in his pocket. It's his personal phone and he seems to use it for routine activities. The other phone, though, is very interesting. It turns out that this is the one that belonged to Dhruva's assistant. It was switched off and kept under the pillow in the bedroom where Rudra was staying.'

'Hmm, two phones for two lives. Looks like he was using

the regular phone for his normal life and the second one for his clandestine activities. Anything else?' I ask.

'Oh yes, sir,' says Bhoomi, beaming. 'Uss kamre mein toh poora khazaana tha. It seems the young man is part of the editorial team at the Maoist journal, *Revolutionary Voice*. He seems to have been in the process of compiling the latest newsletter. We found quite a few printouts.'

'Make some photocopies and put them on my desk,' I say.

Bhoomi holds up a thick folder bulging with papers and places it on my desk. 'Already done, sir.'

'Great,' I say. 'Anything else?'

He holds up a blank sheet of paper. 'I found this lying on a table next to his bed. But there's nothing written on it. Maybe it just got printed out blank?'

'Then it should have been with the rest of the papers. Why was it kept separately? Anyway, please put that on my desk too,' I say. 'Have you been able to unlock his laptop?'

'Not yet, sir. We just need to do a little hand-holding. That will get the job done right away,' says Bhoomi.

'I didn't hear that,' I say immediately. 'Okay. Let me read the printouts now. Report back to me when you get the laptop unlocked.'

The men leave the room. I open the folder and begin picking out pages for reading. The first sheet of paper is titled 'Standing Instructions for All Comrades'.

Standing Instructions for All Comrades

1. All comrades will follow strict discipline. Any breach of discipline will invite strict action.
2. All guerrilla units will move in predetermined formation.
3. After reaching camp sites, guerrilla units must immediately post sentries and then proceed to secure the surrounding area.

4. All weapons must be cleaned regularly and kept in good working condition.
5. All comrades must keep their weapons close by, and within arm's reach at all times. Weapons are not to be handed over to anybody else.
6. Roll call must be taken every morning, followed by a briefing on all important matters.
7. Only comrades capable of hurling objects more than 20 metres are to be given hand grenades for use in action.
8. All comrades are required to read *Revolutionary Voice* and make sure it is read by others.
9. Identified police informers will be arrested and tried in a people's court.
10. If found guilty, they will be given exemplary punishment so that others are not tempted to repeat their crime.

The 5 Pillars of Discipline

1. The relevant committee's orders are to be implemented without question. Usually, a death sentence can only be awarded by a zonal committee. However, in a combat or emergency situation, where the zonal committee is not available for guidance, the local unit commander's instructions will be treated as final.
2. Suggestions can be made and discussions can be held while plans are being formed. But once a plan has been finalised, it must be executed without any doubt or dissent.
3. Whatever material or equipment is seized from the enemy is to be handed over to the party. It will then be reallocated, based on logistical and strategic considerations. No individual claim will be entertained.
4. The weapon allotted to you is to be preserved as carefully as your life.
5. In the course of action, all comrades must strictly carry out

the tasks assigned to them and not deviate from them in any manner.

I take a brief break to call for a cup of tea, then leaf through the pages again. Another document catches my eye. It's titled 'Our Financial Policy'.

Our Financial Policy

In order to improve economic resources and regulate expenditure, it is necessary to have centralised policy and planning. The national-level Central Committee (CC) shall act as the 'nodal agency' to formulate guidelines on financial matters and allocate funds.

The State Committees (SCs) shall examine and ratify the annual budget of the lower-level committees, ranging from the Area Committees (ACs) to Regional Committees (RCs). The SCs shall also maintain state reserves. The Zonal Committees (ZCs) shall allocate funds as per the budget plan and coordinate with various lower-level committees up to the AC and various departments. The basic unit for the collection of funds, expenditure and accounting shall be the ZCs.

Taxes to Be Charged to Finance the Revolutionary Struggle

In order to raise funds to finance the revolutionary struggle, business and economic activity may be allowed in areas controlled by Maoist forces. However, they will be required to make the following contributions:

1. Brick kilns—Rs 20,000/- per year
2. Crushers—Rs 10,000/- per year
3. Compressors—Rs 10,000/- per year (for breaking stones)
4. Rice mills (large)—Rs 100,000/- per year
5. Bauxite mining—20% of total tender
6. Sand mining—10% of total tender
7. Petrol pump—Rs 20,000/- per year

8. Rs 5,000/- for every truckload of coal that is transported, legal or illegal

The trade in tendu leaves, used to make bidis, is a classic example of obscene profits being made, based on oppression of the poor. Our tribal brothers and sisters are forced to slave in sub-human conditions and are paid a pittance for their back-breaking labour while the leaves they collect and pack are sold for crores at auctions. While we will continue to support agitations led by our overground workers and front organisations for better working conditions and wages for our tribal brethren, a rate of Rs 150/- will also be levied per standard bag from tendu leaf contractors.

Levies will also be imposed on Public Works Department contractors, depending on the nature of work and its cost. While it may be as low as 1 per cent in case of construction of schools and drinking water supply schemes, it can go up to 20 per cent in case of works relating to exploration of minerals, building of bridges, roads, culverts and power projects, the railways and industry.

In order to give the local population the satisfaction that they are also helping to finance the revolution, taxes may be collected from households in areas under our control. The amount can vary from Rs 10/- per month to up to Rs 2,000/- per month, depending on the income of the household. In case a family is unable to pay cash, it can be asked to deposit paddy to grain banks set up by the people's government. This paddy can be loaned to poor families in times of distress and need, and also be used to feed our soldiers.

Expenditure Guidelines

Comrade Mao had said that the hallmarks of a good communist are a simple life and hard work. Accordingly, all comrades are instructed to adhere to the following limits for expenditure on personal needs:

Item	Monthly Spending (in Rs)
Pocket money	100
Kurta/shirt	200
Dhoti	190
Pyjamas	150
Lungi	90
Underwear	40
Sari	225
Bag	45
Shoes	200
Petticoat	90
Blouse	60
Slippers	90
Trousers	275

Child revolutionaries aged below 12 years will receive pocket money of Rs 50/- per month. Those aged between 12 and 15 and above will receive pocket money of Rs 75/- per month while those above 15 will receive the full allowed sum of Rs 100/- per month.

Those with weak eyesight and those aged above 50 years will be allowed to use personal two-cell torches, but these must be maintained for as long as possible and used only when essential. Every battle formation will be allotted a couple of flashlights and smaller torches, if required.

Use of mobile phones is strictly prohibited. One phone may be kept with each unit commander and sub-zonal committee head and requested for emergency purposes by any comrade, but the phone must be switched off immediately after use and the team must move out of the area at once. It is entirely the commander or committee head's prerogative to determine whether or not the request to use the phone qualifies as an emergency and refuse permission if he believes that is not the case. Each phone must be kept for at least five years. In case it needs to be replaced before that, an explanation must be submitted to the zonal committee.

'No wonder we were having such a hard time tracking down the mobile that was called to alert them about the patrol leaving camp,' I mutter to myself. I leaf through the papers, and then sit up as I see one with a very interesting heading.

Ensuring Secrecy of Important Messages

Security agencies now have an array of devices and decryption software available that render it unsafe to send electronic messages. While ways can be found around this, for example by using apps like Telegram in which the messages self-destruct, sometimes, the old ways are the best. Very important messages may be hand delivered by overground workers. However, they should either be encrypted, using a previously agreed upon code, or invisible ink should be used.

Given that comrades living in the forest area may not always have access to elaborate materials, it is best to stick to simple ways to make invisible ink. There are two very simple methods.

1. Write with an acidic liquid like lemon juice or vinegar directly on the paper. After the paper is fully dried, apply heat to it, and the writing will become visible. The heat source could be light bulb, a gas stove, or a simple fire (make sure not to accidentally burn the paper, though!)
2. Mix half a cup of water with one tablespoon of baking soda. Use a small paintbrush or cotton swab to write a message on a sheet of paper and let it dry fully. In order to make the message visible, you'll need to apply a reagent. This can be done by thoroughly mixing a half cup of rubbing alcohol with one teaspoon of turmeric. Use a small paintbrush to paint the sheet of paper with the reagent and the message will be revealed.

'Well, well, well, that's interesting,' I mutter. 'I wonder if that's what the blank sheet of paper is about.' I pick it up and sniff to see if I can identify the smell of lemon juice or baking soda, but if it's there, it's too subtle for me to detect.

I call for Bhoomi, hand him the blank sheet and then tell him about the invisible ink. 'Check it out, but be careful. Don't damage the paper,' I say. 'Oh, any luck with the laptop?'

He nods. 'We've got it unlocked, sir. We're looking at the files. A lot of it seems to be genuine research material. Very heavy-duty intellectual stuff. I'll let you know in case we come across anything interesting.'

'Okay, let me know the moment you find something useful,' I say. As Bhoomi leaves, a wave of exhaustion washes over me. My eyes are aching. I lean back in my chair and shut my eyes for a moment.

'Sir, sir?'

I open my eyes and find Bhoomi looking at me, concerned. I realise with a start that I must have dozed off.

'I'm okay, thanks,' I say, rubbing my eyes and sitting up straight. 'Anything interesting?'

Bhoomi hands me the sheet of paper we'd taken from Rudra. It's no longer blank. In fact, it's covered with what looks like bright red paint, under which some writing is clearly visible.

'We tried both methods. The second one worked,' he said. 'A very interesting letter.'

CHAPTER NINE

Dear Comrade P,

As you know by now, we have successfully implemented the plan that was devised in the last meeting of the National War Council. The ambush at Ambuja was a massive blow to the reactionary, oppressive forces and sent a powerful message that reverberated not just in India but across the world. It has served as an impressive demonstration of our power and capability. It has been a huge psychological victory for us, and resulted in a significant boost in new recruits volunteering to join the revolutionary forces.

It is now time to take our campaign to the next level. So far, our major actions have taken place in areas controlled by us. To strike fear into the enemy and drive home the point that no one is safe from us anywhere, we need to stage a massive attack in the national capital. The target must be appropriately high value, in fact, it should ideally be the highest possible value. We can consider taking him down when he ventures out of his stronghold, as he does quite frequently. You are requested to begin exploring how we can 'shorten the chain' of forces arraigned against us, preferably right from the top.

Looking forward to hearing from you, and assuring you of all possible help,

Lal Salaam, S

'So, they're planning an attack in Delhi? But who is the high-value target they're talking of?' I muse. I stretch and walk over to where Bhoomi is sitting, reading though the files on the laptop. Gayaram is sitting next to him companionably, sipping tea.

'The letter was signed "S". Any idea who that might be?' I ask.

Gayaram and Bhoomi exchange glances. 'The zonal committee head in this area is someone called Sooraj, sir,' says Gayaram. 'The letter may have been written by him. Maybe this fellow was going to take the letter to Delhi.'

'It's a thought,' I concede, then gesture at the laptop. 'Anything interesting?'

Bhoomi shakes his head. 'Not so far, sir.'

'Hmm. Have you tried looking at his mails?' I ask.

Bhoomi nods. 'His email ID is RS0105@gmail.com. When you click on the mail icon, it takes you straight to the Gmail home page with his email ID already in the box, but I have no idea what his password is. I asked him, but he flatly refused to tell me. Ulta, I got a lecture on the right to privacy.'

'RS0105?' I ask.

Bhoomi nods. 'His name is Rudra Samant, so that accounts for the RS. As for 0105, well, it could be his birthday. Or it could be the first of May, Labour Day.'

'Hmm. Don't you have any password-cracking software?' I ask.

Bhoomi shakes his head mournfully. 'The cyber cell at Raipur might have it. Sir, you're sure to know someone there. Get them on it, na.'

'Theek hai, karta hoon,' I say. 'But first, let me try something.'

Bhoomi looks at me quizzically, but steps aside so that I can access the laptop. I key in 'Lal salaam'.

It works. 'Waah sir, kya baat hai!' whoops Bhoomi as the inbox opens.

Only, it's empty.

Bhoomi's cry of excitement fades into silence as we stare at the blank screen in dismay.

'Wait,' I say, pointing to the line at the bottom of the screen. It says 'Mailbox twenty per cent full.'

'How can the mailbox be both empty and twenty per cent full at the same time?' I ask, puzzled.

Bhoomi sits up. 'Check his trash, sir,' he says. 'Lots of people delete mails only once. They don't realise that it will lie around in the trash for a few more days unless you go there and delete it again.'

Sure enough, the trash contains several mails. 'Waah Bhoomi, first time tumne kaam ki baat ki hai,' I say approvingly. Then I turn to the screen and begin reading the mails.

To: PP1967@gmail.com
Re: Threat at Ambuja

Dear Comrade P,

I am writing to you on the urging of Comrade S as a worrying situation is developing in Ambuja. As you know, revolutionary forces often have to deal with cruel and oppressive officers of the state machinery. Such officers actually help our cause, because they make it easier for us to arouse the public against the state. However, the real threat arises from officers who attempt to drive a wedge between the local populace and revolutionary forces.

One such challenge has arisen in Ambuja. In the past, the police and CRPF had confined themselves largely to the boundaries of the district while the people's army held undisputed sway in the forest areas neighbouring the town. However, an IPS officer on deputation with the CRPF, Darshan Kumar, is actively attempting to alter the balance of power. He has launched an outreach to the common people, and is organising medical camps for the local populace and classes for young students. At the same time, he has begun area-dominating exercises in strength, pushing in further and further into our stronghold. And he is also attempting to squeeze our sources of revenue dry.

If his efforts prove successful, they will not only severely damage our cause in Ambuja, but may also embolden others elsewhere to follow suit. We must not only execute him, it must be done in such a way that no one else will ever dare to undertake similar measures after seeing the fate that befell him.

We have already set our plan in motion and infiltrated his classes. In his naivete, the fool does not realise that we are now aware of most of his movements. Sooner or later, he will venture out on another jungle patrol. Whenever he does, we will be ready to strike with maximum impact.

We have even identified a suitable ambush site. It offers multiple advantages, like a narrow path in which people can only move in double file, abundant vegetation cover on both sides in which to conceal our soldiers and a nearby hillock with a clear line of fire. The path can easily be mined. Once the ambush is launched, we can easily funnel the enemy into a killing zone.

However, to make sure that the operation is a total success, we need to deploy as many fighters as possible. We also need to equip them with the best possible weapons and munitions. Comrade S has already sent out word to units in neighbouring districts to start moving towards Ambuja. We have also established contact with an arms dealer and indicated our requirements to him. He has quoted a price that is beyond our capacity. You are requested to look into the matter urgently and, if possible, sanction funds from the central pool for the same.'

Lal Salaam, R

I look at the reply, noting that it is dated a couple of days later.

To: RS0105@gmail.com
Re: Threat at Ambuja

Negotiations done. Money arranged. He'll be in touch with you shortly to finalise pick up.

Lal Salaam, P

The third and final mail in the chain followed close to three weeks later.

To: PP1967@gmail.com
Re: Threat at Ambuja

Mission accomplished. PFA a video you might like. We are showing it to all our cadres and young recruits as a motivational tool. It is always received with cheers and applause.

Lal Salaam, R

I click on the attachment. It begins opening, but it's a heavy file and the process is slow. As I wait for it to open completely, I feel my lower back cramping slightly. I rise to my feet and stretch, then walk around a bit. Suddenly, I hear a gasp from Bhoomi. I turn towards him. He's staring at the screen.

Darshan is propped up against a tree, dead. His face and body have been mutilated, but they are still hacking away at him. Men gather around him, brandishing weapons and flashing V signs. One of them raises two fingers behind Darshan's head, as though to give him horns.

My body has gone numb, but I can hear the blood pounding in my heart, salty tears flooding my mouth. I pull out a handkerchief and mechanically wipe my face clean. Pure murderous rage floods through me, calling out for justice for Darshan and punishment for his killers. A red mist settles on my brain. I find myself walking towards Rudra's holding cell.

Rudra looks up as I enter. 'Back for more questions?' he sneers. 'Can't you get it into your thick skull that I'm not going to talk unless there's a lawyer present? And you can be certain that he'll hear about how your goons forcibly unlocked my laptop ....'

He's still talking when I reach him. I grab him by the hair and slam his head hard onto the table. He yells, a mixture of fear, shock and pain. I lift him off his feet—I register rather detachedly that he's quite light for his size—and hurl him against the wall. He smashes hard into the wall and falls in foetal position to the ground.

I pick him up again and slap him hard on his right cheek. His skin splits and blood pours out. He instinctively covers his face and I punch him in the stomach. He clutches his belly and sinks to his knees. I cuff him hard on the head. He rolls to the ground and curls up. I kick him on his ribs, back, legs, anywhere my feet can get at him.

Dimly, I realise that I'm yelling. 'You butchered him like an animal! Why? Just because he wanted to teach some kids? What did he do to deserve such a death? He was worth more than the whole worthless bunch of you put together.'

There is a flurry of footsteps and I feel hands pulling me away. 'Sir, sir, what are you doing? You'll kill him,' says someone. I can't make out who it is. The voice seems to be coming from very, very far away. I break loose and kick Rudra, who has managed to get onto his hands and knees, sending him smashing into the wall again. Once again, I'm dragged away. I growl in frustration.

'Sir, please don't do this. Get hold of yourself. If you want to give him the third degree, there are other people to do it. Tell us what questions you want asked,' a voice hisses in my ears.

Questions. The word penetrates through the mist that has settled on my brain. I can't kill him. I need to ask him some questions.

'Calm down, sir, please. Are you okay now?' Dimly, I realise that it's Keshav speaking. I take a deep, shuddering breath, not yet trusting myself to speak.

'Take sir to his office. Get him some water, something to cool him down. And get a doctor, right now! We can't afford to have Rudra die here,' orders Keshav.

I look around and see people staring at me, their faces reflecting shock, surprise and curiosity at the sight they've just witnessed. A glass of water is handed to me and I drain it in one gulp.

Rudra is hauled to his feet. His face is a bloody mess. He's taking deep, ragged breaths and wincing every time he breathes. Tears are streaming down his face and he's shaking like a leaf in a gust. I step towards him and he flinches, backing away.

'Sir, please. You need to get back to your desk. I'll take care of things here,' says Keshav. He turns to the men flanking Rudra. 'Arrey, you lot! Why are you still here?' he bellows. 'Bola na, take this chap to the doctor.'

I'm led away to my office and slump down in my chair. This is the first time I've raised a hand on a prisoner. But I have no regrets. As I think about those images of Darshan, my fury rises again. I shut my eyes tightly, trying to will the memory away.

I force myself to breathe deeply, trying to calm down. But the visuals are seared in my brain.

I lose track of how much time has passed before there's a knock on the door. I open my eyes and find Bhoomi looking at me, a curious expression on his face.

'Come in, Bhoomi,' I say, trying to keep my voice calm.

Bhoomi nods and walks into the room. I nod at him to sit down. He does so silently.

'How's he?' I ask.

'Pretty badly wounded, but he'll survive,' replies Bhoomi.

'Good. He still needs to answer several questions. Like who is this PP1967,' I say.

'I can tell you that right away,' says Bhoomi. 'I've been doing some background checks. It's a big fish. Ek baar system se check kar lijiye. Baad mein problem ho sakti hai.'

'Big or small, just give me the name,' I snap.

Bhoomi shrugs, as if to say it's on my head. 'Rudra is actually working on a PhD from DU. His guide is Prakash Padmanabh.'

I sit bolt upright. 'Prakash Padmanabh? Professor Prakash Padmanabh?'

Bhoomi smiles grimly. 'Naam toh suna hi hoga. There is a lot of stuff on him. Here, I printed some off the internet for you.'

I quickly leaf through the articles, which supplement whatever I already know about the man. Prakash Padmanabh is dark and stocky, with piercing eyes and a thick moustache now flecked with grey. A brilliant student, born to an impoverished, barely literate farmer. The first person in his family to study beyond Class VI, his entire education was funded through grants and scholarships. He first shot to fame as a fiery orator and charismatic student leader in Osmania University, where he did his PhD.

He then went on to teach in Delhi University. He also served as visiting faculty in several prestigious colleges in the US and UK, where he befriended many world-renowned academicians and even a few Nobel laureates. He's now confined to a wheelchair thanks to a debilitating disease, but remains as active as ever. One of the articles describes him as an 'inspirational figure who has made light of the challenges posed by his disability to devote his life to the cause of uplifting the dispossessed and the downtrodden'.

'Prakash Padmanabh,' I mutter. 'Well, that explains the PP. And 1967?'

'Could be his birth year?' suggests Bhoomi.

'That's possible,' I agree. 'Though something else happened in 1967.' I quickly do a Google search. A couple of minutes later, I read the result that pops up.

The Naxalbari uprising was an armed peasant revolt in 1967 in the Naxalbari block of the Siliguri sub-division in Darjeeling district, West Bengal, India. It was mainly led by local tribals and the radical communist leaders of Bengal and further developed into the Communist Party of India (Marxist–Leninist) in 1969.

'The Naxalite movement was born in 1967. If it's a coincidence, it's an interesting one,' I say.

Bhoomi nods. 'Very interesting, sir.'

There's something about his tone that seems a little strange. 'Is something the matter?' I ask him.

Bhoomi looks me straight in the eye. 'You should've confided in us, sir.'

'Meaning?'

'After you exploded, I wondered why that video affected you so much. I did some research on Darshan Kumar too. A few pictures on his social media feed were available for public access. His graduation, his marriage, stuff like that. There was a familiar face in many of them,' he says.

There's no point denying it. 'Yes, he was my friend,' I acknowledge.

'A very close friend, it seems. And you haven't told anybody. Do you realise that this whole investigation has become tainted now, sir? Nobody will ever believe that you're capable of handling the case objectively, not after this.'

His voice is mild but his words hit me hard, especially because I know that they're true. The DG had posted me to Ambuja because he trusted me to be objective. But if he hears of this, he'll never let me handle the investigation. And I'm determined to see it through, come what may.

'Who else knows?' I ask.

Bhoomi shakes his head. 'I haven't told anyone else. But that's not to say that people won't put two and two together, like I did.'

'I'll tell people eventually, when I feel the time is right,' I say, relieved that I still have some time. 'But for now, let's go get Prakash Padmanabh.'

'I still think it's a good idea to ask the higher-ups,' says Bhoomi.

'Pehle, complete the investigation. That's when we'll check with them,' I retort. 'Ask the team to pack their bags. Next stop, Delhi.'

CHAPTER TEN

Prakash Padmanabh's home is a pleasant little red-bricked house with a small cottage garden in a quiet locality in the vicinity of Delhi University. The setting sun adds to the idyllic feeling.

This place seems a rare oasis of peace and tranquillity in the bustling national capital. A couple of steps lead up to the veranda where we are standing. There's a ramp with a steel railing next to the steps. Clearly a more recent addition to the house.

We'd reached Delhi in the afternoon. Rudra had been admitted to the hospital under tight security—I didn't want him to make a getaway while undergoing medical treatment. From his mails and other files, it had become clear that Padmanabh functioned as a sort of coordinator and fundraiser for the Maoists. He was also an ace recruiter—he identified and radicalised idealistic young students and then drafted them to the Maoist cause. Rudra himself had come under his sway while studying at the university.

Our first port of call was the local police station; we had to let them know that we'd be picking up a person suspected of being a senior Maoist leader. The harried officer had his hands full with other cases and barely registered what I said. He asked perfunctorily if we needed any assistance and looked visibly relieved when I assured him that we could manage by ourselves.

Standing at the doorstep, I reach for the bell. Then I pause, doubt creeping into my brain for the first time. Are you sure, a voice whispers in my head. Once you do this, there is no turning back.

Bhoomi sees me hesitate. 'Ab aa hi gaye hain to baja bhi doh, sir. Dekha jayega,' he says.

I smile wryly at how our roles have reversed and press the bell firmly. For better or worse, I'm committed now. Dekha jaayega.

The door opens and a woman in a kurta and jeans steps out. Her long hair is tied back in a bun. There are streaks of grey in it, and tiny wrinkles around her eyes and mouth, but she looks youthful otherwise with her slim frame.

Her eyes widen when she sees us in uniform, but her voice is steady when she speaks. 'Yes? What is it?' she asks.

'We are here for Professor Padmanabh,' I say.

'You can speak to me. I'm his wife, Bhanumati,' she says. I recognise her now. She'd been frequently mentioned in the articles that I'd read on Padmanabh online.

An accomplished academician herself, she'd written a couple of books with him, but then let her career take a backseat and devoted herself to caring for him after he developed amyotrophic lateral sclerosis, a progressive nervous system disease that affects nerve cells in the brain and spinal cord, which caused him to be confined to the wheelchair.

'Our work is with the professor,' I reply.

'He's busy with some students right now. Do you have an appointment?' she asks.

'Ma'am, I think our work needs to take priority. We're here to arrest him,' I say calmly.

'What! Do you know what you're saying?' she asks, startled. 'Why are you doing this? Is it because he's written articles criticising the government's policies in tribal areas? My husband has always been anti-establishment. But surely that's no reason to start arresting people?'

'No, ma'am. We're here to arrest Professor Padmanabh on charges of being a Maoist leader, being involved in the ambush that killed seventy-six CRPF men in Ambuja, and for being part of a conspiracy to carry out attacks on high-value targets. We have an arrest warrant for him. Now, I request you to kindly step aside and let us do our job,' I tell her.

My voice is still calm and steady.

'You do know whom you're talking about? My husband is an internationally renowned academician.' Her voice is equally calm, though there is an undertone of anger.

'What's the matter, Bhanu? Is everything okay?' A male voice rings out from inside the house.

She turns to reply, creating a small space. I deftly step through, and into the drawing room. There is very little furniture here, the idea clearly being to create as much space as possible for Padmanabh to manoeuvre his wheelchair. The few chairs and stools have an ethnic look. There's a dining table to one side.

Padmanabh is seated there in his wheelchair. Three earnest-looking youths—two men and a woman—are seated at the table with him. They seem to have been taking notes. All four have teacups next to them, along with a couple of plates of biscuits and chips. They're all startled at the sight of me.

'Good evening, Professor. We're here to arrest you for your involvement with the Maoists. Please cooperate with us and come peacefully,' I say.

'Please, just look at him. He needs special care. What sort of medical facilities do you have in jail? Who'll take care of him there?' asks Bhanumati.

'It's okay, Bhanu. Let me speak to the officer. I'm assuming you have all your paperwork in place?' he asks politely. He's talking to us as though we're guests who've dropped in for tea, without the slightest hint of stress or agitation.

I nod. 'We have an arrest warrant for you, duly authorised by a magistrate. Your arrest memo is ready too. I need you to countersign it, and we need a witness to sign as well.' I gesture at the three students. 'Any one of you will do.'

The young woman rises to her feet, a furious look on her face. 'This is absolutely outrageous,' she says.

'It's okay, I'm sure it's all a misunderstanding,' says Padmanabh in a soothing tone. 'We'll have it cleared up in no time. Let's cooperate with the officer. Please, give me the paper to sign.'

I hand over the paper to him. As he signs, I notice that there's a pronounced tremor in his hand. He catches me looking at it and smiles wistfully. 'Ah, the torture this disease puts one through. Nobody ever truly appreciates good health unless it's gone forever. There, my signature is done. Can one of you also please sign this? And Bhanu, will you please pack all my medicines and write down on a paper when and how many I'm supposed to take?' He smiles at me apologetically. 'I'm so used to her popping up every few hours with my pills that I've never bothered to remember the details.'

Bhanumati bustles away and comes back a few minutes later with a medicine kit and a piece of paper. There's tenderness in her eyes as she bends towards him. He whispers something to her.

'What's that?' I ask, my antenna instantly alert. I lean in to hear their conversation.

'Give them some privacy, you brutes,' screams the female student suddenly.

Startled, I look at her. She launches herself at me, clawing at my face with her nails. I jerk my head back just in time and grab her hands to keep them away from my face. As we struggle, I hear both the young men shouting as well.

The young woman is screaming abuses at me, spraying my face with saliva, struggling wildly. If she had been a man, I would have taken care of the situation in a second. I could have easily taken her down, but I'm reluctant to use force. I grimly hold on to her wrists, hoping she'll tire out.

I feel a hand on my shoulder from behind and react instinctively, pushing the girl away and shoving hard at whoever is trying to grab me. As my hand connects, I realise I've just made contact with a woman. A second later, I hear a cry of pain.

I whip around and find Bhanumati on the floor. Prakash Padmanabh is sprawled next to her. How and when did he get there?

'Everybody just calm down,' I yell.

'You hit me. I was trying to separate the two of you and you hit me,' says Bhanumati.

I spread my hands in apology. 'I didn't mean to. I didn't realise it was you,' I say.

'And you and your men attacked my husband too. Get him an ambulance right away,' she snaps, her calm demeanour fraying.

'What! We never touched him. He doesn't need an ambulance. We'll just get him back on his wheelchair right away,' I say.

Lokesh and Gayaram rush to help him. Bhanumati immediately covers him protectively with her own body. 'Don't you dare come near him,' she says.

'Ma'am, please step aside. We need to take him to the police station,' I say.

'If you want to arrest him, you'll have to arrest me first,' she says. Then she looks around. 'But I don't see any women officers with you.'

It's true. We hadn't brought any women officers because I'd foolishly never anticipated that something like this would happen. Silently, I curse myself for my stupidity. Then, suddenly, I realise that the two male students have their phones out and are busy recording the whole drama. I point at them. 'Hey, stop doing that! Somebody, take those phones away.'

The young men hastily back away, simultaneously jabbing at their screens before putting the phones away. I turn back and glare at Bhanumati and Padmanabh.

'Ma'am, I'm asking you politely one more time. Please step aside and let us do our work,' I say.

She shakes her head stubbornly. 'He's physically challenged and he needs special care. And I don't trust you goons with him. If you're sick enough to attack a handicapped man, who knows what else you might do to him.'

'Let me say this one more time, we never laid a finger on him,' I say. I'm starting to get really irritated by now.

'Oh yes, he just fell to the floor all by himself,' she shoots back sarcastically.

'Actually, I think that's exactly what happened. And I think you and your young friends here have staged an elaborate show for the benefit of the video camera. But I came here to do a job and I'm not leaving without finishing it. So please move.' My voice is up a few decibels by now.

'Fine, then arrest me and you can move him,' she says. There's a triumphant note in her voice. She thinks she has me cornered. But she doesn't realise I can get very stubborn too.

'Have it your way,' I say. 'I'm going to call the local thaana and ask them to send some women cops. You can keep lying on the floor till they get here, and then they'll arrest you and we can all proceed to the lock-up.'

Padmanabh stirs slightly at my words. 'Please let me speak to my wife,' he says. 'And I'd really appreciate it if we could have a conversation without you trying to eavesdrop.'

They have a hurried conversation in low tones and then Bhanumati finally looks at me and nods grudgingly. 'He'll come to the police station. But we have a van specially modified for his needs. I'll drive him there myself. One of your men can accompany us in the van if you like.'

I nod, careful not to let the relief show on my face. As Padmanabh is settled into his wheelchair, I tell him, 'In case you wish to notify a lawyer, please do so now. We leave for Ambuja tomorrow morning, and we'll take you straight to the court for your hearing once we reach there.'

He smiles at me benignly, but there is a cold look in his eyes as he looks at me appraisingly. 'Oh, I very much doubt I'll be spending the night in jail. Or going to Ambuja for that matter.'

CHAPTER ELEVEN

We're about five minutes away from the local thaana when the phone rings. I hurriedly fish it out of my pocket and look at the name flashing on the screen.

Devika Doria.

I frown in surprise. I've been so busy in the past few days with the investigations that I haven't spoken to her or messaged her at all. Why is she calling out of the blue? Well, only one way to find out.

I press the green button to answer. 'Well, this is unexpected ....' I begin.

'Are you out of your mind?' she asks, her voice frantic with worry.

'I'm sorry?' I say, genuinely puzzled.

'What were you thinking? Wait, were you even thinking?'

'Devika, what's going on? Can you please stop speaking in riddles?' My befuddlement is growing by the minute.

She draws a deep breath, as if calming herself, and then says, 'There's a clip of yours that has gone viral. It shows you manhandling one woman and then shoving another to the ground. Meanwhile, a handicapped man is lying on the floor and writhing in agony. Then you threaten some students who are filming this on their mobiles. And then it turns out that this handicapped man is none other than Professor Prakash Padmanabh—and you and your men have attacked him!'

'What? That's complete nonsense. We did no such thing. It's a set-up,' I splutter.

'It looks pretty convincing,' she replies. 'I got the clip a few minutes ago and you can bet that all the major newspapers, TV channels and websites will have got it too by now. For your sake, I hope you have a convincing explanation ready.'

'We did not attack anybody. It's a set-up. He and his wife are perfectly fine. They're following me in their own vehicle. I'm not saying this as an officer to a journalist. I'm telling you this as a friend. I don't lie to my friends,' I say. I suddenly realise that it's really important to me that she believes me.

She's silent for a long moment. 'Fine, then let me also give you some advice as a friend. Don't even think of bringing them to Ambuja. Register whatever case you have to, ask them your questions, then leave them there and come back. All hell will break loose if you try bringing them back with you.'

I'm about to reply when the phone rings again. I look at the screen. It's DGP Satyadev Chandrakar. 'I'm sorry, I've got to go,' I mumble.

'I understand. You take care,' she says and ends the call.

Chandrakar's voice booms into my ear. 'Vikram, what the hell is going on? Why are you in Delhi? Did you check with anyone before going there?'

'It's part of the investigation into the Darshan Kumar case. We have enough evidence to nail Padmanabh,' I assure him.

'To hell with your investigation. This is a nationally sensitive matter. And you didn't even see fit to keep anyone in the loop? Get back to Raipur right away and brief me,' he yells. 'Oh God, the CM's calling. This is a bloody disaster. Salvage the situation as best you can. Okay, bye.'

He hangs up abruptly. I glare at the phone, fighting the urge to bang it hard on the dashboard. It's not the phone's fault. Then I look at the rearview mirror and frown. There's no sign of Padmanabh's vehicle. I call Bhoomi, who is accompanying them.

'Kahaan ho?'

'Sir, we're stuck at a roundabout. Madam says we'll reach in about five minutes,' he responds.

'Sambhaal ke. They may have more tricks up their sleeve,' I say.

Beside me, the driver curses softly. I look up to find the entire road in front of the police station jammed with press vehicles and OB vans. Several reporters from different TV channels are speaking animatedly into their mikes.

The driver honks furiously and repeatedly, managing to manoeuvre us through the gate. As I get out of the vehicle, one of the cameramen yells out, 'Yeh toh wahi video clip waala hai.'

The whole gaggle of reporters rushes towards me, mikes outstretched. The questions rain down thick and fast.

'Sir, aapne Professor Padmanabh ko kyon maara?'

'Is he safe? What are the charges against him?'

'Is he being targeted because of his outspoken anti-establishment interviews and writings?'

'Where's he right now? Is it true that you are going to get him in an encounter?'

I walk through the crowd grimly, not saying anything, Gayaram and Lokesh flanking me. An officer appears at the entrance. I realise it's the DCP in charge of the area.

'Ek minute, ek minute, please,' he yells at the reporters pursuing me, and pulls me aside. 'Arrey yaar, tum kamaal karte ho. It's one thing to court danger and controversy, it's another to bring it to my door! Where's the professor?' He is speaking in a low tone that only I can hear.

'He and his wife are following in their vehicle. One of my men is with them,' I mumble back.

'What?' Recovering quickly, he hisses, 'Call your man right away and tell him to turn back before this bunch realises they're here. Otherwise, they'll hold an impromptu press conference in front of my station and it'll go live nationally. Do it now.'

'He's a suspect. I need to question him,' I argue.

'Bhai merey, you've put us in a tough spot. I'm attempting damage control here, and you are more interested in your questioning? Go back to the backwaters that you came from before things heat up further. We can figure out everything else later.'

He steps out and addresses the reporters. 'Your attention, please. Professor Padmanabh is safe and well, and so is his wife. A Special Investigation Team from Chhattisgarh has come down to meet him. There was an unfortunate misunderstanding, for which we respectfully apologise.'

'Will they take him back with them? Can you assure us there will be no encounter on the way?' yells one of the reporters.

'No, he will not be taken back. If we need to speak to him, we will do it right here. And I can assure you no harm will come to him. I appeal to all of you, please don't spread rumours and misinformation,' he says.

He turns around and walks back to me. 'Well, did you get it sorted?'

Before I can answer, Lokesh speaks up. 'Yes, sir. I called them. They're headed back.'

'Oh, thank God!' says the DCP and stomps off. I give Lokesh a reproachful glare.

'Sorry sir, it was the right call to take,' Lokesh says.

'Phir kisi din unse nipat lenge,' says Gayaram soothingly.

I nod, not trusting myself to speak. Grudgingly, I concede to myself that Lokesh did the right thing under the circumstances, even though I'm livid with him for doing so. Finally, when I've regained my composure somewhat, I open my mouth to speak. Right on cue, the phone rings.

'Wonderful,' I say, yanking out my phone and looking at the screen. It's Chandrakar.

'Update?' he asks. I fill him in quickly. He hears me out, then sighs. 'This is a real mess you've got into.'

'I'll come to Raipur tomorrow and brief you, sir,' I say.

'No, you need to be in Delhi tomorrow. The Supreme Court has stepped into the matter. An international NGO called Friends of Liberty approached the court, alleging major human rights violations. They're asking for anticipatory bail for Padmanabh and also demanding that all charges against him be squashed.'

'If they want bail, shouldn't they go to the lower courts and the High Court before approaching the SC?' I ask.

'Well, the SC appears to be willing to give them a hearing. The case is listed for tomorrow in Justice Behramjee's court. You've heard of him, right?' asks Chandrakar.

'Yes, sir,' I reply.

Justice Behramjee has a well-deserved reputation for being a stickler for the rule of law and due process. Over the years, many unfortunate police officers have been at the receiving end of severe tongue-lashings from him.

'It gets even better. The lawyer representing Prakash Padmanabh is Jitendra Goyal,' adds Chandrakar.

My eyebrows shoot up. Goyal is one of India's top defence lawyers. He charges more for one hearing than Chandrakar and I together get paid in a year.

'Padmanabh's friends are really rolling out the heavy artillery,' I observe.

'He has very powerful friends, with connections in extremely high places. You've stirred a hornet's nest, Vikram. I hope it doesn't come back to bite you. Well, all the best at the hearing,' says Chandrakar and hangs up.

Goyal is tall, about 10 kg overweight, has a receding hairline and sports a goatee. Justice Behramjee, in contrast, is thin to the point of being emaciated, with a thick mane of brownish hair which has one white streak running prominently through it.

The preliminary hearing is taking place inside the judge's chamber so that we can—as he puts it—'avoid the media circus'. He peers at us through glasses resting halfway on the bridge of his nose, then nods as if satisfied.

'Right, gentlemen. Now that everybody's here, let's commence proceedings,' he says. 'Mr Verma, what are the charges against the professor?'

The prosecutor, a mousy-looking individual with thick glasses, clears his throat and begins. 'Your Honour, there are extremely serious charges against Professor Padmanabh. He is accused of being part of the Maoist leadership, raising funds for them, recruiting and indoctrinating young people into their cadres, and most worryingly, being part of a conspiracy to carry out attacks on high-value targets in urban areas.'

Justice Behramjee raises his eyebrows. 'Those are serious charges indeed. I'm sure the prosecution will have enough evidence to substantiate them?'

'Well, Your Honour, most of it is in Ambuja, since the original plan was to take Professor Padmanabh for trial there,' Verma replies.

'Hmm.' The judge rubs his chin thoughtfully, then turns to Goyal. 'Mr Goyal, let's hear what you have to say.'

'Your Honour, my client is a scholar of international repute. The police, on some trumped-up charges, not only arrested him but also roughed him up. For good measure, they also assaulted his wife. This is an absolute outrage. The actions of the police have not only sullied the uniform, they have shamed India in front of the entire world. You can be certain that the shocking images that we all saw have been shared around the world, and the impartiality and integrity of our system of justice will be called into action,' thunders Goyal.

'I suggest you worry about your client and let me worry about the system of justice,' says the judge tartly. 'If you have a point, please get to it.'

I supress a smile. It's good to see that the judge is even-handed with his withering sarcasm.

Goyal looks a bit taken aback, but quickly composes himself. 'Your Honour, we request that you please grant the professor bail till you are in a position to see this evidence for yourself and determine whether the police actually have a case. We fear for the professor's safety and well-being in case the police are allowed to take him to Ambuja. We apprehend that he may not reach there alive,' he says.

'That's ridiculous,' I burst out spontaneously.

Goyal swivels to look at me. 'SP sahab, you may be used to being the lord and master of all you survey in the boondocks, but may I remind you that over here, you are not supposed to speak unless you're spoken to.' He turns back to Justice Behramjee. 'As I was saying, Your Honour, we fear that some convenient accident may befall Professor Padmanabh. Or, who knows, he may be shot dead trying to make a dramatic getaway.'

'Oh please,' says the prosecutor, unexpectedly showing some spirit. 'He's confined to a wheelchair. How is he supposed to try and make a dramatic escape?'

'Exactly!' says Goyal triumphantly. 'Not only is my client well known, he also unfortunately suffers from a disease that has left him immobile. He is hardly in a position to suddenly vanish. Besides, given the fragile state of his health, he needs constant medical attention and care. I request you to grant him bail and also transfer all legal proceedings to this city.'

'Hmm, that seems reasonable enough to me,' says the judge. 'Bail is set for Professor Padmanabh at Rs 50,000. He is not to leave the city without seeking the police's permission till such time as the case is on. In a week from now, I'll review the prosecution's argument and decide whether it should be quashed or trial should be allowed to proceed.' He looks meaningfully at the prosecutor. 'I look forward to seeing just how substantial the evidence against him is.'

CHAPTER TWELVE

'So, let me get this straight. The first link in the chain of evidence is the mobile phone?'

Goyal is looking at me quizzically, his head cocked to one side. This time, we're in a proper courtroom, which is completely packed. Several reporters are busy taking notes. The prosecution has presented its case, and I'm being cross-examined.

'That is correct,' I reply. On the advice of Verma, the prosecutor, I'm deliberately keeping my answers as short and to the point as possible, because Goyal is famous for seizing upon the slightest ambiguity and tying up the witness in knots.

'Hmm, so just to make sure that I've understood things properly, let me recapitulate. This is the mobile phone that was used to inform the Maoists that the CRPF patrol had left the camp?'

'Yes,' I say tersely.

'Well, that's a very crucial piece of evidence indeed,' says Goyal. He strolls over to his seat, taking his time. 'So I gather you asked the mobile service provider to give you the call detail records of this phone, and that's how you traced its ownership?'

'Yes, I did,' I say.

'And, of course, you formally wrote to them asking them to provide the records, as is required?' he asks.

'Of course I did,' I begin, and then pause. I know I meant to, but did I get around to actually doing so?

'Take your time, think about it carefully. We wouldn't want you to commit perjury. That's a very grave offence, you know,' says Goyal.

I frantically try to recall if I actually wrote that damn mail. I know Bhoomi reminded me to. But then, something or the other kept coming up.

'We're waiting, SP Vikram Singh,' Goyal reminds me. His sugary tone is really starting to get on my nerves.

'I don't recall,' I say, which is the most honest answer I can come up with.

From the corner of my eye, I see Verma visibly slump.

'I understand. You have so many responsibilities to worry about, how can you be expected to recall something so trivial?' soothes Goyal. 'Well, allow me to assist you. I made inquiries from the mobile service provider and they never received any such request. I believe they will be taking action against the employee who shared the information with you without following due process.' He turns to the judge. 'Since the information was procured illegally, the defence requests the court to kindly rule it inadmissible as evidence.'

'But ... but that's just a technicality,' I splutter.

'These technicalities, as you put it, are very important, SP Singh,' says Goyal. 'If the police gets into the habit of ignoring them, then who knows what "other" short-cuts they may start taking to come up with convenient results?' He turns to Justice Behramjee. 'Your Honour?'

The judge wrinkles his brow in thought, then nods slowly. 'Defence's request is granted. The CDRs will not be admissible as evidence.'

Goyal bows. 'Thank you, Your Honour.' He turns to me. 'By the way, was the phone we're referring to retrieved from Mr Rudra Samant in person?'

'No, it was found hidden in his room,' I reply shortly.

'So ... it's entirely possible that it was planted there by the police?' asks Goyal.

'Objection, Your Honour,' says the prosecutor instantly.

'Sustained. Counsel will please refrain from speculative allegations,' says the judge.

Goyal holds up his hands apologetically. 'Forgive me, My Lord.' He turns back to me. 'There was another phone found on Rudra Samant, was there not?'

'Your Honour, is this case about Prakash Padmanabh or Rudra Samant? Why is the counsel constantly bringing him up?' asks the prosecutor.

'Because the whole so-called case against my client rests on material that was allegedly taken from Rudra Samant, and I believe there are grave doubts about its authenticity. Please answer the question, SP Singh.'

'Yes, another phone was found on him,' I acknowledge.

'I see. And what did the investigation into that phone reveal?' asks Goyal.

I shrug. 'It was a normal phone. There was nothing untoward about it. Just the usual calls and messages that you'd expect a student to make.'

'Was it used frequently?' asks Goyal.

'A lot more frequently than the other phone,' I respond.

'So there was nothing incriminating in the phone he used regularly, but there was in a phone that had gone missing a year ago, and was used only sporadically thereafter, and which was not even found on his person?' asks Goyal.

'It was found in his room,' I point out.

'No, it was found in a room where he had been sleeping, after he had already been arrested and taken away from the premises. Can you say with one hundred per cent certainty that it was not planted there by somebody else?' asks Goyal.

'Objection,' says Verma again, instantly. The judge looks thoughtful for a very long time before he finally says, 'Sustained.'

'All right then. So you set off to arrest my client. Before you did that, did you consult any of your seniors?' asks Goyal.

'No. It was a straightforward investigation. I didn't see the need,' I reply curtly.

'You set off to arrest an internationally renowned academician and you didn't even see the need to discuss it with anybody? Were you worried that saner minds might tell you to stand down? Or did you just not want to share the glory and the medals that might follow?' asks Goyal.

'Objection, Your Honour. Counsel is badgering the witness,' says Verma.

'I'm badgering him? My friend, have you seen what the witness does to people who don't answer his questions?' says Goyal mockingly. 'Anyway, I have no further questions for the witness right now, but he may be required later. Witness may please be requested to not leave the courtroom.'

As if I can do so while the case proceedings are underway. I give him a short nod and leave the witness box.

'Your Honour, the defence would now like to call DSP Keshav Rai as its witness,' says Goyal.

Keshav looks decidedly nervous as he shuffles up to the box and takes the oath. Goyal smiles at him benignly. For some reason, I'm reminded of a shark smelling blood.

'DSP Rai, a certain episode took place in the lockup after Mr Samant was arrested. Would you care to tell the court about it?'

'I'm not sure what you mean,' says Keshav hesitantly.

'Let me jog your memory. It involved Mr Samant and SP Vikram Singh. Do you remember now?' says Goyal.

'I ... er ... uh ....' Keshav stammers. I stare at him horrified, feeling as though I've been hit in the stomach with a hammer.

'DSP Rai, let me remind you that you are in a court of law and have sworn to tell the truth. What happened that day?' asks Goyal. 'Answer me or I'll have to conclude that you're deliberately withholding crucial information.' His voice is stern now and there is not even a hint of cordiality.

Keshav looks at me pleadingly, as though to say that he's helpless. I nod slowly.

'We're waiting, DSP Rai,' says Goyal.

Keshav takes a deep breath. 'I heard loud noises coming from the interrogation room. I rushed there and saw Rudra lying on the floor. He was curled up against the wall.' There's a buzz in the courtroom as Keshav says the words.

'Order, order,' says the judge. 'Silence in the court.' He waits for the buzz to subside, then nods at Goyal. 'Please proceed.'

'Thank you, Your Honour. Now, DSP Rai, could you please tell us what SP Vikram Pratap Singh was doing? The truth, and only the truth, if you please.'

Keshav shuts his eyes for a moment and then says something in a voice that is barely a whisper.

'Again, please, DSP Rai. We couldn't hear you,' says Goyal.

Keshav speaks up, loud and clear. 'He was kicking Rudra all over his body.'

The court erupts in bedlam, as if everyone is speaking at the same time. All eyes are on me. I stare straight ahead, stone-faced, bitterly regretting losing my cool that day.

'Order, order,' says the judge, banging his gavel. 'Any more interruptions and I'll have the courtroom cleared.' As the din subsides, he gives me a cold, hard look.

'Right. So you found the SP beating Mr Samant. What did you do next?' asks Goyal.

Keshav fidgets with his collar and clears his throat. 'I held him back and pleaded with him to stop. Then I suggested that we send Rudra to the hospital for medical attention.'

'And was that done?' asks Goyal.

Keshav nods but doesn't say anything.

'I commend you for intervening that day, DSP Rai. You may just have saved an innocent life. And what did the doctor have to say about Mr Samant's injuries?' asks Goyal.

'He said they were pretty bad and he needed to be admitted to the hospital,' says Keshav.

'Oh, come now, DSP Rai. That's such a sweeping generalisation. Let's get a little more specific,' says Goyal. He walks over to his desk, pulls out a paper and begins reading. 'Did the medical report not mention that the patient was severely concussed, had a black eye, large bruises all over the body and a couple of fractured ribs?'

There's an audible gasp from the audience. Goyal holds up the paper and looks grimly at Keshav. 'We can always call the doctor as a witness to refresh your memory, if you need.'

'Er ... yes, I think the medical report noted something like that,' concedes Keshav.

'Thank you for your honesty, DSP Rai. I'm glad some police officers still have a conscience,' says Goyal. It's hard to tell whether or not he's being sarcastic. There's a grave look on his face as he gazes at the packed courtroom, drawing out the moment, turning from side to side. Momentarily, our eyes meet. He stares intently at me. I stare right back, refusing to give him the satisfaction of looking away. Goyal's expression hardens and he turns away to face the judge.

'Your Honour, what we have here is a truly horrifying story of police excess. A promising, idealistic student, the kind of young person any country should be proud of, whose only crime is that he has a social conscience, was arrested on trumped-up charges. We are told that he was very conveniently carrying lots of documents that apparently revealed many Maoist secrets. Given everything that we have seen of the case so far, who is to say that these documents were not written by some overactive mind in the police and planted on this young student? Can we be sure that these documents are not as false and made-up as this whole case itself?'

Goyal pauses for a second, letting that sink in, then continues. 'This young man was brutally tortured. This torture was conducted by SP Vikram Pratap Singh. The same SP Vikram Pratap Singh who then turned up in Delhi to arrest an internationally renowned academician and attacked him and his wife as well. The SP seems to have a very interesting style of investigation—when in doubt, hit out.'

A brief titter runs through the courtroom but quickly subsides.

'Please, this is no laughing matter,' says Goyal. 'It is a matter of deep shame for all of us as concerned citizens of this country that the police feel free to violate basic human rights with such impunity. God alone knows how many more such cases happen every day, deep in the interiors, without ever coming to light. Your Honour, not just this country, the eyes of the whole world are riveted on this case. This honourable court represents the only hope of justice left for my client. I beg of you, please throw out the charges against my client with the contempt that they deserve.'

I glance around the courtroom. The audience is riveted by Goyal. Many seem to be on the brink of tears. I feel the bile rising in my throat, choking me, and force it down. Even before the judge pronounces his verdict, I know what's coming.

'This whole case rests on what can, at best, be described as extremely shoddy investigation. No compelling evidence exists to substantiate any of the charges wilfully and recklessly bandied about by the investigative team. The court dismisses all the charges against the accused and orders that they be freed with immediate effect.'

As the judge finishes reading his statement, there is an uproar. Reporters scramble for the exit, pulling out their mobile phones as they race to break the news. I sit there frozen, unable to move, feeling like my mouth is full of ashes. My hopes of securing justice for Darshan and punishment for his killers lie in tatters.

After a long time, I rise, leadenly putting one foot in front of another. Suddenly, there is a hush. Dully, I wonder what's going on and then realise that I'm standing right in front of Padmanabh. His wife is standing protectively next to him.

He gives me a lazy grin. 'Bad luck, SP. Now go back under the rock from where you crawled out,' he says. I stare back, unable to speak, rage clogging my throat.

Then his wife speaks. 'Come on darling, let's go home. There's no need to waste any more time on these low-lifes.'

I swivel around and walk away, but I can feel his gaze burrowing into my back, his smile mocking me every step of the way.

CHAPTER THIRTEEN

'What could I do, sir? That lawyer put me in a tight spot by summoning me as a witness. I could not stand in court and lie. Kahin naukri chali jaati ....'

Keshav is sweating profusely. It's the first time I've seen him since the day in court, his testimony dealing the final blow to our case against Prakash Padmanabh and Rudra.

Following that fiasco, I was summoned to Raipur by Chandrakar and given a thorough dressing down. I took it quietly, without saying a word. There was nothing he could say or do to me that would be any harsher than the self-hatred I'd been heaping upon myself.

Chandrakar's last words, though, took me by surprise. 'Fortunately for you, you have had an exceptional record up till now and a lot of goodwill within the department. That is the only factor saving you. You deserve to be given a punishment posting. But honestly, what could be worse than the posting you already have? You stay put in Ambuja and try to fix the mess you've created. But for heaven's sake, don't pull another stunt like this one or it will be impossible to save you.'

And that's how I find myself staring silently at Keshav as he stammers in his desperation.

'Relax, Keshav,' I say finally. 'You only told the truth. Nothing wrong with that.'

'Ji, sir. Thank you,' he says, bowing low.

'So what has been going on while I've been away? Are FIRs being filed or not? Have we made progress on any of the old cases?' I ask.

Keshav looks around to make sure we're alone before venturing, 'Sir, please don't take this the wrong way. I'm saying this for your own good. You've just had a narrow escape. Just let things be for a while. Why play the hero?'

I'm about to reply when Bhoomi comes dashing in. 'Sir, we just had an urgent call. Mangtu has been found.'

'What?' I leap up. 'Where is he?'

'There's a river about thirty kilometres from here. Once you cross it, you enter what the Maoists call the "liberated zone". They have complete control over there. A CRPF patrol came across a group of Maoists near the river and there was a skirmish. Two of the Maoists were killed and one was wounded. The others fled. When they went to capture the wounded man, they realised it was Mangtu,' says Bhoomi.

'Are they sure it's Mangtu?' asks Keshav.

'His dhaba's been right outside their camp for years,' replies Bhoomi. 'I'm sure they won't make a mistake in recognising him.'

'Has he said anything?' asks Keshav.

Bhoomi shakes his head. 'He's unconscious. They've brought him to the main hospital in Ambuja.'

'Right, let's go talk to him,' I say.

'I'll come with you, sir,' says Keshav instantly.

'Why don't you stay here and handle things while I'm out, Keshav?'

'Please sir, the last time, things went out of control. I'd like to be there,' says Keshav.

I think about it for a moment, then relent. 'Okay. Bhoomi, get Lokesh and Gayaram. Let's go.'

I jump into the driver's seat. The driver, used to my ways by now, quietly moves to the back. I floor the accelerator as we race towards the hospital. 'Sir, please, sambhaal ke,' pleads Gayaram as I swerve to avoid a herd of cattle on the road.

'Arrey, relax, Gayaramji, we're going to the hospital anyway,' I tell him.

'Sir, I'd prefer not to arrive as a patient,' he says.

At my laugh, he smiles back, 'Arrey sir, you'll understand my fears better once we get there.'

The building comes into view. I stop the vehicle and step out, looking disbelievingly at the sight in front of me. People are sprawled on the roadside, flies buzzing all around them. There is an overpowering stench of sweat and urine. Many are moaning in pain, or in a delirium brought on by fever. Others are staring listlessly into the distance, as though they've lost all hope.

More people are sprawled along the hospital corridors as we enter. Only a few of them are lying on sheets, the rest are on the bare floor. A rat darts in and out, nibbling at the garbage that litters the floor.

I'm stunned. 'What the hell is going on here?'

'Too many people, too few beds, sir,' says Bhoomi. 'This is why most of the local population doesn't even bother to come here. They simply go to some ojha or witch doctor. I'd say the chances of recovery are about the same.'

Keshav grabs a harried-looking doctor who's racing by. 'Excuse me, we need some help. Could you please tell us where Mangtu is? The CRPF would have brought him in?'

The doctor frowns for a moment, then nods. 'Oh yes, the gunshot victim. He's in the ICU. But he's in a coma right now. I'm afraid you can't speak to him until he recovers consciousness.'

'How long is that likely to take?' asks Keshav.

The doctor shrugs. 'It's hard to say with these things.'

'Can we at least see where he is? We need to post a guard,' I say.

The doctor gestures towards a lift. 'Second floor. Room at the end of the corridor.'

I nod my thanks. Keshav and Gayaram are already by the lift door, waiting for it to open. Lokesh and Bhoomi take the stairs and sprint up, disappearing from view in seconds. I decide to follow their example when the lift door opens and Devika Doria steps out.

'Oh, hello,' I say. 'You here?'

She nods, and I notice that her expression is strained. 'Baba had a heart attack.'

'I'm so sorry to hear that. How is he now?'

She makes a face. 'Not good. He's in the cardiac care unit right now, though it's pretty basic. Ideally I'd shift him to a better place, but that's at least six or seven hours' drive away, in Haripur, and the doctors are saying he's in no shape to make the journey. And God only knows whether the ambulance will even have the equipment required.'

'If I can help you in any way, please let me know,' I say. 'If you need an escort vehicle when he has to be moved, I'll be happy to provide it.'

'Thank you, I appreciate that,' she responds.

'Arrey, anything for a friend,' I say.

A smile appears on her face, even though it's only a wan one. 'I haven't been much of a friend to you, have I? You've been going through a bad time. A lot of my colleagues in the media raked you over the coals, in many cases quite unfairly, I thought.'

I shrug. 'That's okay. They don't know me. You do.'

'Still, I didn't even call you or come to meet you. In fact, this is the first time we're talking since ... well ... the day I called to yell at you over the phone,' she says.

'That was the first of many I got over the next few days,' I say wryly. I see her looking contrite and hasten to reassure her. 'Please, don't feel bad about it. You have far bigger things to worry about right now. Focus on getting your father back to good health as quickly as possible. I have yet to savour that special dish he makes for you.'

She smiles, a much fuller one this time. 'Aapke mooh mein ghee shakkar.'

'Ghee shakkar? Bas? And here I am, salivating over mutton curry.'

She laughs out loud and punches my arm. 'Mutton curry it is.'

I smile back at her and then realise that Keshav and Gayaram are still waiting by the lift, looking at us curiously.

'Right, duty calls,' I sigh. 'I'll see you soon.'

'Okay. I have to go talk to the doctor anyway. See you,' she says.

I wave goodbye and start walking towards the lift. Just then, Keshav's phone rings. He takes the call and an expression of concern appears on his face. 'Kab? Kahaan? Kitne log hain?' he asks. He listens briefly, then says, 'Theek hai. Update dete rehna,' and disconnects.

'What's up?' I ask.

'A group of villagers is blocking the main road just outside town. They're alleging that the Naxals were killed in a fake encounter and want the bodies handed over to them.'

I resist the urge to groan. 'Where are the bodies?'

'In the mortuary, sir. A post-mortem has to be conducted before they can be handed over. It's a legal requirement,' says Keshav.

'Well, can't we just tell the villagers that?' I ask.

Keshav shrugs. 'Someone needs to go tell them. And it needs to be done fast. The situation can deteriorate rapidly.'

I nod. 'I'll go. Tell the SHO to send an armed contingent, but there should be absolutely no engagement with the protesters till I get there. You take care of things here.'

Keshav nods and starts to get into the lift. 'Sir, take Bhoomi. He speaks the local dialect well,' says Gayaram.

'Okay, send him down immediately. I'm waiting here,' I say.

A couple of minutes later, Bhoomi comes charging down, taking the stairs two at a time.

'You don't believe in taking the lift?' I ask.

'Not if I'm in a hurry,' he responds. 'When God has given us two legs, why rely on an ungli?'

'Good man,' I say approvingly. We race to the jeep and I get into the driver's seat. Bhoomi quickly puts on the seatbelt and I hear him mutter something that sounds like a prayer. I ignore him and floor the accelerator.

CHAPTER FOURTEEN

A little later, we reach the spot. Policemen wearing body armour and holding shields and laathis are standing on the road, blocking a group of villagers shouting slogans. A tall, elegantly greying man wearing a kurta-pyjama and a sleeveless Nehru jacket stands out from the rest. When he sees Bhoomi and me, he waves and begins walking over towards us.

'That's Rajan Sahai, sir,' says Bhoomi.

'Why's that name so familiar?'

'He's a tribal rights activist. Very well known. Runs an NGO that has won lots of awards,' explains Bhoomi in an undertone.

'So how's he connected to this?' I wonder out loud. 'Well, let's just ask him.'

'Namaskar,' says Sahai as he reaches us. 'I'm Rajan Sahai.'

'I know who you are,' I reply. 'I'm SP Vikram Pratap Singh.'

'I know who you are too,' he shoots back with a smile. 'I'm sorry we couldn't meet before. Too bad it had to be under these circumstances.'

I smile in agreement. 'May I ask what you are doing here?'

He smiles back. 'Straight to the point, just like your reputation has it. Well, I heard there was trouble brewing here. I thought I would come and try to calm down the villagers. I'm glad to say that the tribals here consider me a friend and my words carry some weight with them.'

'That's very noble of you,' I say. 'So, can you please explain to them that the bodies will be respectfully handed over as soon as the post-mortem is conducted?'

He sighs. 'You don't understand, SP sahab. They're convinced that all evidence of torture will be covered up under the pretext of a post-mortem.'

'That's ridiculous,' I say.

'Really? What world are you living in, SP sahab? Do you think such things don't happen here?' he asks. 'It'll do you good to get out of your office and get to know these people. Try to understand why they are angry, instead of just declaring every protester a Naxal.'

'I'm not declaring anybody a Naxal,' I say. 'I'm just requesting that they clear the road and disperse peacefully.'

'Why? They're just holding a non-violent protest. They're perfectly within their democratic rights to do so,' he says.

'I thought you wanted to calm the situation. It sounds more like you're aggravating it,' I say.

'I'm just conveying their demand—which I think is perfectly valid. If you accept it, we'll have a solution and we can all go home peacefully,' he replies.

I'm just about to reply when an SUV with a 'vidhaayak' sign on it comes screeching up, followed by a police jeep and a couple of other vehicles. The local MLA, Rajesh Kashyap, steps out, followed by a posse of guards including policemen and civilians.

'Waah, this seems to be turning into one big circus,' says Sahai wryly. On this, at least, I find myself in agreement with him.

'Rajan Sahai! But of course. Wherever there's trouble, one can be sure to find Shri Sahai.' Clearly, the MLA is no fan of Sahai.

'Magar aapko dekh kar mujh ko toh bahut aascharya ho raha hai,' says Sahai. 'I'm astonished that you managed to find time from sucking up to your rich brother-in-law and his crony capitalist friends to come here.'

Kashyap's face hardens at the jibe. 'I go wherever the people of my constituency need me,' he says.

'Even those who've never voted for you and never will?' Sahai continues to needle him.

'Gentlemen, please. This isn't helping. Can we please discuss possible solutions?' I intervene hastily before their conversation turns nastier.

Kashyap nods. 'You're right. But can we please involve some of the village elders in the discussion? They should also be part of it, don't you think?'

'Waah, Kashyapji. You seem to be very concerned about these people. I wish those friends of yours who're making money off their land, water and jungles were as caring,' says Sahai snidely.

Kashyap reddens, but before he can retort, Sahai quickly walks back to the villagers and speaks to them. A couple of village elders step out with him and walk towards us. A quick discussion follows, in which they reiterate their demands. After a while, Kashyap pulls out his phone.

'I may be able to offer a compromise,' he says, and sends a message. Nothing happens for a while after that.

'May I ask what your offer is?' I ask when the silence becomes uncomfortable.

'I've messaged the CM's office. I'm suggesting that we offer to video record the post-mortem and share its full findings with the villagers. If they want, we can also ask for a judicial probe into the encounter,' says Kashyap.

Almost as soon as he finishes speaking, the phone rings. Kashyap turns to one side, covers his mouth with his palm and speaks in a low, urgent tone. All eyes are on him.

Suddenly, from my peripheral vision, I notice a blur of motion on the villagers' side and a large stone comes hurtling at Kashyap. 'Look out,' I yell and start to move towards him, but Bhoomi gets there first and shoves him aside. The stone targeted at Kashyap strikes Bhoomi's head instead.

Some of Kashyap's guards immediately surround him. Others raise their weapons and point them at the villagers. The unmistakable sound of guns being cocked fills the air.

'Wait. Nobody shoot,' I yell frantically. It's a tinderbox and one spark could set it ablaze. I turn to the village elders. 'Tell your people not to do anything stupid. Do it now!'

They shout urgently at the villagers, gesticulating for them to calm down. I try to see if I can identify the stone-thrower, but whoever it was has melted back into the crowd.

I turn to address Kashyap's guards. 'Get the MLA out of here.' As his men start to hustle him away, I ask him, 'Was your suggestion accepted?'

There's a mixture of shock, alarm and anger on his face, but he manages to recover enough to say 'yes' before he's shepherded into his SUV, which zooms off at top speed.

I notice that Bhoomi is bleeding profusely. 'Are you okay?' I ask.

He starts to nod, then winces. 'I'm feeling a bit giddy,' he says, and then suddenly slumps.

I grab him before he falls to the ground. 'Take him to my jeep. There's a first-aid kit there. Give him some treatment and then drive him to the hospital,' I yell. A couple of men step forward and lead him away, his arms wrapped around their shoulders.

I give Sahai and the village elders a long, hard look. 'I suggest you accept the solution proposed by the MLA and take your people away. We all need to act responsibly, otherwise this could turn into a bloodbath,' I say. 'And I want the stone-thrower handed over.'

Sahai and the villagers confer urgently. Then Sahai turns to me. 'They're willing to accept the offer and leave. But don't ask them to hand over the stone-thrower right now, in front of everybody. It will put them in an impossible position.'

'He almost triggered a major clash here. He has to face the consequences,' I insist.

'You're right. But he is one of them. They can't just hand him over to you and walk away. They will deal with him in their own way, back in the village.'

I shake my head stubbornly. Sahai sighs. 'Look, just let it go for now. You can always go to the village and make inquiries later.'

'By then, he'll have vanished into the forest,' I say grimly.

'SP sahab, josh se nahin, hosh se kaam lijiye. We can salvage the situation now, or you can wreck it with your stubbornness. Meet them halfway, compromise. In any case, the man must have run away by now. He won't just be standing around.'

I think about it briefly and reluctantly come to the conclusion that Sahai is probably right. 'Theek hai. Ask them to leave without any further drama,' I say.

Sahai and the elders walk back. There is a quick exchange. A few seem to be objecting to the agreement, but others shout them down. Thankfully, the majority seem to be in favour of withdrawing before the situation deteriorates further. After a while, they start moving away.

I heave a long sigh of relief once the road is clear and realise that my whole body is rigid with tension. I move around, stretching my neck and shoulders, trying to ease out the kinks. I start walking towards my jeep and am startled to find that it is missing. Then I recall that I had sent it away with Bhoomi.

The Inspector who'd led the policemen to the site comes up to me. 'I think we can go back now, sir,' he says.

'Yes. You and your men did a fine job. Well done,' I say. 'By the way, can I get a ride with you back to town?'

'Of course, sir. I'll send a vehicle to drop you back to the office,' he says.

Keshav is pacing up and down when I get there. The look

on his face tells me he has bad news to impart. 'Out with it,' I command. I can't take the suspense and I'm in no mood to play guessing games.

'Mangtu didn't make it out of coma. There were already two CRPF guards posted at the door. They started arguing about us posting additional guards. Before we could resolve it, the doctor informed us that it was a moot point because Mangtu had died.'

'Damn! Why didn't you call or message?' I ask.

'You were already managing a tense situation. I didn't want to add to your stress. There's nothing you could have done about it in any case,' says Keshav.

'Thanks for the consideration,' I say dourly. 'Any word on Bhoomi?'

Keshav nods. 'He threw up a couple of times on the way to the hospital and was complaining of a headache. The doctor said he's probably suffered a mild concussion and told him to rest for a few days. Apart from that, he's fine. He's gone home. I told him to take it easy for a while. I hope that's okay.'

'Yeah, sure. Hope it's nothing serious,' I say.

'The doctor didn't seem to think so. He said a couple of days' rest should do the trick. At least, that's what Bhoomi told me.'

'Okay. Were we able to get any details about where Mangtu was all this while?'

'Obvious hai, sir. He was the Maoists' informer. Went back to them the minute he thought we were onto him,' says Keshav.

'Yes, but who was the mystery caller who tipped him off? How did he know about our plans? We need to find out more. By the way, are we keeping track of what Rudra is up to these days?' I ask.

Keshav looks at me incredulously. 'You still want to go there? Despite all that's happened? Forget him, sir.'

I shake my head. 'Our method was wrong, but not the case. And I don't repeat my mistakes. Sooner or later, he'll slip up. I want us to be ready with a cast-iron case when he does. Keep an eye on him.'

'Yes, sir,' says Keshav, his tone carefully neutral. 'Anything else, sir?'

'No, let's call it a day.'

Keshav salutes and leaves. Through the door, I overhear him muttering something about my stubborness. Momentarily, I feel a flash of anger. Then I force myself to calm down. I'll convince the sceptics eventually. But it won't happen in a day. Fortunately for me, I've never been scared of hard work, though I could definitely do with a good, long night's sleep right now.

'Go home, Vikram Pratap Singh,' I tell myself. 'Tomorrow is a new day.'

I'm so exhausted, I literally drag myself to my jeep. The driver starts to move over, but I wave at him, indicating that he should drive. He stares in surprise for a brief moment as I get in and pull on the seat belt.

As the vehicle starts to move, I wonder how Devika's father is. I dial her number. The phone rings and rings. Nobody responds. After a while, the recorded voice on the phone informs me that the person I am trying to reach is not answering the call.

'I can make that out myself,' I grunt, irritated. I try calling her again. The same thing happens. I feel a twinge of anxiety. Suddenly, on impulse, I turn to the driver. 'Hospital chaliye, please.'

The driver nods and turns the vehicle onto the road that leads to the hospital. All along the way, I keep trying her number. There's no response. By the time we reach the hospital, I'm seriously worried.

There seems to be an even longer line of people sleeping on the road outside and in the hospital corridors, but I barely notice as I sprint to the CCU, my exhaustion forgotten.

Devika is sitting slumped on a bench outside, her head in her hands. Her bag is next to her. Occasionally, a soft beep emanates from within it, her mobile phone informing her of calls and messages. They don't seem to register with her at all.

'Devika,' I say softly.

She raises her head and glances at me. One look at her and I know what has happened. Her hair is dishevelled, her eyes are red and her face is streaked with tears.

'Baba left us,' she says, confirming my suspicion. 'He seemed to be getting better. We even talked for a while. I stepped out to get a coffee, and he had another massive heart attack and he ... he ....'

Her voice chokes and she stops, unable to go on. I walk up to her and tentatively pat her on the shoulder, though it seems like a hopelessly inadequate gesture in the face of such overwhelming grief. She grips my shirt in both her hands, pulls herself up and buries her face in my chest, her shoulders shaking with silent tears.

For a moment, I'm too stunned to react. Then I gently stroke her hair, silently offering her whatever strength and support I can provide, and let her cry her heart out. No words are exchanged. There is no need for them.

I'm not sure how long we remain standing like that. Time seems to work differently at moments such as these. I hear a sound behind me. Reluctantly, I turn my head. Anjali and Purshottam Sethi, flanked by a couple of guards, are staring at us. Bhoomi is standing behind them, a bandage around his head.

For a fleeting second, I wonder what they'll make of what they're seeing. Then I dismiss the thought. Devika has already lost her mother, and now her father is no more. Having witnessed the death of both my parents, I can relate to what she's going through. She needs a friend to lean on, and I happen to be here. If people choose to misinterpret that, it's their problem.

Devika senses the slight change in my posture and looks up quizzically. I tilt my head slightly to indicate that we have company and then gently step back. She lets go of my shirt and disengages, wiping her face.

'We came as soon as we heard. I'm so sorry, sweetie,' says Anjali, stepping forward and enfolding Devika in a hug. I exchange nods with Sethi, then turn towards Bhoomi. He salutes me formally, then glances first at Devika and then back at me, raising an eyebrow inquisitively. I return the salute and shake my head silently, indicating that there's nothing to talk about. He doesn't look too convinced, but nods, and then steps past me to offer his condolences to Devika.

CHAPTER FIFTEEN

'So Anjali was saying you probably haven't got the shirt I wept on washed yet.'

I look at the text on my phone and stifle a smile. Keshav, Bhoomi, Lokesh and Gayaram exchange glances but stay silent.

'And why is that?' I message back. Then I turn to Keshav. 'Sorry, please continue.'

'Yes, sir,' says Keshav. 'As I was telling you, things seem to have quietened down somewhat. We haven't had any serious incidents this month. We're also keeping an eye on Rudra, but there's nothing much to report. As for the sarpanch ....'

The phone beeps. It's Devika again. 'What do you mean "why"? That must've been the very first time a girl clung to you and cried her heart out. I think you should keep that shirt as a memento.'

'Yeah, right,' I snort. Then I realise that the others have fallen silent again and are looking at me, half amused and half irritated.

I hold up a hand in apology. 'Sorry, let me just put the phone on silent and we can talk in peace.' I quickly type, 'In a meeting. Will talk later' and hit send.

'Haan haan, take your time. No need to act pricey,' she responds promptly.

I turn to focus on Keshav, but my mind keeps wandering to Devika. It's been a month since her father died. For the first fortnight or so, she'd been a shell of herself, all the emotion drained out of her. The only time I saw a flash of her old self was at the funeral, when someone objected to a woman performing the last rites.

Devika had let it be known in no uncertain terms that no one but she would light her father's pyre and dared the person to try and take the flame away from her hand. He had hastily subsided, and the rest of the funeral had proceeded uneventfully.

After that episode, Devika had become quiet and withdrawn again. Her friend Anjali had moved in soon after, bringing with her two burly bodyguards and a house help, and taken over the household.

She made sure that Devika had her meals on time. Left to herself, Devika would probably not have bothered to eat. As it is, she picked at her food listlessly and only ate when Anjali nagged her. She also made sure that her bodyguards, who usually kept vigil on the porch, were well looked after and were served all their meals, including snacks, on time. Having often observed the casual callousness with which the privileged treat the less fortunate, I was impressed by her thoughtfulness.

'You take good care of your friend,' I said to her once, when Devika had excused herself to go to the washroom. I'd begun to visit her almost every evening, unless it had been a very long day at work.

'I could take better care of her if she'd agree to stay at my place. But you know how she is. She refuses to leave this house even for a few days,' sighed Anjali. 'Says it has too many memories and she can't bear to be parted from them.'

'It's not a very big house, is it? It must get a little cramped for five adults,' I ventured.

'There's a company guest house nearby where the bodyguards sleep,' she said. 'They're just a phone call away if needed.'

'Still, you're putting yourself to a lot of inconvenience for her.'

'She's been my best friend since school. And she was there for me after Dhruva passed. It's the least I can do.'

Devika had returned then, and we changed the subject. But that little chat gave me a rare insight into Anjali—the girl hardly ever talked about herself.

Of course, I'm not much of a talker myself, so we usually just sat around quietly, nursing a cup of tea or coffee. Sometimes Anjali would try to get the conversation going, but her efforts usually wilted quickly under my monosyllabic replies. One day, after I'd thwarted the fifth or sixth such attempt, she finally got exasperated. 'What's the matter? You never utter more than fifteen–twenty words when you come here. You have a word limit for when you're visiting?'

'Anjaliji, I can go for days without speaking that much. What you see here is me being talkative,' I defended myself.

Suddenly, Devika laughed, startling both Anjali and me. It was the first time in weeks.

'What's so funny?' asked Anjali.

'The two of you,' said Devika. 'You are probably the two quietest people I know, and watching you struggle to make PC is just hilarious.'

She lapsed into silence for the rest of the evening, but somehow seemed lighter, as though a weight had been lifted off her. The next day, she actually welcomed me with a smile. 'Let's all go out for coffee.'

'Why, is my coffee so bad?' asked Anjali.

Devika leaned across and patted her hand. 'No, sweetie, you actually make pretty good coffee, thanks to your teacher.' She turned to me and winked. 'I taught her how, right after school, when she was getting ready to leave for college, you know. Till then, madam didn't even know how to boil water.'

'Oh, please, stop embarrassing me,' Anjali muttered. 'It's all my parents' fault, they spoilt me rotten.'

'Yes, but luckily for you, friends like me keep your feet on the ground,' retorted Devika. 'Anyway, I want to go out for coffee because I'm getting a little bored sitting around at home all the time. I think a change of scene will do us all good.'

'They actually have coffee shops in Ambuja?' I asked, trying for a joke.

'You can count them on one hand. The best one is Anjali's dad's. But there I have to fight to get the bill, they keep insisting that my order's for free,' Devika said.

'It's okay. The moment we get there, I'll tell them that they should present the bill without any fuss. And we'll go dutch. I hope that's okay. Devika is very prickly about these things,' said Anjali, looking at me questioningly.

'Sure,' I agreed immediately, encouraged that Devika was ready to start venturing out of the house again.

The coffee shop was small but packed with people and served surprisingly good coffee. Sitting there, one could easily imagine that one was in a metropolis, though the prices were considerably lower, I noticed wryly.

Before long, Anjali was reminiscing about some teenage memories while Devika laughed and egged her on. Listening to them, it suddenly dawned on me just how good Devika was at drawing out people, even natural introverts like Anjali and me, and making us feel comfortable enough to share our thoughts and feelings. Darshan had the same quality, I suddenly realised.

'Penny toh nahin hai, athanni chalegi?' Devika asked suddenly.

'Sorry?' I responded, startled.

'You're really lost in thought. What's got you brooding like that?' she prodded.

I hesitated briefly, a small part of me still self-conscious about revealing vulnerability. Then I plunged ahead, deciding to risk it.

'I was thinking about a very good friend. He was a lot like you.

He could really get people to open up,' I said, leaning over to place my coffee mug on the table, so I wasn't looking at her as I said the words. After a moment, I glanced up. She was looking at me with a tenderness that vanished the moment our eyes met.

'Haan bhai, all your friends must be extroverts like me, with all the requisite social skills to get you to talk. Otherwise, it'd be the hermit's life for you,' she teased.

'Yes, he definitely had the knack of pulling me out of my shell. He'd also back me up for sure and tell you that this is my most talkative avatar,' I smiled ruefully.

'Oh, I'm so sorry,' Anjali said softly, perhaps picking up on something in my voice.

I shrugged, ready with the platitudes. 'All of us have lost loved ones. I don't think we'll ever forget them. But however hard it is, we have to pick up the pieces and go on with our lives.'

'True that. Pick up your pieces, I mean cups, everyone,' Devika said. When we obliged, she raised her own cup and proposed a toast. 'To old friends and new beginnings.'

'Sounds like you're ready to make one of your own,' Anjali smiled.

'What does that mean?' Devika asked, her face colouring slightly, but Anjali only shook her head.

The next morning, on my way to the breakfast table, Sharmaji, the ancient cook who had been working at the SP's official residence for at least twenty years, gave me an indulgent smile.

'What's the matter, Sharmaji?'

'You're in the news, sahab.'

'What are you talking about?'

He disappeared into the kitchen, then returned with the newspaper. He opened it with a flourish to a page that featured Devika and me laughing together in the coffee shop. Anjali had been cropped out of the picture.

I quickly scanned the accompanying text. Luckily, it didn't say anything scandalous, apart from noting rather pointedly that I was one of the town's most eligible bachelors and had been spotted having coffee with 'firebrand journalist Devika Doria'.

'Pah, what nonsense!' I put down the paper. 'Can I have breakfast please, Sharmaji? That poha you make so well?'

'Sure, sahab. Would you like some coffee as well?' he asked, fighting to keep a straight face, but began to laugh as he walked into the kitchen.

While waiting for my breakfast, I sent the picture to Devika. 'Look who's in the papers,' I said, adding a smiley.

A couple of minutes later, she pinged back with, 'This is awful. It's terrible, it's disgusting,' along with several angry emojis.

'What happened?' I asked, taken aback by her vehemence.

'This kind of stuff is really bad for my reputation.'

'Arrey, I'm such a local celebrity, I thought being seen with me would enhance people's reputation, not lower it,' I wrote, trying to defuse the situation.

She took her time to reply. 'As a woman professional, this is horrible for me.'

'Horrible as a professional or horrible as a woman?' I keyed in. Then, thinking it might not be such a great idea, I quietly deleted the message before leaving for work.

That evening, I decided not to see Devika, unsure of my welcome. Just as I was getting ready to leave for the day, my phone beeped. I noted with some surprise that the message was from Anjali. 'Hope you're coming over?'

'Should I? Not sure,' I replied.

'You absolutely must. Act totally normal. And don't say I messaged,' she wrote back.

Though tempted to ask why, I decided to leave it be. Later that evening, I presented myself at Devika's place as usual. Her face seemed to brighten momentarily, but she fell silent after a quiet greeting. In the long, awkward pause, I cleared my throat uncomfortably. She looked at me, a question in her eyes. I hurriedly looked down.

Just as the silence was getting unbearable, Anjali piped up. 'Should we go get coffee?'

Devika and I stared at her, and then all at once, all three of us began laughing. I'm not sure why—it wasn't particularly funny—but we roared with laughter until the tears poured down our cheeks. Mostly, I felt a huge sense of relief that the subject had been brought up and we'd got it out of the way. After a while, Anjali wiped her eyes and retired to the kitchen to make coffee—and we resumed our now established routine.

Since that day, Anjali had begun to tease Devika about me. Underneath that quiet exterior, she had quite a sharp wit, and she used it at my expense, trying to set us up. This latest one about the shirt was the most obvious one. Or maybe she'd said other stuff to Devika that had not been passed on to me?

Suddenly, I realise with a start that Keshav is done speaking and everyone is looking at me expectantly. I've been so busy mooning about Devika that I haven't registered a word.

'Hmm. All right. Thank you. Let's break for now,' I say, hoping desperately that nothing important has been said. They all file out obligingly, their faces expressionless, though I think I detect a hint of a smile on Gayaram's face. When I look at him closely, though, he quickly looks away and exits the room.

Well, since you spent so much time thinking about her, you might as well message her, I tell myself. I reach for the phone and key in a message. I read it and wrinkle my nose. Too boring. I delete the text and try again. Now I sound too familiar. I give it one more shot. This one just seems downright needy.

Arrey yaar, you'll spend the whole day like this, I tell myself. Finally, I send a simple 'Want to talk?'

My phone rings right away. 'It's a good thing you messaged just now. I was about to tell you I might be busy for the next few hours,' Devika tells me.

'Kyon, kya hua?' I ask.

'Well, Anjali's going back to her house today. I overheard her mother asking her the other day whether she should just send all her stuff over, and I realised that I can't expect her to stay with me indefinitely,' she says.

'Oh, so you're going to be all alone? Won't that feel lonely?' I ask, concerned.

'I'll have to get used to it,' she responds. 'But you're right, I thought it might feel strange to be all by myself. So I've decided to tackle all the things I've been putting off. For one thing, I really should sort out Baba's papers. The room has been untouched since ... well ... since that day. And then, I should look at my mails. They must've been piling up all this while. Maybe I'll start working on a story or two as well. I've been out of the game for far too long.'

'Arrey baap re, that's a month's programme being planned to fit into a day!'

'That's the idea,' she laughs. 'So I might be a little preoccupied for the rest of the day.'

'Good for you,' I say, but I feel a little pang at the thought of her being too busy to talk to me. Stop being selfish, I scold myself. This is an essential part of her healing. You should be happy for her.

'Are you all right?' she asks. 'You sound a little ... umm ... bothered?'

'Haan, main soch raha tha, meri evening coffee ka kya hoga? I think I've got addicted to the way it's made at your place.' I'm only half joking.

There's a long pause, and then she says, 'Well, Ambuja has lots of other delights to offer. Remember Foodie's Paradise?'

'Foodie's Paradise? Er ... oh wait, the guys who make the Chilli Manchurian Paneer?' I recall.

'That's it. They also do a killer masala chai and cheese omelette. Maybe it's time you sampled some of it. We could go tomorrow for breakfast? It's a Sunday, so you should be able to have breakfast peacefully,' she suggests.

There's an even longer pause from my side. Finally, she breaks the silence. 'What? Are you scared I'm trying to poison you?' Beneath the humour, there seems to be a touch of nervousness.

'Just to be clear, this is just a foodie introducing some good khaana to a boring friend. And one more thing, haan, we'll only go if you pay for it. I'm absolutely broke right now,' she says, her voice firming up.

'I don't mind paying at all, but I thought you always liked to go dutch. At least, that's the impression I got from Anjali,' I say.

'Yes, but very very occasionally, I'm okay with making exceptions. You have a problem?' she asks.

'No problem at all. I'm honoured you're making an exception for me,' I assure her hastily.

'Yeah, okay. I'll see you in the morning then, at around 9.30, at Foodie's Paradise?' she says casually.

'Sure. And I'll give you a call in the evening just to make sure you're doing fine?' I say, trying to match her nonchalance.

'Sure. Chalo, talk to you later.' She cuts the call abruptly, leaving me staring at the phone with a huge grin on my face.

What if the local paparazzi take another picture, though, I'm tempted to ask her. Then I shrug it away. If she's not worried about it, why spoil her mood unnecessarily?

The next few hours go by in a happy haze. At around 5 p.m., I call her again.

'All good?' I ask.

'Yes. I've found a cracker of a story! But it's damn sensitive stuff, and I need to do a lot of work on it,' she says.

'Arrey! How did you come up with it in a couple of hours?' I ask.

'Bas, aa gayi. Sometimes the best stories are sitting right next to you, waiting for you to see them,' she says. But somehow, her tone worries me. Instead of sounding excited, she sounds downcast.

'Is everything all right? It seems as though something is bothering you,' I ask, concerned.

'Umm, yeah, I'm fine. I guess, sometimes, it's just disappointing when you realise that people spend so much of their time wearing masks. And it's even more disheartening when you see what lies beneath.'

'Now you've really got me intrigued. Do you want to tell me what this is about?'

'Sorry, no. That would be unprofessional. You'll just have to wait to read it with the rest of the world,' she says.

'Okay, I can respect that,' I say, though I can't help feeling a little disappointed.

'Actually ... I might need your help. There are some old files that I'll probably need to see,' she says.

'I see. I'm at your service,' I tell her, somewhat sarcastically.

'Since you brought it up ... can I bring my laptop and work over there? Woh kya hai na, the light's rather crazy here. By the time the electricity switches from the mains to the generator—or back—my concentration's fried.' She laughs teasingly, starting to sound more like her usual self. 'And if you serve the files with a side of tea and biscuits, I'll be set.'

'And I'm sure you'll write stories on the zaalim police raining atrocities on the innocent junta.'

'As a reporter, it's my job to write the truth,' she says.

'Kya baat hai! That's some nerve you've got, attacking the police while sitting in my office, tucking into my chai-biscuit! There's a C-word that describes this well,' I say feelingly.

'Chutzpah? Haan, I'm full of it!' she laughs.

I let it pass. 'On a slightly serious note, this one-way traffic won't do. You need to tell me what's going on.'

'Hmm, okay, I'll tell you a little bit tomorrow, face-to-face. But you have to promise not to fly off the handle and start arresting people left, right and centre before I finish my story,' she warns.

'Oh, so we're still meeting tomorrow? Shukar hai. I thought that had been nixed in favour of your investigation,' I say.

'Arrey nahin! I never say no to good food, woh bhi free ka,' she says promptly. 'Don't think you can wriggle out of buying me a meal. And let me tell you, I can work up quite an appetite. Don't be fooled by the amount you saw me eating in the last month or so. I wasn't in form then.'

'No problem. You can empty out Foodie's Paradise as far as I am concerned,' I say gallantly.

'Ha! You'll regret that,' she says. 'Okay, back to work for me. I'll see you tomorrow at 9.30.'

'I'm really looking forward to it,' I tell her, and I mean it.

'Me too,' she says. 'I have lots of things to tell you.'

'It's a date,' I say, but only after she's ended the call.

Back at home, I try to read a file, but I'm barely able to focus. Stop acting like a teenager, I scold myself. I close my eyes and take some deep breaths. After a while, when I'm feeling a bit more focused, I try reading again. Within seconds, I let out a huge yawn.

I abandon my efforts at reading and decide to go to bed. I usually fall asleep the moment my head touches the pillow, but not tonight. My mind is restless, and the thoughts come flying thick and fast. I wonder what she wants to talk about. The story she's working on? But she said she had 'lots' to talk about. Could it be something personal?

I punch the pillow, frustrated by the lack of sleep. My thoughts wander. What if she says nothing? What if she's waiting for me to make the first move? What if I'm completely misreading her? Is she going through the same torture? I snort—she's never been shy of expressing herself.

I'd never really considered a long-term relationship, but had always vaguely assumed it would be with someone as quiet and reserved as me. Devika is the very opposite of that.

I roll over, still restless. A couple of minutes later, I sigh, give up, and have a glass of water. Sometime in the night, I manage to fall asleep. A short while later, I wake up to an orange glow in the horizon. Dawn is breaking. I get up and wince. My neck is aching. I must have slept at an awkward angle.

I try to recall the last time I worked out. It's been a while. 'Not done, Vikram Pratap Singh. You'll soon be getting a paunch at this rate,' I mutter. I change into a T-shirt and shorts and start a brisk warm-up, then segue into kata—a detailed pattern of movements meant to be practised alone.

Okay, now to get the heart rate really pumping, I tell myself. I drop to the floor and begin a series of push-ups. My body protests, but I goad it on.

'Forty-five, you got this. Forty-six, don't stop now. Forty-seven, almost there. Forty-eight, two to go. Forty-nine, come on! Fifty, yes! Aaaaaaahhhhh!'

I sink to the floor, panting. My shoulders and arms are on fire. Sweat runs down my face. I blink and shake my head, trying to get rid of the salty irritation in my eyes. My heart is pounding. I take deep breaths to slow my racing pulse. As my heartbeat gently settles down, I become dimly aware that someone is knocking on the door.

I frown and look at the time. Who could it be this early in the morning? I haul myself up and open the door. A constable looks at me apologetically and salutes.

'Sir, something big has happened,' he says.

'What's it now?' I ask.

He starts to answer, then clams up. 'Sir, you should take a look yourself,' he says.

I stare at him, nonplussed, but he doesn't say anything more. 'Where?' I ask.

'Right on the main road,' he says.

'Okay,' I say. 'Give me five minutes.'

I shower and change. It had to happen today of all days, I mutter to myself grumpily. I'd better let Devika know I may get delayed. She probably won't let me hear the end of it.

I pick up my phone to call her when I realise that the battery is completely dead. I usually recharge my phone the moment I get home, but I was so preoccupied last night that I'd completely forgotten to plug it in.

I pick up the landline and dial her number from memory. As I do so, I can't help smiling. In this day and age of mobile business cards, if you actually remember someone's number, it shows they really matter to you.

The number rings and rings. There's no response. I try again. The same thing happens.

Great. She's already playing hard to get. I'm definitely in for an earful when we meet, I grumble to myself.

The constable shifts impatiently, though he doesn't say anything. I hang up and head out, deciding to plug my phone into the car to revive it enough to send her a message.

As we near the outskirts, I see that a big crowd has gathered. People are talking excitedly to each other. Others seem stunned. I see an old man shaking his head sorrowfully. A few policemen yell at the onlookers and gesture to them to move, opening a path for the vehicle.

My phone lights up just then, coming alive. I have a message waiting for me in my voicemail. I play it.

It's Devika. She says, 'Vikram, I really need to tell you this ....' Then her voice suddenly goes silent, as though someone has put a hand over the phone. There's a muffled exchange, but I can't make out what is being said. Then the call is disconnected.

I stare at the phone, nonplussed. Just then, the car door opens.

I realise that we've stopped. Lokesh opens the door for me and salutes. There is a strange expression on his face.

'Will someone tell me what's going on?' I ask, exasperated.

Lokesh simply turns and points towards a lamp post. I look in that direction. A wave of horror washes over me. I feel the gorge rising in my throat and desperately force down the urge to throw up.

This can't be real, a voice says desperately inside my head. This can't be happening. It's a nightmare. Any moment now, I'm going to wake up.

But it's all too devastatingly real. Slowly, leadenly, I walk forward. I want to look away. I want to shut my eyes. But I don't do either. I keep walking, eyes wide open, taking in every harrowing detail.

Devika Doria and I will never have that breakfast we had planned. Nor will we ever get to do any of the things that might have followed. Because she is hanging from the lamp post. Her face is badly bruised and contorted, as though she died in agony. A big sign has been hung around her neck. It says, 'Sarkar ki Kuttiya'.

CHAPTER SIXTEEN

'Is this entire neighbourhood populated by the blind and the deaf, damn it? How's it possible that nobody saw anything or heard anything!' I'm ready to punch the wall in frustration.

'It's a small town, sir. Everyone's indoors by nine, watching TV. Even the shops are closed.' Gayaram's explanation feels like an apology.

I glare at him and he hastily looks away. A part of me still can't believe that this is really happening. But here I am, standing outside Devika's house, my regular adda. Only, it's turned into a potential crime scene.

'Okay, let's try to retrace her last few hours. Who was the last person to speak to her?' I ask.

There is complete silence. I look around. Everybody avoids my gaze.

'Kya baat hai? Seedha jawaab do!' I command.

Bhoomi clears his throat. 'According to her phone records, that would be you, sir.'

I feel my face flush. Bhoomi hastily goes on. 'She may have met someone in person after that, but none of her neighbours saw anybody go over during the day.'

'Ask for transcripts of all her phone chats in the last few days,' I say.

'Sir ... are you sure?' asks Bhoomi.

I give him a furious glare. 'What's that supposed to mean?'

'You had come to be good friends with her, sir. Ambuja is a small town, people notice these things,' says Bhoomi.

'What rubbish, Bhoomi!' exclaims Keshav.

'Nahin. Kehne do. Let's hear what he has to say.' My voice is a deathly whisper.

'Sir, I'll get the transcripts, but I hope there's nothing that discredits you or Devika,' says Bhoomi.

I glare at him, speechless with rage. Bhoomi looks at me for a moment, then looks down at the floor. There is a long, strained silence. Finally, Keshav speaks. 'Sir, shall we go in?'

I nod and everybody visibly relaxes. As we start to walk inside, I turn to Bhoomi. 'Get those transcripts.'

'Sir,' is all he says.

We walk inside and look around. Everything looks exactly as it was the last time I was here. It's such a familiar scene, I half expect Devika to walk out with a welcoming smile.

I start to turn away, and then I stop. There is a chest against a wall. I walk up to it and gaze down.

'Kya hua, sir?' asks Lokesh.

I point at the floor. There is a little patch of dust right next to the chest. Everyone looks at me quizzically.

'Look at the rest of the floor. It's clean. That chest has been moved very recently. Someone was in the house. They took pains to put things back exactly as they were, but they slipped up here,' I say. 'Do a thorough search for any clues. Right, who's the last person who saw her alive?'

'Most probably Anjali Sethi, sir,' says Bhoomi. 'We've spoken to the maid who comes in to do the sweeping and cleaning. She says Anjali was staying with Devika and left only yesterday afternoon, after lunch.'

'Yes, that's right. Well, I guess I'll go talk to her. Have we found anything on Devika's phone or laptop?'

Keshav shakes his head. 'They aren't here, sir.'

I'd already started to move towards the vehicle, but stop mid-stride. 'What was that?'

'There's no sign of any mobile or laptop in the house, sir,' repeats Keshav.

'And we didn't find them with her, either,' I say, slowly.

'That's right, sir,' says Keshav.

'Do a sweep of the house again, very slowly and carefully. Make sure we don't miss anything. If we find her devices, let me know,' I say. Then I head out to Purshottam Sethi's residence.

Prashant greets me with a namaste and ushers me into the tastefully decorated living room, with ethnic furniture. Sethi rises to his feet as I enter.

'Welcome to my humble abode,' he says. 'I'm truly sorry it had to be under such tragic circumstances. Devika was like a second child to me. This is just so shocking and heartbreaking,'

'Yes, it is,' I agree. 'I'd like to speak to Anjali, please,' I add.

Sethi spreads his hands. 'SP sahab, we'd love to help you in every way possible, but Anjali is really fragile right now. I don't know if it would be a good idea to speak to her in this state ....'

'It's okay, Papa. I'll speak to him,' says Anjali. We all swivel around as she comes out of one of the adjoining rooms. Her eyes are swollen from weeping and she has huge dark circles that appear even more prominent because of her pale skin and delicate bone structure. I remember the last time I saw her, at Devika's home, and how she had smiled and teased me. It seems a lifetime ago.

Anjali looks at me. There is pain and grief in her eyes, and another emotion. After a moment, I realise it is sympathy. In the midst of her own sorrow, she actually feels for me. She walks straight up to me and places her hand on my arm. 'I am so sorry.'

I feel a lump forming in my throat and hurriedly clear it so that

I can speak without emotion clogging my voice. 'Thank you. I am very sorry for your loss too. She was your best friend. I know this must be very hard for you.'

She nods, then gestures to a chair. I take a seat and she sits next to me.

'Can you please tell me everything that happened yesterday? I'm really sorry to do this, but it could be important,' I ask.

'Well, I didn't want to leave Devika. But she insisted that she had to get used to living alone. "Kabhi toh start karna padega" were her exact words.'

'Okay. Was she behaving normally?' I ask.

'Yes. It seemed like she was doing her best to be upbeat. Then she said, "Okay, let me sort out Baba's papers", and went into his room. She was there for quite a while. And then ....' Anjali's voice tapers off.

'And then?' I prompt.

'She was in there for quite a long time. Her mood had changed when she came out. She was excited, like she used to get when she was tracking a big story. I even commented about it. She told me, "I've come across a story that'll shake Ambuja to its very foundations." It was like seeing the old Devika again.'

'I've found a cracker of a story!' Devika's words ring through my head. 'Did she tell you what it was?' I ask.

Anjali shakes her head. 'No, she said it was still at a very early stage and she needed to do lots of research to be sure of it. She said, "I'll need to confirm it one hundred and ten per cent before I make it public."'

Pretty much what she had told me too. 'Okay, now think very carefully. Are you certain that her mood changed only once she went into her father's room? Not before that?' I ask.

Anjali wrinkles her brow, as if concentrating. 'Yes, I'm quite sure.'

'Okay. And then?'

'We had lunch. And then, as I was leaving, she gave me a tight hug and said, "I love you, sweetie. Always remember that." Those were the last words she said to me,' says Anjali. Suddenly, her eyes well up. 'Oh God, poor Devika. If I'd only known what would happen, I'd never have left her.'

She buries her face in her hands, crying silently, shoulders heaving. Sethi instantly goes to her and wraps his arms around her.

'I think that should be enough for today, SP sahab,' he says, quietly but firmly. 'My daughter is distraught and will need some time to grieve. In case you need to talk to her again, you can always send us a message.'

I nod and rise to my feet. 'Thank you for your help.'

'Oh, please, there is no need for such formality. We will be happy to help you in every way we can. Devika hamaari bachchi jaise thi. Please bring her killers to justice at all costs,' he says.

'I will. You can count on that,' I say grimly.

Bhoomi and Keshav are waiting back at the station. 'Okay gentlemen, hope you've got some useful leads,' I say.

'Kuch information toh hai, sir. Can't say how useful it is,' says Keshav.

'Give me the information. I'll figure out whether it's useful or not,' I say curtly.

Keshav nods. 'Her post-mortem report is in, sir. One small mercy, no sign of rape.'

I wince and he hurriedly says, 'Sorry, sir, didn't mean to ....'

'It's okay,' I say. 'Please carry on.'

'Er ... yes.' Keshav clears his throat and goes on. 'Lingering traces of chloroform. Sounds like she was drugged.'

I nod slowly. 'Yes, but chloroform doesn't work like it's shown in the movies. It's not that someone just sniffs a handkerchief soaked with chloroform and passes out right away. It can take far longer—anywhere from two to five minutes—and so the person who's being attacked would definitely struggle. There's also a real danger that you could end up killing the person.'

'But it's there in her system, sir,' says Keshav.

'Okay, so let's assume someone used it to drug her. What else do we have?' I ask.

'A couple of her nails are chipped,' Keshav goes on.

'That could happen if she was struggling to free herself. She might have clawed at someone's wrist or face or chest,' I say. 'Did they find any blood or skin cells on her nails?'

'Sir, woh level ka forensics TV shows mein hota hai, Ambuja mein nahin,' says Keshav.

'I wonder when Ambuja will join the rest of us in the twenty-first century,' I grumble. 'Which is the closest forensic unit? Phone lagaao. Ask them to collect the evidence. Seal off the area completely till they get here. Any blood stains that weren't hers?'

Keshav shakes his head mutely. I grunt in frustration, then ask, 'Well, did the report say anything else?'

'Yes, sir. There's also severe bruising on the left side of her face and a deep gash on the right side of her forehead.'

I jerk upright as a thought strikes me. 'Did they check her brain?'

Keshav raises an eyebrow. 'What makes you ask, sir?'

'If she has bruising on the left and a gash on the right, there's a strong possibility that somebody hit her hard on the left and she fell and hit the right side of her head on something,' I say.

Keshav looks at the report, then nods. 'You're absolutely right, sir. She had a skull fracture, severe trauma to the brain and heavy internal bleeding. She was dead long before she was hanged.'

I shut my eyes for a second and take a deep breath to calm myself. Then I turn to Bhoomi. 'What have you got?'

'She got a message from her bank with an OTP to confirm a

transaction. She had booked a room in a Raipur guest house for two nights—Monday and Tuesday,' says Bhoomi.

'Today is Sunday. So she planned to be in Raipur tomorrow. Any idea what she wanted to do there?'

'Ek chat transcript hai, sir,' says Bhoomi. 'With Mr Shravan Kumar Mathur.'

'He's a senior IAS officer,' I say. 'He handles the PWD, if I'm not mistaken.'

'That's him,' says Bhoomi.

'Let's see the transcript,' I say, extending my hand. Bhoomi hands it over.

DD: Good afternoon, sir. This is Devika Doria. Hope you and the family are doing well

SKM: Yes, thank you. I heard about your father. My condolences. Madho was a good man and very well respected by all who knew him

DD: Thank you. He always spoke warmly about you and said you were one of the most efficient and approachable DMs Ambuja ever had

SKM: That was so long ago ... He could really badger govt officers. But we always knew his heart was in the right place. So, how are you doing?

DD: It's taken me a while, but I'm starting to pull myself together. Thank you for your concern

SKM: In my experience, work is the best medicine. Keep yourself busy. It will help

DD: You're so right. Actually, I'm messaging you regarding a story. I needed to speak to you. Would it be possible to meet sometime?

SKM: You can ask me over phone, if you wish

DD: It's sensitive stuff. Needs to be done face-to-face

SKM: Must be quite a story if you're willing to drive down eight hours for an interview

DD: It is. You'll understand when we talk about it

SKM: That sounds intriguing. Does tomorrow lunch work for you?

DD: I'm so sorry, but I have a really important breakfast meeting that I don't want to cancel/postpone. Any other day?

SKM: Well, I'm free Tuesday morning for around 30 mins from 11 a.m. on. Can you be in Raipur then?

DD: Sure. Will be there. Thank you so much

SKM: Okay, take care

I finish reading and look up at Bhoomi and Keshav. 'Let's pay Mathur sahab a visit.'

'Sir, please tread carefully,' says Keshav. 'Not only is he a senior officer, he's very well connected.'

'Arrey bhai, we're not accusing him of anything. We'll just be asking him about a murder about which he might be able to give us some useful information,' I say.

'Toh phone pe baat kar lijiye,' says Keshav.

'I want to see his expressions when we talk,' I reply.

'But if he's not accused of anything, then why ...?' begins Keshav.

'I've made up my mind. Can we please not argue about this?'

Keshav sighs. 'Theek hai, sir. As you wish.'

'Thank you. It's quite late now, so I'll call him tomorrow morning and set up an appointment. Waise, going by the transcript, he should be free on Tuesday morning,' I say.

'I wonder who that breakfast meeting was with. The number is saved as Khadoos,' says Bhoomi. 'But the person seems important to her.'

I feel a flash of pain. I know exactly who it was with. But there's no need for anyone else to know that.

'Did we find her laptop and phone?' I ask, changing the subject.

Both of them shake their heads. 'I think we can safely say that they're with the Maoists, sir,' says Keshav.

'Yes, and so is whatever story she was working on. Did we find any fingerprints at least?'

'Quite a few on her body, sir. We're checking the database to see if they match with any records. But none in the house,' says Keshav.

'No fingerprints on any of the surfaces in the house? Were any papers or clothes disturbed?' I ask.

'No, sir. There was nothing,' says Keshav.

'But I'm one hundred per cent sure that someone searched the house,' I say. 'So what does that tell you?'

Keshav and Bhoomi look at each other in mutual incomprehension, then shake their heads.

'Arrey bhai, put those brains of yours to some use!' I snap. 'If the person didn't leave behind any fingerprints, it means he—or they—were professionals who knocked her out, did a thorough search, then took her away and handed her over to someone else.'

'That makes sense, sir,' says Keshav.

'Okay, so if someone took her away after knocking her out, they must have had a vehicle of some sort. A car, a jeep, a van, something. Isn't there any sort of CCTV footage of the neighbourhood available that will give us a lead? Also, it means she died somewhere else. That means we have not seen the primary crime scene.'

Bhoomi shrugs helplessly. 'Sir, even if there were cameras, I highly doubt if they were functioning properly.'

'Damn it, Bhoomi, don't give up without even trying!' I say. 'Go back to the neighbourhood. Ask around quietly if anybody has any sort of footage or saw anything. If nobody wants to officially become a witness because they're scared of the Maoists, that's fine. But at least see if they'll give us some leads to work with, even if it's off the record.'

'Okay, sir. I'll get going,' says Bhoomi. He salutes and leaves. As he walks out of the room, I feel a wave of exhaustion wash over me suddenly, and slump into my chair.

'Are you doing okay, sir?' asks Keshav, concern colouring his voice.

'I want this case solved, Keshav. I want the men who did this,' I say.

'Karenge sir, zaroor karenge. But you need to look after yourself. It won't help anyone if you fall sick. Go home and get some rest. We've already done whatever we could today,' he reassures me.

'Hmm, okay,' I say. I haul myself out of my chair, supressing the urge to let out a weary sigh, and head home.

Sharmaji is waiting to serve me dinner. Dimly, I try to remember when I last had a meal. Then it strikes me, I haven't eaten the whole day. But the thought of food fills me with nausea.

'Rehne dijiye, mann nahin hai,' I tell him.

He looks at me sympathetically. 'Sahab, kuch soup ya chai hee le lijiye?'

'Theek hai, thoda sa soup de dijiye,' I answer.

He serves me and leaves me alone. I sit there, desultorily pushing the soup around with my spoon. What a day it's turned out to be. How very differently I'd imagined it when I woke up.

I have a couple of spoons of soup and nibble at the bread half-heartedly, but finally give up the meal as a lost cause. Unbidden, Darshan's face comes to mind. In all the time that he'd known me, I had never ever wasted food—the result of my parents' strict insistence that no meal could be left unfinished—and he used to tease me mercilessly about it.

'It will be Armageddon the day you give up food—or, maybe, when you fall in love,' he was fond of saying.

'Yaar, I think it's both today,' I tell him aloud. It's the first time I've acknowledged just how much Devika had come to mean to me. As the realisation hits me, I feel tears stream down my face. I look around to make sure no one can see me, then retreat to my bedroom. I kick off my shoes and flop face-down on the bed as a sense of utter desolation and loneliness overwhelm me.

First Ma, then Darshan, now Devika. I've lost them all. I'd always scoffed at the term 'heartbreak' as a flight of poetic fancy but now, I feel an actual physical ache in my chest. With all this turmoil, I don't expect to get any sleep, but I'm clearly more exhausted than I realise. I wake up to a faint hum. It's my phone vibrating on the wooden table, creating a knocking sound.

I snatch up the phone and peer at it. It's barely dawn. Now what's happened for Keshav to be calling me at this hour? I bring the phone to my ear.

'Yes?' I ask.

His voice is breathless. 'Sir, Purshottam Sethi has just been shot in the head while taking his morning walk. He's dead.'

CHAPTER SEVENTEEN

A bullet wound to the head is not a pretty sight. Purshottam Sethi looks as if someone's battered his head with a hammer. There's a small entry wound at the front, and huge hole at the back where the bullet exited. Most of the soft brain tissue is splattered on the ground like a thick pink jelly. Pieces of brain tissue and skull litter the ground.

His assistant, Prashant, is shaking badly, even though he has a blanket wrapped around him. 'We'd just started our early morning walk when there was a sound like a cough. And then Sethi sahab's head just exploded. There was blood spraying everywhere. It was just horrible ...' He trails off, the tears pouring down his face.

I look at Keshav. There are dark circles under his eyes, and he looks every bit as exhausted as I'm feeling. Neither of us has got much sleep of late. 'Sniper shot?' I ask.

Keshav nods. 'We've sent the bullet for analysis, sir.'

'He was shot right here, right?' I ask.

'Yes, the body is exactly where it fell. No one has moved it,' says Keshav.

I look around, taking stock of my surroundings. Sethi's bungalow has a lush, manicured garden in front and a small vegetable garden at the back. There's a huge garage, bigger than most apartments, and an independent outhouse. Circling the complex are a walking track and a large boundary wall with spikes on top. There's a tall building opposite Sethi's home, at a distance of about half a kilometre. The rooftop looks into the front garden.

'There,' I say, pointing. 'The sniper would have fired from there. What is that building?'

'It's an office complex of some kind, sir. I've already sent Lokesh and Gayaram to check. Oh, here they are.'

Lokesh salutes as he walks up to me. 'The building had a guard, sir. We found him unconscious, his hands and feet bound.'

'Brilliant. Multiple layers of security around Sethi. And just one guard for the building that provided a clear shot into his home. What was his security in-charge thinking?' I fume.

'Sir, with all due respect, Maoists don't usually use snipers. The security arrangements for Mr Sethi were according to the threat perception,' says Keshav.

'Did you revive the guard? Did he see anything?' I ask.

Gayaram shakes his head. 'He says it was a normal night. He was doing his duty when suddenly something hit him hard on the head. The next thing he knew, he was tied up and looking at us. I have a feeling the attacker clubbed him when he was already asleep.'

'Did the attacker leave any clues? Any trace of who he might be?' I ask.

'Yes, sir. We found this spray-painted on one of the walls of the rooftop,' says Gayaram. He shows me a picture he's taken with his phone. A big, bold 'Lal Salaam', in red, painted on the wall.

'Well, he's certainly left a message,' I mutter. 'It's an office building. I hope it will have CCTV cameras. Can we please try to get hold of some footage?'

'Ji, sir. Bhoomi sir is talking to the office administration. He'll get hold of whatever footage they might have,' says Lokesh.

'Okay. Let's go talk to the family,' I say.

'Neither Mrs Sethi nor Anjali are in any shape to talk right now, sir,' says Keshav. 'I'm told Anjali took it really hard. She was absolutely hysterical and had to be knocked out with a sedative.'

'I'm not surprised. She had barely recovered from the death of her husband, and now her best friend and her father are gone in such shocking circumstances, and that too, one after the other. Anyone would break down,' I say.

My phone rings. Truecaller informs me that it's Rajan Sahai. I frown, puzzled. Why would Rajan Sahai be calling me?

'Kahiye, Sahai sahab,' I say.

'SP sahab, what's going on in this town?' he begins without a preamble. He sounds tense, anxious. 'First Devika, now Sethi sahab. It seems as though anybody can murder anyone at will. It seems law and order are just ideas you people talk about!'

'I didn't know you were so concerned about Mr Sethi's well-being,' I snap back, nettled.

'I may have ideological differences with many people, but that doesn't mean I wish them ill. Why don't you keep these ill-advised opinions to yourself and do some actual work,' he says.

'That's exactly what I was in the middle of,' I say as icily as I can manage.

He pauses, perhaps realising that he's pushed me too far. When he speaks again, his tone is conciliatory. 'I'm sure you're doing your best. We're all counting on you.'

'Thank you. You can rest assured that I will leave no stone unturned,' I tell him and cut the call.

'Chaliye, time to hand over the crime scene to forensics. By the way, did they get to Devika Doria's case?' I turn to Keshav.

He shifts uncomfortably. 'Er ... sir ... the nearest unit is two hundred kilometres from here. They refused, citing an already heavy workload.'

I'm about to explode in anger when the phone rings again. It's the DGP this time.

'Vikram, what the hell is going on? Two murders in two days!'

'I'm on the scene of the second one right now, sir,' I respond.

'Are the two linked in any way?' he asks.

'I don't know yet, sir,' I respond truthfully. 'I haven't found anything that connects them, but it seems like too much of a coincidence.'

'You need to get some results fast, Vikram,' says Chandrakar.

'Sir, it's been barely a few hours. I've only just begun,' I say.

'Yes, but the news has gone viral. All the news channels are talking about how the Indian state no longer has control over Ambuja. The CM has called me. Sethi was the biggest businessman in those parts. If people like him can be killed at will, then nobody will be willing to bring any investments into the state. You need to do something, fast. If you need any help or resources, just ask,' says Chandrakar.

'Well, I could do with a little help, sir,' I say.

'What is it?'

'Sir, I'd asked for the nearest crime scene unit to come down and do a forensic probe of Devika's home. But they say they're too busy. It would be really good if they could come down for the Sethi investigation. But I'm worried they may still be too busy,' I say.

'What the hell! They're killing high-profile people as if they were flies, and these guys have nothing better to do than indulge in babugiri! I'll arrange for a team from Raipur via chopper. They should be with you later today.'

'Thank you, sir,' I say.

'Don't thank me, just get this damn thing solved. I'll call you again in a couple of hours. I want an update on everything you've gathered by then.'

He cuts the call abruptly. I scowl at the phone and put it in my pocket.

'Some trouble, sir?' asks Keshav.

'DGP sahab wants instant results,' I vent.

Keshav looks around to make sure no one can overhear us, then says conspiratorially, 'Perhaps he's trying to give you a hint, sir?'

'What do you mean?'

'We could round up a couple of suspicious characters and orchestrate an encounter. Known bad characters, not law-abiding citizens,' he says, speaking even more softly.

I stare at him, speechless. Misunderstanding my silence, Keshav goes on talking. 'This will pacify the media and allow us to carry on the investigation without the pressure.'

'I see. And how many cases have you solved like this in the past?' I ask.

'Forget the past, sir. We have a problem right now. This is a quick fix,' he says.

'You really think this is what the head of the state police wants?'

'Who knows, sir. It's not like he can give us a direct order. You need to read between the lines,' says Keshav with the conspiratorial air of someone who is well-versed in such things.

I'd carefully kept my face expressionless all this while. Now, I let the disgust and anger show. Keshav takes one look at me and hastily steps back.

'Just a suggestion, sir. Only out of concern for you. Please don't take it the wrong way,' he mumbles.

'Don't work yourself up worrying about me,' I say. 'And the next time I hear such a suggestion, you're getting a suspension on the spot.'

'Yessir, yessir, I'm very sorry sir. Galti ho gayi,' he stammers in a rush.

'Let's get back to office and take stock of whatever we've come up with so far,' I say curtly, turning away.

'The bullet was fired by a Heckler & Koch PSG1A1. It uses 7.62X51mm NATO rounds,' says Keshav, reading out the forensics report. His tone is noticeably subdued.

'It's the updated variant of the PSG-1, isn't it? The PSG-1 was the first sniper rifle designed from scratch for law enforcement use. They started designing it in 1971 and fast-tracked it after the failure of German security agencies to rescue hostages kidnapped during the 1972 Munich Olympics. PSG is an abbreviation for some German term.'

Darshan had been a real firearms freak and often bored me with long, detailed histories of various weapons.

'Präzisionsscharfschützengewehr. That's German for precision sniper rifle, sir,' says Lokesh. He holds up his phone. 'I just looked it up.'

'Waah! From paper clippings to online searches, you've come a long way, Lokesh,' I say wryly. 'What else have you found in your search?'

'Hmm? Well, it costs a bomb. And it's extensively used by security agencies around the world. In India, it's used by the NSG, the Army, the Marcos Navy commandos, the Octopus commando force in Andhra Pradesh and Telangana and ... oh, interesting.'

'What's so interesting?' I ask.

'It's also used by the Greyhounds,' says Lokesh.

'That's the special forces unit operating in Andhra Pradesh and Telangana. They specialise in operations against the Naxals,' I say.

'It's possible that our sniper could have got it from there. It's fairly common for these Naxals and Maoists to keep the weapons of those they kill or capture. And the rifle could have made its way here for a special operation,' says Bhoomi.

'Definitely an angle worth considering,' I say. 'Let's see if we can find out whether any military or paramilitary organisation has lost a sniper's rifle in the recent past. Even if they have, they're unlikely to be forthcoming about it. Anyway, let's follow the lead. What about the building from where the shot was taken? Did it have any CCTV footage?'

'At the entrance, and then inside the lifts. But the killer was smart. He didn't use the lifts. So the only shot we have is of him entering the building. And his face was covered. So you can't really see much,' says Bhoomi.

'Show me,' I say. Bhoomi dutifully runs the footage. A slim figure clad in a black track suit and wearing a balaclava mask on his head makes his way into the lobby. He has a bag slung over his shoulder and an iron bar in his hand. He glances briefly in the direction of the camera, then walks up to it and smashes the camera with the bar. The screen goes black.

'This is totally like those Japanese-style killers, what are they called? Ninjas!' says Gayaram. 'Ambuja ka ninja,' he chortles. 'Kya baat hai, that's a story I'd read!'

I glare at him and he subsides. 'Sorry, sir,' he mutters as the others titter.

'A little focus here, please,' I say sharply, rapping the table. Everybody immediately falls silent. 'Is that all the footage we have of him?' I ask.

'Yes, sir,' says Bhoomi.

'Okay. What time was the entry?'

'About 4.30 a.m., sir,' says Bhoomi, checking the time stamp.

'All right. And what time was Sethi shot?' I ask.

'Don't know the exact time, sir. But Prashant said they usually began their walks at 5.30 a.m. sharp,' says Keshav.

'Okay, so let's try to put ourselves in the killer's mind. He came in at around 4.30 a.m. and got himself into position well in time. There's no rifle visible in the video. So, most likely, he brought all the parts in the bag, assembled it after he reached the roof, then got into position and took the shot,' I say. 'Chances are the bar he used to smash the camera was the same one with which he knocked the guard down. By the way, where was the guard positioned?' I ask.

'Outside, sir,' says Lokesh. 'He says he was on his night round when it happened.'

'And where did you find the guard?' I ask.

'In the lobby, sir. He says he was dragged inside and left there,' says Lokesh.

'But this guy came in alone, not with the guard. So he knocked him out, came in, smashed the camera, then went out again and brought him in. Why leave the guard alive? Why not just kill him too?' I think aloud.

'He wasn't the target, was he? By that logic, why not kill Prashant too?' asks Lokesh.

'Precisely. This guy was only interested in killing Sethi, not in harming any innocents,' I say.

'Hmm. Professional lagta hai,' says Bhoomi. 'Sirf target pe focus.'

I'm about to answer when the phone rings. It's Chandrakar. I groan inwardly. No doubt he is calling about his update. I gesture to the others and they quickly file out of my office.

'Tell me,' he says, without any preamble.

I bring him up to speed. He listens intently without interrupting, then asks, 'Okay, so what's the next course of action?'

'Well, first of all, we need to try and figure out where the weapon came from. I was thinking of sending out a message to all forces and paramilitary forces that use them, asking if they have lost any such weapon to Maoists. But it might be better if such a message went out from your office. There's a chance of actually getting a response,' I say.

'Fine,' says Chandrakar. 'And any headway on the Devika Doria case? It turns out a lot of editors at the foreign newspapers and websites she wrote for thought very highly of her. Her death is actually attracting a lot of eyeballs globally.'

'Well, I don't think the forensics team has arrived yet,' I say.

'They'll get there. It's just taking a while to get things organised. Now tell me, do you have any other leads?' asks Chandrakar.

'Well, Devika's last chat on WhatsApp was with Mr Shravan Kumar Mathur. In fact, she was supposed to meet him tomorrow morning. We'd requested him for an appointment to talk to him regarding that. I need to check whether he's agreed to our request or not,' I say.

'S.K. Mathur? You're going to question him in a murder case? Did you learn nothing from the last time? He's very well respected, not to mention connected,' says Chandrakar, irritated.

'We're not questioning him as a suspect, sir. We just want to have a chat with him regarding the case. Who knows, he may be able to tell us something that might help,' I say.

Chandrakar sighs. 'These simple chats always stress me out. Anyway, let me know when you're to meet him.'

'Actually, why don't I just check and find out? Will you give me just a second?' I walk out of my office and reach Keshav's. He's engrossed in his mobile screen. I knock on his door. He doesn't react. I knock again, harder. He's still lost in the screen.

'Keshav,' I snap, walking into the room. He leaps up, startled, hastily putting his phone away. 'Sir, you should've called me,' he says.

'Mathur sahab ke appointment ka kya hua?' I ask.

'Sir, he said he was busy and would get back to us. We haven't heard anything from him since then,' says Keshav.

'What? When were you planning to inform me?'

'Sorry, sir, it slipped my mind,' he says sheepishly.

I resist the urge to give him an earful, remembering that Chandrakar is on the line and can hear everything. Instead, I shoot him a poisonous look, then turn around and return to my room. 'Sorry, sir, it seems we don't have an appointment yet,' I say.

'Yes, I gathered that,' he says dryly.

'Sir, can't you use your good offices and get me some time with him? I'll be on my very best behaviour. You have my word.'

'Hmm, let's see. The chief secretary is hosting a reception for his daughter and newly acquired son-in-law tomorrow night. If I see him there, I'll put in a word,' he responds.

'Sure, sir. Thank you very much,' I say.

'One last thing,' he says, then clears his throat. 'Your MLA has been bombarding me with calls and messages. And he's getting his friends in the ministry to do so as well.'

'Rajesh Kashyap? What does he want?' I ask.

'Sethi was his brother-in-law, remember? He's terrified about his own safety now that Sethi has been killed,' says Chandrakar.

'He has a mini army guarding him. I don't think he needs to worry,' I say.

'Well, we thought Sethi was well guarded too. And look how that turned out,' says Chandrakar.

Can't argue with that, I think. 'So what would set his mind at ease, you think?'

'He was very impressed with one of your boys. He apparently pushed him out of the way and got hurt himself. Unusual name for a man. What was it? Ah yes, Bhoomi. He wants Bhoomi added to his security detail,' says Chandrakar.

I can't stop myself from groaning. 'Seriously, sir? Kashyap can get trained security personnel from anywhere. I hardly have any decent guys to work with over here. I can't afford to lose the people I do have.'

'Is that so? What exactly does this fellow do?' asks Chandrakar.

'Well, he's sort of my tech expert,' I say reluctantly.

'And what great tech wizardry has he done that's provided you with a major breakthrough?' asks Chandrakar.

I'm silent, because the truthful answer is, none at all. It's just that I've become fond of all these guys, I realise with a start. Bhoomi, Gayaram, Lokesh—whatever their idiosyncrasies, they're my team and I've got used to having them around.

'Well, that settles it,' says Chandrakar, interrupting my reverie. 'The situation is really delicate here, and if the MLA for Ambuja asks for one guy by name, I'm certainly not going to reject his request. Tell Bhoomi he is to report to Kashyap's security detail immediately.'

'Yes, sir,' I say grimly. Chandrakar cuts the call and I stride to Keshav's room. This time, he's on his feet the moment I step in.

'Aisa phone pey kya tha?' I ask him. 'Porn?'

He flushes. 'Sir, a video has gone viral online. It was made by somebody in the crowd when Devika Doria was hanged. I was trying to see if we could get any leads out of it. Nothing there, I'm afraid.'

'Send it to me,' I say.

'You might find it a little disturbing, sir,' he says.

'Send it, Keshav. I've seen enough death and violence in my life,' I mutter.

Keshav nods and picks up his phone. A few seconds later, my phone pings.

I nod and leave the room. Once I'm back in my office, I take a couple of deep breaths and click on the link.

A close-up of Devika's lifeless face fills the screen. It hits me like a punch in the gut. Slowly, the camera zooms out to show her entire body, dangling from the lamp post. Then the view changes and the crowd gathered there becomes visible. Some faces have a terrified expression, others look sad. Some sparkle with sick, voyeuristic delight. I see one young man pointing towards the body and talking excitedly, as if he's describing some tourist landmark.

Vultures, I think. Always ready to witness a tamaasha, vanish when we need help.

Suddenly, my stomach clenches and I feel the bile rising in my throat. I try to clap my hand over my mouth, but I'm too late. The bile shoots out, through my fingers, leaving them stained. I fall to my knees, coughing and retching. A small puddle forms on the floor, and a sour taste fills my mouth. A mixture of fury and frustration washes over me. I punch the ground hard. The pain that floods through me is almost a relief.

'Are you okay, sir? Arrey, yeh kya hua?' Gayaram comes rushing in and pats my back solicitously. His nose wrinkles at the sour smell blooming in the room.

'Looks like a touch of food poisoning,' I tell him. 'Please get it cleaned.' I rise to my feet and walk away, avoiding his curious gaze. In the loo, I wash my hands with soap and rinse out my mouth. Then I splash some water on my face. I wet my handkerchief under running water, then shut my eyes and spread the wet cloth over my face, savouring the cool sensation. I take a couple of deep breaths, the handkerchief still on my face, and feel a sense of calm descend upon me.

'I will find the men responsible for your death, Devika, and I will make them pay. No matter how long it takes me, no matter what it costs. I will bring your killers to justice,' I vow silently to myself.

CHAPTER EIGHTEEN

'She was such a lovely girl. I knew her when she was an earnest student, diligently tagging behind her father, scribbling away in a little notebook, almost his mirror image. And now, both of them are gone, just like that. It's truly shocking what's happened to her. What a ghastly death for such a wonderful young girl.'

Shravan Kumar Mathur shakes his head solemnly. He's a lanky man with a receding hairline, artfully combed to conceal the bald patch. His formal shirt and trousers are perfectly pressed and a jacket is draped over his chair carefully to ensure that it doesn't get crumpled. His shoes are polished so brightly, they could be used as mirrors. 'You knew her father too?' I ask politely. I'm seated in Mathur's office thanks to Chandrakar's intervention. The latter had called me back the night after we spoke and told me that Mathur had agreed to meet me.

'But go alone. And make sure that it's a polite conversation, nothing more. Remember it won't be your thaana and you will not be interrogating him,' Chandrakar had admonished me sternly.

'Of course, sir. I'll be politeness personified,' I'd assured him. Chandrakar had snorted at that, but refrained from further comment.

So far, though, the meeting has been extremely cordial. Mathur has been a gracious, if slightly condescending, host.

'Oh yes, I knew her father. A good, old-fashioned patrakaar.

Honest, fair and always willing to speak his mind. He used to work for this regional daily that was very big back in the day. Sadly, it's gone the way of the dodo,' he says.

'And how exactly did you come to know him?' I ask.

'I used to be the DM of Ambuja. He was always around, asking questions. My wife used to complain that I spoke to him more than I did to her,' Mathur guffaws. I smile politely.

'Did you keep in touch after you left Ambuja?' I ask.

'Oh, you know, the usual. Diwali and New Year greetings, that kind of stuff. Every now and then, if I had to go down to Ambuja on official business, we'd catch up over chai or something,' he replies.

'And you knew Devika through him?' I ask.

'Oh yes. Like I said, she was always following him around like a little cub reporter. I remember the last time I met him. She was with him. He told me that he had retired but she would keep the family flag flying high. "You've been very kind to me all these years. Please do give her your blessings and support." That's what he said to me,' recalls Mathur, a faraway look in his eyes.

'And she corresponded with you regularly?' I ask.

'Oh yes, she made it a point to stay in touch, and not just for stories. She was very old world in that sense. Today's kids, they only ever call you when they want some news out of you. But the older lot believed in building relationships and maintaining them. She was a lot like her father that way. Learnt from him, I guess. We only tailed off a bit in the last few months, but I suppose she had too much on her plate. Can't really blame her, poor girl,' says Mathur.

'Now, coming to her last conversation with you, apparently it was regarding some story she wanted to do? Would you have any idea what that story might have been?' I ask.

Mathur spreads his hands helplessly. 'I'm every bit as puzzled as you are, believe me. I was quite intrigued, for what kind of story would make someone drive down such a distance, just for a chat? In fact, I must confess I was quite looking forward to the conversation. It was a nasty shock when I learnt that she'd been executed in that brutal fashion.'

'Could you hazard a guess about what she wanted to discuss with you? Something to do with your current posting? Or perhaps something to do with the time when you were posted in Ambuja?' I ask.

Mathur shakes his head slowly. 'I'm sorry, I really am. I truly wish I could help you. But I'm completely clueless about this.'

I hadn't expected much else, but I still feel a pang of disappointment. Mathur clears his throat. 'Is there anything else? I'm due for another meeting soon.'

'Just a couple more questions, please,' I say. 'Did you know Purshottam Sethi?'

'Yes, of course. A thorough gentleman. Again, I knew him from the Ambuja days, and we'd kept in touch. Another horrible death. Two in such quick succession, it's just unbelievable,' says Mathur. He leans forward. 'Do you think there is any connection between the two?'

'That's exactly what I'm trying to find out,' I reply.

'Well, all the best to you. I wish I could do more to help, but I'm afraid I've told you everything I know. Now, if you'll excuse me ....' he says.

I take the hint. 'Thank you very much for your time,' I say, rising from my seat. Just as I'm about to leave, I pause. 'One final question, if you don't mind. Did you mention to anybody at all that you'd had this chat with Devika?'

'Well, I obviously mentioned it to my wife. And, oh yes, interesting now that you bring it up. I'd run into an old acquaintance at the club that day—Kailash Shukla. He used to be the SP in Ambuja when I was the DM. I remember telling him that it seemed to be the day for old memories from Ambuja to come calling, because I'd just had a chat with Devika and she was coming to interview me about some big, hush-hush story.'

'Kailash Shukla? I think I've heard of him. Isn't he retired now?' I ask.

'Yes, retired a few years ago. We haven't really kept in touch. Just occasionally, when we bump into each other at the club. This was one of those days,' says Mathur.

'I see. Did you have a long conversation with him?' I ask.

Mathur shakes his head. 'Not really. To be honest, and please don't quote me on this, when one meets him in the evenings, he's rarely in a sober state. I usually exchange some pleasantries and move on.'

'Well, thank you once again,' I say, and leave. As I step out of his office, I pull out my phone, which I had kept on silent during the meeting, and check for messages or missed calls. There's one message from Chandrakar. It says, 'Come and brief me as soon as you're done.'

But when I reach Chandrakar's office, I have to cool my heels for a while because he's busy with a call. 'Sorry about this, sir,' says his staff officer. 'He's really getting bombarded with calls today.'

'No major problem, I hope?' I ask, concerned.

The young officer leans forward and speaks in a conspiratorial whisper. 'There was a raid last night on a very exclusive establishment that offers very expensive wine and women to its clientele. They netted quite a few big fish, including a netaji who apparently has impressive stamina. He's been known to disappear into a room early in the evening with three–four girls, the younger the better, and only emerge late the next morning.'

'What a hard-working politician,' I quip. 'That must make life really convenient for his security detail.'

Before the staff officer can answer, Chandrakar's door opens and he peers out.

'Ah, Vikram. Sorry to have kept you waiting. Please come in,' he says.

'There isn't much to tell you, sir, to be honest,' I report, once we're both inside his office and the door is shut. 'Mr Mathur says he was only sporadically in touch with Devika, and he has no idea what she wanted to meet him about. The only other people who knew he was meeting her were his wife and Kailash Shukla, whom he met at the club.'

'Kailash Shukla? Oh yes, quite a sad story. His wife died some years ago and he stays by himself now. He's developed a bit of a reputation for loving the bottle. You'd better be careful. Those who spend a lot of time alone seem to turn out that way,' says Chandrakar.

'Doesn't he have any family?' I ask.

'An IT engineer son who's doing quite well for himself in the States but has no time to visit his father. I meet Shukla sometimes at reunions and get-togethers. He seems a very sad, lonely man,' says Chandrakar.

'His old colleagues don't try and cheer him up?' I ask.

'Some drunks are cheerful. Others are painful,' says Chandrakar. 'Anyway, why are we even discussing him? Aapka investigation kahin bhi aage badha?'

'No, sir. The forensics guys didn't come up with anything. There was one video of Devika Doria hanging that had gone viral. I've been trying to track where it originated from. But it's been forwarded so many times, it's hard to get a fix on who shot it. In any case, it could have been any bystander there. I'm afraid I've run into a bit of a dead end,' I say.

Chandrakar frowns. I brace for the yelling that I know is coming, but before he can say anything, there's an urgent knock at the door and his aide pops in.

'I'm really sorry to interrupt, sir,' he says hurriedly. 'But we just got an alert and I thought you'd like to know. A retired police officer has been found dead in his home. A gentleman by the name of Kailash Shukla.'

CHAPTER NINETEEN

Chandrakar and I exchange startled glances. Then he turns to his aide. 'What happened? How and where was he found?'

'Shukla's cleaning lady goes there in the afternoons to clean and cook. She rang the doorbell a few times. When there was no response, she pushed the door and it swung open. He was lying on the floor. There was a shattered bottle of alcohol beside him. She panicked and ran to the neighbours, who called us,' says the aide.

'Sir, I need to get there right away,' I say.

Chandrakar swivels back towards me. 'You're a long way from Ambuja, Vikram. It's not your jurisdiction,' he says.

'It's the third death linked to Ambuja in a few days, sir. Somebody else can do the investigation, but I need to be there, at least as an observer. Please sir, it might be important,' I plead.

Chandrakar strokes his chin thoughtfully, then nods. 'All right,' he says. He gestures to his aide. 'Call the local thaana. Let them know that SP Vikram Pratap Singh is on his way there. He is to be given all cooperation.' Then he wags his finger at me. 'And you, try to remember that it's not your investigation—yet.'

Shukla's house is a two-storey villa in a quiet, leafy colony. The houses all come with gardens, each one separated from its neighbour by a brick wall marking the boundary. A small crowd has gathered outside his house and is busy pestering the constable at the gate. He looks at me inquiringly as I start to walk past him.

'Aap kaun?'

'SP Vikram Pratap Singh. Aapke officer ko mere baare mein khabar kar di gayi hai,' I tell him.

He salutes. 'Ji sir, aaiye, please.'

The small garden in the front would be pretty if it wasn't overrun with weeds. The house itself looks shabby and run down, as if the owner stopped taking care of it a while ago. I walk in and find a photographer taking pictures of the scene. The officer in charge, a portly Inspector, walks over to me and salutes.

'Kya pataa chalaa?' I ask him, returning the salute.

'He was drinking alone. Seems to have died suddenly, perhaps of a heart attack,' he says.

I step gingerly towards the body. Glass shards from a bottle are scattered on the floor and the alcohol has dried into a pale yellow stain. Shukla is in his pajamas, lying face-down in the middle of this mess. There is a centre table, a solitary glass on it. There's a chair lying on its side.

I peer closely at the floor. Shukla seems to have stepped on some of the spilled alcohol, because his footprints are clearly visible in a zigzag pattern.

'Who was the last person who saw him alive?' I ask.

'His neighbour, sir,' says the Inspector. 'Around 9 p.m. he was returning from a walk when he saw Shukla sahab seated in his balcony. They greeted each other and then Shukla sahab said he was retiring for the night. The next person to see him was the cleaning lady. She found him like this.'

I notice an inhaler lying on a table near the entrance. 'Lung problem?' I ask.

The Inspector nods. 'Asthma.'

There's a glassware cabinet to one side. I look at the glass on the table, then glance at the cabinet. There are four more such glasses on a shelf. I walk across to the cabinet and count the glasses again.

'Four glasses there, one here,' I say. 'Where's the sixth?'

'Sir?' says the Inspector, confused.

'This is a set of glasses,' I explain. 'And sets normally come in even numbers. So where's the sixth glass?'

The Inspector shrugs. 'Kabhi kabhi glasses toot jaate hain ya kho jaate hain, sir. Not every set has to be complete.'

'True. But consider a few things,' I say. 'The door was not locked from inside. The cleaning lady was able to walk in, right?'

'Yes, sir,' says the Inspector.

'Theek hai. Now look at him. He's in his pajamas. Clearly, he was going to sleep after he'd finished his drink. So why did he leave the door unlocked? If you knew you were going to bed, wouldn't you latch the door before settling down for the night?' I ask.

The Inspector thinks about it. I can see him starting to make the connection in his head.

'Look at his footprints,' I point out. 'Look at the furniture. He stood up, walked around disoriented, collided with furniture and grabbed at the table as he fell. In the process, he knocked over the bottle. But the two glasses stayed on the table.'

'But why are you so sure there were two glasses, sir? And if there were, woh doosra glass gaya kahan?' asks the Inspector, a puzzled furrow on his brow.

'Because I'm pretty sure he wasn't drinking alone,' I reply. 'Get an autopsy done on his body. They'll probably say lung collapse. That would be natural, given his asthma. But ask them to also check for poisoning. And also get the alcohol that was in the bottle tested. Get a thorough check done of the table surface. There might still be a mark left by the second glass that's not visible to the naked eye.'

'Aapki theory kya hai, sir?' asks the Inspector.

'Somebody came to meet him. Somebody he knew. He opened the door for him and brought him to the living room. They opened a bottle, sat down for a drink together. For all you know, the bottle may have been a gift from the visitor. After all, Shuklaji's drinking habit was hardly a secret. Are you with me so far?'

The Inspector nods slowly and thoughtfully.

'Good. So, at some stage, the visitor slipped poison into Shuklaji's drink. Maybe Shuklaji went to the loo, maybe the visitor diverted his attention somehow. Whatever he did, for a brief while, the drink was unguarded and that's when the poison was slipped into it. Shuklaji returned, had the poisoned drink. Once the reaction set in, he collapsed. The visitor then cleaned up all evidence of his ever having been here. So, the murderer was clearly a professional who knew what he was doing. But the second glass posed a problem. It would have immediately let us know someone had come calling, and we might have been able to get DNA samples from it. So he simply took it with him. By now, it might be lying in pieces in some garbage dump in the city,' I explain.

The Inspector gapes at me, open-mouthed. 'Sir, yeh toh Sherlock Homes ke jaise case solve kar diyaa!'

'It's only a theory,' I say. 'But get the tests done, please. And let me know as soon as the results come in.'

'Yes, sir, definitely,' he says.

'One more thing,' I say. 'Don't breathe a word of this theory to the press or anybody who's not connected with this investigation. For official purposes, he died a natural death and we have no reason to suspect foul play.'

I return his salute and leave. If this is indeed murder, and I'm willing to bet it is, then it's just too much of a coincidence. Something links the three deaths that have taken place in rapid succession. But what could it be?

'So what you're telling me is that there's a killer on the loose and he's going around knocking off people who are all linked to Ambuja in some way?' asks Chandrakar when I return to his office and brief him.

I nod. 'Like I said, sir, let the reports first confirm poisoning. But yes, I believe that the three deaths are all linked, and there's a common hand behind all of them. I told the IO that we should officially say Shuklaji died of natural causes. If there is indeed one killer behind all three deaths, then I don't want him to know that we've established a link. Oh, and it might not be a bad idea to discreetly give Mr Mathur some special security, if he doesn't already have it.'

Chandrakar looks at me, thunderstruck. 'You think he might be in danger as well?'

'He spoke to two people connected to Ambuja and both of them died shortly afterwards,' I say. 'Perhaps it's best not to take any chances when it comes to him.'

He starts to nod, and then frowns as there's a knock on the door and his staff officer enters. 'This better be important,' says Chandrakar. 'I thought I'd asked to not be disturbed.'

'I'm sorry, sir, but I thought you might like to hear of this,' says the young officer. 'The forensics guys called. When they started to remove Shukla sir's body from the crime scene to conduct the autopsy, they heard a crinkling sound from one of his pajama pockets. They found a note tucked in there. It had two words written on it.'

'Let me guess,' I say. 'Lal Salaam.' From the startled look on the young man's face, I know immediately that I'm right.

CHAPTER TWENTY

'Presence of barbiturates in the alcohol and bloodstream. It reacted with the liquor and turned into poison. There's no doubt that it was a case of poisoning.'

I jerk upright as the message pops up on my phone. I'm back in Ambuja, having returned after extracting a promise from the IO to keep me posted on all developments. Now I'm wondering if I should go back and seek permission to investigate the matter further. But even as I'm thinking about it, my door opens and an unusually animated Gayaram steps in.

'Sir, I've got a tip-off. A small party of Maoists stayed overnight in the village from where we picked up Rudra,' says Gayaram.

'Ab yeh tip-offs kahan se aane lage, Gayaramji?' I say, surprised. 'I thought no one was willing to be an informer for us.'

He leans in close. 'I'll tell you, sir, but let's keep it just between us. An innocent life is at stake.'

Mystified, I nod. Gayaram speaks in little more than a whisper. 'You remember the little boy who was acting as a courier for Rudra? The one who used to carry chits from him to Mangtu every day?'

'Arrey haan, woh doosra chottu. Kya naam tha uska?' I wrinkle my brow, trying to remember.

'Forget the name, sir. I've struck up a friendship of sorts with him. To be honest, he reminds me a little of my grandkids. Anyway, I thought, no point letting this rapport go waste. So I meet him once a week secretly near the school, give him some chocolates and ask him what's going on in his village.'

'Waah, well done, Gayaramji,' I say. To be honest, I hadn't expected him to show so much initiative. Just goes to show that people are always full of surprises.

'There's more. Apparently one of the women in the Maoists' party that stayed overnight in the village is expecting.'

I raise an eyebrow. 'Is that allowed? I thought they were pretty strict about women members not getting pregnant?'

'Usually they are, but sometimes there are exceptions,' says Gayaram. 'Especially if it's someone senior.'

'Okay, so do you think they brought her there for her delivery?'

Gayaram shakes his head. 'I'm not sure, sir. But there's a doctor couple who visit the villages here every now and then, and do free check-ups as social service. They may have taken the woman to them for a consultation.'

'Who are these doctors? Have we investigated them for Maoist links?' I ask.

'Pataa nahin, sir. That's above my pay grade,' says Gayaram.

'Hmm, aap chalo. I'll get this going in a bit so that no one links it with our conversation,' I say.

Gayaram salutes and exits. I wait for about five minutes, then call Keshav into my room.

'Is there a doctor couple who goes around the villages treating people?'

He nods. 'They're very well known, sir. Dr Shakuntala Kamte and her husband, Dr Brijmohan. They have a big set-up in Raipur but they travel to the tribal areas a couple of months a year.'

'Don't they worry about the Maoists?'

'So far, no one has done anything to them, sir. They are left to do their work. They serve these areas of their own volition, you see. If the Maoists harass them, it would backfire,' says Keshav.

'And we've never questioned them either?'

'Dr Shakuntala's father was a legendary social worker. He won many prestigious awards, both national and international. Her father-in-law is a former state minister. For all you know, she could get a Nobel Peace Prize one day, or at least a Magsaysay award. And she and her husband often treat our boys for free. So, no sir, we've never officially questioned them.'

'Well, let's go meet these angels,' I say. 'And let's take along a proper party. I don't want to stumble upon a nest of Maoists.'

By the time we get there, though, the Maoists have already left. But we do meet the doctors, a couple in their late fifties or early sixties, who've set up a rudimentary clinic inside a large tent. The husband, Brijmohan, is slim, mild-mannered, and has an air of quiet competence. His wife, Shakuntala, is plump without being obese, wears her grey-streaked hair in a bun and has a brisk, grandmotherly air that makes me want to check if I've washed behind the ears.

'Did any Maoists come to consult you?' I ask.

The lady gives me a severe look. 'I don't ask my patients about their political beliefs, young man. I treat them all alike, as human beings who need my help. Though, to be honest, sometimes I wonder why I even bother, given how hell-bent everyone here seems to be on killing each other.'

'Aren't you worried that they may harm you?' I really am curious.

'So far, no one has,' she replies.

'You saw a pregnant woman today. How far along is she?' I ask.

She crosses her arms and purses her lips in disapproval. 'That is between me and my patient.'

'Ma'am, I'm merely asking you this because in case she's due any time soon, wouldn't it be better for her to have stayed back for the delivery?'

'I would always like my patients to have the best medical facilities possible. I advise them accordingly. It's up to them whether they choose to follow the advice or not,' she replies. I get the distinct impression that she's not too happy about a pregnant woman trudging around the forest.

'Well, could you at least tell me how long ago they left? I'm sure that doesn't violate any patient confidentiality,' I ask.

She hesitates. Before she can speak, Lokesh pushes aside the flap that serves as the tent entrance. 'Sir, a word with you, please,' he says.

I walk across to him. He speaks in a low tone. 'I've spoken to some of the villagers quietly. There were eight of them, including three women. They left barely an hour ago, on foot. The pregnant woman was walking, but they were also carrying a stretcher in case they need to carry her. They couldn't have gone very far. The woman's husband is apparently a senior Maoist leader in the area, Sudhakar. He was with them too.'

I whistle softly. 'Good work. Let's go.' Then I turn to the couple and raise my voice. 'Will you be staying a bit longer?'

They exchange glances. 'We were planning to move to the next village in an hour or so,' says the husband.

'Please stick around here today. Your services may be required.'

As I start to head out, Dr Shakuntala calls out, 'SP sahab.'

I turn back, an eyebrow raised in inquiry.

'Try not to harm my patient, please. Or the life she's carrying inside her.' I am taken aback by the depth of concern in her voice.

'I'll try my best to keep them safe. You have my word,' I say. Now, it's her turn to look surprised. I nod to the couple and rapidly exit the tent.

We pile into our vehicles and race down the rough jungle track, the wheels churning up dust. The journey is carried out mostly in silence, the only sound being that of the roaring engines. Then a thought strikes me. 'Are you sure we're not being led into a trap, Lokesh?' I ask. 'What if this road is mined?'

Lokesh and Gayaram, sitting in the rear, exchange uneasy glances.

'Toh kya karein, sir? Waapis chalein?' asks Gayaram.

'How trustworthy were the people you spoke to, Lokesh?'

'I don't know them, sir,' he says. 'They could have been telling the truth. Equally, they could have been telling me what Sudhakar told them to, and we could be headed straight for an ambush.'

I glance at my watch. We've been driving for about fifteen minutes. We haven't been moving too fast, but even so, we should be catching up with the party any time now.

A sparkling river comes into view. Just ahead of it, there's a grove of palm-like trees.

'There's a bridge a couple of kilometres ahead, sir,' says Gayaram. 'Once you cross it, you're in Maoist territory. I don't think any government officer has ventured that side in a decade.'

'What trees are those?' I ask, pointing at the grove.

'Salfi, sir. The sap from the tree is a natural beer, very refreshing. Maybe we can have some and then go back,' says Gayaram hopefully. 'We'll have accomplished something from the trip. But you need to have it fresh. It can turn poisonous if it gets old.'

Lokesh says something that I don't quite hear. I lean towards him—and at that precise moment, a bullet slams through my windscreen, passing through the exact spot my head had been a microsecond ago. It ricochets inside, clangs and bounces off the sides before embedding itself in the seat. Miraculously, nobody is hit.

'Shit,' I yell. 'Everybody out! Take cover.'

Luckily, the driver has the presence of mind to turn the vehicle to one side so that it is not facing the grove head on. While the right side is directly in the line of fire, the left side is shielded from it.

Having done so, he slams the brakes and turns off the engine. We tumble out of the vehicle, the guys who were seated on the right side quickly crawling out without exposing themselves. All of us shelter behind the jeep.

The vehicles behind us follow our example. Cautiously, I stick my neck out and try to peer at the grove. A bullet clangs into the fender. I hastily withdraw.

There is complete silence for a moment. And then, a low, agonised moan from a woman fills the air before it is hastily cut off, as though someone has clamped a hand over her mouth. The pain in the voice sends a shiver down my spine.

'What the hell was that?' I ask.

'Sir, sounds like labour pains,' offers Gayaram with a wrinkled brow. Of the four of us, he's the only one with children.

'Damn. How long will it take for delivery?' I ask.

Gayaram shrugs. 'You never can tell, sir.'

'Oh my God. If she doesn't get to a doctor fast, could she die right here?' I ask.

'Yes sir, it's possible,' says Gayaram.

Another moan floats towards us, and is again hastily cut off. I make up my mind. 'Sudhakar,' I yell out at the top of my lungs. 'Has your wife gone into labour?'

There's no response. Then a figure tries to scurry out from the grove towards the distance, where the bridge is. A volley of shots rings out from our side. He scuttles back into the cover of the trees.

It's a stand-off. If we try to move towards the grove, we become easy targets. But if they try to emerge out of the grove and head for the bridge, we can pick them off. Of course, we have one huge advantage in our favour—we don't have a woman who's probably about to have a baby in our party.

The silence continues for a while. Then the woman makes another sound. This time it's a short, sharp cry.

'Sudhakar, your wife needs urgent medical attention. Her life could be in danger. Surrender now and come out peacefully. I promise none of you will come to any harm and we'll rush her straight to the doctors at the village,' I yell.

A couple of shots ring out and slam into the jeep. I sigh.

'Don't be a fool. You're risking her life,' I yell again.

Silence. When it stretches on for about five minutes, I cautiously peer out from behind the jeep. Nothing happens this time. I start to rise and duck right back when a shot is fired. It clangs into the side of the jeep.

'This jeep is going to need a lot of work when we get back,' I growl.

After a couple of minutes, a constable who's taken cover in the van behind us starts wriggling along the ground. A puff of dust rises up a few feet ahead of him. He freezes on the spot, then rapidly rolls back.

I lean against the jeep and gaze up at the sky, trying to figure out what to do next. The sky is a clear, idyllic blue. The warmth of the sun on my face is pleasant.

A sense of calm settles upon me. It's absolutely quiet now. In the stillness, a bird begins to chirp. Suddenly, the whole situation seems completely ridiculous. In the midst of all this natural beauty, why are we busy trying to kill each other?

'Sir, sir, jaage hain ki so gaye?' asks Gayaram, breaking my trance.

'Don't worry, Gayaramji. I'm very much awake,' I say. As I speak, I cough. The dust from the dirt track is irritating my throat. I look around. 'Paani hai kya?' I ask.

'Gaadi mein hai, sir. Nikaalta hoon,' says Gayaram. He opens one of the doors, leans in, pulls out a canteen and hands it over. I take a sip and roll the water around in my mouth, trying to get rid of the dryness. No point taking big gulps, there's only a little bit to go around.

'Aur kisi ko chahiye?' I ask.

They all nod. I pass the canteen around. The shadows are starting to lengthen. I look at the spot on the ground where the bullet had slammed in, ahead of the constable, and a thought occurs to me.

'Ek cheez notice ki? The last couple of bullets have been fired well wide of us. It's almost as if they don't want to hit us, they just want to keep us pinned down,' I say.

'Or maybe they're just really bad shooters,' says Lokesh, dryly.

'At least some of them over there must have spent years fighting our forces. They can't all be that bad,' I say.

'Chaliye, aapki theory test karte hain,' says Lokesh. Before I can stop him, he rises and steps out from behind the jeep. Immediately, a shot is fired, but the bullet passes by harmlessly.

Lokesh calmly strolls back and nods at me. 'Yes, I think that was a deliberate miss.'

'Paagal ho kya? You could have been killed. What the hell were you thinking?' I'm furious.

'Arrey, seniors pe itna toh bharosa hona chahiye, sir,' responds Lokesh with a smile.

'So, they're not really trying to hit us, but they're also not letting us move ahead. What the hell are they playing at? Is there any other way to cross the river, apart from the bridge?'

'Only if you swim across,' says Gayaram. 'The river flows behind the grove.'

'That's it! One or two of them must have stayed back to keep us pinned down while the rest cross the river. But the ones who stayed behind don't want us to get angry in case they're captured, or if they eventually surrender,' I say.

'But there's no way a woman in labour is going to be able to swim across that river,' says Gayaram. 'Unless they have a raft or something.'

'Weren't they carrying a stretcher? They could try floating her across in that,' I point out.

'That's risky, but doable. If they're desperate, they might just try it,' concedes Gayaram.

'That makes sense,' says Lokesh. 'Toh ab?'

'Let me try again,' I say. Raising my voice, I yell out, 'It's not too late. You can still surrender. Nobody has been killed or wounded. I promise no harm will come to anybody who surrenders peacefully.'

There's another bullet in reply. Lokesh frowns. 'Looks like they're not interested in your offer, sir,' he says.

'Hmm, all the bullets only seem to be coming from one direction and one weapon,' I say. 'Lokesh, when I say the word, do that stunt of yours again, but don't expose so much of yourself this time. Just a quick peek out and back in, okay?'

He nods. I pick up his rifle—my revolver doesn't quite have the range I'll need—and say, 'On my count of three. One, two, three, go!'

Lokesh steps out for a second, then retreats. As he does so, I lean out from the other side. Sure enough, there's a flash from the grove and a bullet whizzes towards Lokesh, but passes by harmlessly. I whip up the rifle and fire in the direction of the flash. A second later, there's a wail of anguish and then a panicked cry. Then we hear the sound of running feet, trampling on leaves.

'Looks like they're trying to make a dash for it,' I say, leaping to my feet.

'Wait, sir. It could still be a trap,' says Lokesh. 'Let me go first.'

'We'll step out together,' I say. 'I'll go from the front side of the vehicle, you go from the other side. Ready? Now.'

I step out around the vehicle, feeling like a turtle whose shell has been removed. Lokesh does the same from the other side. Nothing happens. I signal to the others and they all emerge from cover.

'To the grove,' I yell and begin running. The others follow. There are no shots.

As I enter the grove, I see a prone figure. Instinctively, I point my revolver at it. Then I see that it's a heavily pregnant woman, curled up in agony. Tears are running down her face.

'You've killed him,' she sobs. 'You've killed Sudhakar.'

The others burst into the grove behind me, ready to open fire. 'Don't shoot! Hold fire!' I yell frantically.

There's a body lying near the woman. He's bleeding from the temple. Lokesh squats and then looks up, startled. 'Sir, he's still breathing!' he says. 'He's unconscious, but he seems to be alive.'

'Let me see.' I bend over and look at Sudhakar. I gently run my fingers over his head, searching for the exit wound. There isn't any.

'The bullet is still lodged in there,' I say. 'I'd heard of cases like this, but I'd never actually seen one.'

'Can he still make it?' asks Lokesh.

I shrug. 'Only a doctor can tell us that. The best we can do is get his wound cleaned and bandaged.'

Lokesh nods, then points at the ground around us. There are lots of footprints and the soil is disturbed. 'The others can't be too far off,' he says. 'We might still be able to catch them.'

'Take some men and head for the river,' I say. 'But be careful not to rush into an ambush. The rest of you, please pick up these two and take them to my jeep. We have some lives to save.'

CHAPTER TWENTY-ONE

A newborn's lusty wails fill the air. Gayaram, Lokesh and I spontaneously break into relieved smiles. We've been pacing here—'here' being the village headman's house, which we've commandeered as a makeshift surgical ward—ever since they took the woman into the OT. The house had been close enough and big enough for our purposes. We'd requested Dr Shakuntala and Dr Brijmohan to tend to the couple—they already knew their case histories. Just about the time we'd sorted this out, Lokesh had joined us.

Following our departure from the grove, he and some men had raced to the riverbank and spotted someone swimming in the river. Lokesh had debated whether to go after him, but as they were already more than halfway across, he sensibly decided against it and drove back to the village instead. There, he'd joined Gayaram and me in our tense vigil.

'Thank goodness!' says Gayaram. 'I wasn't this worked up when it was my own children.'

I laugh and slap his shoulder. Just then, Dr Shakuntala steps out, looking absolutely exhausted. She removes her surgical mask, heaves in a couple of deep breaths and looks at us. 'Anyone have a beedi or cigarette?'

We gape at her. 'But you're a doctor,' objects Lokesh.

'Yes. And right now, I'm also an extremely tired, extremely irritable human being,' she says grouchily.

'I'm sorry, I don't smoke,' I say. Gayaram shakes his head too. 'I quit some years ago,' he says. 'Doctor's orders.'

'Right, rub it in,' growls the doctor.

I look inquiringly at Lokesh. 'Sir, main toh athlete aadmi hoon. Cigarette bidi se kya kaam? Haan, but I can definitely offer madam some water,' he says, proffering a bottle to her.

'Good lord, what saintly policemen,' she grumbles, but takes a deep swig from the bottle. She keeps the water in her mouth for a couple of seconds, savouring it, then gulps it down. She does that a couple more times, then nods gratefully and hands the bottle back to Lokesh.

'Thanks. I needed that. And I'm glad you guys don't smoke. I've been doing my best to quit and a puff now would have undone months of effort,' she says.

'We're happy to help. Er ... doctor sahab, how are the mother and child doing?' I ask.

She smiles. It's the first time I've seen her not looking grumpy or surly, and it transforms her face. 'They're both okay, thank God. It was touch and go for a while. You got Saroj here in the nick of time. The baby wasn't due for another couple of months. I was worried about her, but she's a little fighter and she should be okay. Mind you, an incubator would be nice, but Brij will do some jugaad and rig up something to help. He's quite resourceful.'

'So the mother's name is Saroj?' I ask.

Her smile vanishes. 'Yes. Now I suppose you'll have to arrest her or something?'

'It depends. I don't think she's wanted for any major crimes, though I'll have to check. What about Sudhakar? How is he?'

She shakes her head. 'He's in coma right now. He'll need a very complicated surgery and neither Brij nor I are competent to perform it. Even if he gets operated and survives, it's hard to say what long-term damage he might suffer. He could spend the rest of his life hooked up to a machine, he could suffer complete memory loss, he could be in a wheelchair, or he could just start walking and talking and be absolutely fine apart from the occasional headache. The brain is a funny thing. Until we can get him to a surgeon, all we can do for him is to try and keep him as stable and comfortable as possible.'

'Is it okay if I talk to Saroj for a while?' I ask.

'Okay, but try not to make it too long. She's very tired and needs rest,' says the doctor.

I turn to Lokesh and Gayaram. 'I want the strictest possible security cover for Saroj as long as we're here. Nobody apart from the doctors and the three of us goes in or out of the room. I want either one of you to personally be here and monitor this at all times.'

'Yes, sir,' they chorus. I nod and step into the room.

Saroj is lying on the bed, the baby peacefully nestled against her. She is looking at her infant lovingly, managing to simultaneously look completely exhausted and utterly radiant.

She turns at the sound of my footsteps. Her expression changes to one of hatred.

'You!' she spits out. 'What do you want? You've practically killed my husband anyway. Have you come back to finish the job?'

I take a step back, shocked at her vehemence. 'Why would I want to do that? I kept yelling at him to surrender! He didn't listen.'

'Yes, because he was certain that if he did, you and your goons in uniform would finish him off in a fake encounter, since he's such a high-ranking Maoist. And you know the real irony? We were on the run from the Maoists ourselves!'

'What?' I say, puzzled. 'How is that possible?'

'Sudhakar had a bitter falling out with the head of the zonal committee, Sooraj. Both of us had been getting steadily disillusioned for some time. We'd joined the Maoists because we'd thought it was a noble movement. But over time, we came to realise that while many of the cadres lived in extreme hardship, the so-called revolution had just become a lucrative business for many of the leaders. When Sooraj took over from Santoshji a few years back, we thought things would get better. But he proved to be even more corrupt and brutal than his predecessor.

'A few days ago, Sudhakar and Sooraj got into a fierce argument in front of the whole camp. Sooraj is not the sort of person who tolerates dissent. That night, some of his men attacked our tent. Luckily, we were expecting something like that, and managed to escape with a few of Sudhakar's closest comrades. But we knew it was only a matter of time. Either the police would get us or the Maoists would. Well, congratulations. You got there first. I hope you're very happy.'

I stare at her, trying to figure out what to say. But before I can open my mouth, the doctor steps in.

'You have no business yelling at this man, young lady,' she says, wagging her finger admonishingly at Saroj. 'If he hadn't come racing back with you, your baby would almost certainly not have survived. You'd probably have bled out and died too.'

I'm not sure who's more startled by the doctor's outburst, Saroj or me. But before either of us can react, the doctor takes a deep breath and resumes. 'I've seen the world. I've seen lots of people. This is a good, conscientious officer. He didn't have to bring Sudhakar back. If he wanted to finish him off, he could have simply put one more bullet into his skull. He didn't have to bring you back either. But he did. And this is how you thank him?'

Saroj opens her mouth to reply but the doctor holds up a hand. 'Don't interrupt me. I'm not done talking yet. All these years, when Sudhakar was terrorising innocent people and killing cops, you didn't have a problem with it. Now that you've had a baby and you've come face-to-face with your own mortality, you've suddenly become all concerned about the sanctity of life? You chose a life of violence and lawlessness for yourself. What did you expect, that you'd get to waltz off into the sunset with your baby and Prince Charming? Well, wake up, this isn't a fairy tale, it's the real world. Actions have consequences. You have only yourself to blame for whatever has happened to you and your family.'

The doctor pauses to catch a breath. She's gone very red in the face. Before she can resume, Saroj bursts out crying.

'Oh God, spare me the waterworks. They're not going to achieve anything. If you want to make amends, do something constructive, like maybe talking to this man,' says Dr Shakuntala. She looks at me sternly. 'Can you help this woman and her baby in any way?'

I stare at the doctor speechlessly. I'm deeply moved by her intervention on my behalf, more so because it was so unexpected.

'Oh, quit goggling at me like a fish out of water. Do you have anything helpful to contribute?' she asks waspishly.

I hastily pull myself together. The thought crosses my mind that Dr Shakuntala is a bit of a coconut, with a tough exterior concealing a tender core, but I keep it to myself. Instead, I turn to Saroj. 'If you genuinely want to surrender, I can help,' I say. 'But I'll need your full cooperation. There are rehabilitation schemes for surrendered Maoists. You could get a new identity and go away somewhere far from here. I'll have all charges against you dropped and help you get a brand new identity, if you like.'

'And what would I do? Become a manual labourer somewhere or work as a maid in someone's house?' she asks bitterly.

'What are your options?' I ask. 'Will you go back into the forest? How long will you survive now that Sooraj has turned against you? Bringing her up without any facilities, always fearing for her safety—is that really the life you want for this child? Or growing up in a prison, for that matter?'

Dr Shakuntala reaches for her hand. Saroj looks at her

apprehensively, but the doctor now speaks gently. 'Saroj, I know people who run welfare homes for women and help with skill development. I can speak to them. You're very bright and you can build a better life for yourself. More importantly, you can offer your child a far better life than she would otherwise get. Think about her too, not just yourself.'

'And what would I have to do in return?' she asks.

'Nothing much. Just answer a few questions,' I reply.

She looks at me speculatively. 'What about Sudhakar?' she asks.

'I'll ensure he gets medical treatment,' I reply. 'Beyond that, I can't promise anything. There are too many serious charges against him. If he recovers and becomes an informer, the government may be willing to offer him some sort of amnesty or reduced sentence, but that's not a commitment I can make at my level.'

'What if any information I give you is useless? Will our deal still hold?'

I hesitate, then answer as honestly as possible. 'I want to help you. I really do. Please help me help you.'

She stares into my eyes, perhaps trying to gauge my sincerity. I look back at her wordlessly. Finally, she nods. 'All right,' she says. 'Ask your questions.'

'Fine,' I say. 'Why was Purshottam Sethi killed?'

She shakes her head. 'That wasn't us. We were as mystified by that as you seem to be.'

'What? Are you sure about that?' I ask.

She nods. 'If it had been us, I would have known for sure. Sudhakar would have told me. It wasn't us.'

'And what about the journalist? Devika Doria?' That's the question that I really want answered.

She looks troubled. 'Sudhakar wasn't involved with that. Sooraj's men were supposed to bring her into the forest. But something went wrong and she got killed instead. Sudhakar was very upset. It was one of the reasons he had his tiff with Sooraj. He said that Devika Doria had always been fair in her coverage and there was no reason for us to get involved in her abduction, especially since it went so horribly wrong. Sooraj simply told him that it was important for Devika to be silenced and Sudhakar didn't need to know everything.'

This isn't terribly helpful, I think. Saroj has a faraway look in her eyes. 'I got quite a shock when I heard about Devika. I'd met her father years ago, you know. He'd come to stay with us for some time, to do a detailed article. Madho uncle was very friendly, spent a lot of time with the children and teenagers in the camp. I think he was fascinated by our lives. He often spoke about Devika to us—and how she would have really liked me and Mahua.'

'Mahua?' I ask.

Saroj nods. 'She was my best friend. An orphan. Her father was the legendary Maoist commander Bhadru, who fell in love with a village school teacher. If I'm not mistaken, Devika's father had met Bhadru a few times, which is why he spent so much time with Mahua and Kranti when he ran into them in our camp. Anyway, after Bhadru met his lady love, he surrendered, served a short sentence and became a farmer.'

'The Maoist leadership allowed him to just walk away?' I ask.

'Santoshji would never have allowed it, but the zonal committee head then was a different person. Bhadru gave him his word that he would never betray the movement in any way and would continue to work for the poor in that area. He gave his blessings to Bhadru to surrender,' explains Saroj.

'So what happened then?' I ask, intrigued by this story of how a Maoist commander's life was transformed by love.

'They started a family—they had Mahua and her younger brother, Kranti. There was some talk of Bhadru launching a political career—apparently he was quite popular with the people of that area. But he and his wife got killed one day in a crossfire between the police and our forces. So Mahua and Kranti came to stay with us in the forest.'

'How old were they then?' I ask.

'Mahua must have been about sixteen, around the same age as me,' she says.

'If you don't mind my asking, how did you end up joining the Maoists at such a young age?' I ask.

She sighs and seems to sag into the pillows. 'There was a Maoist party that visited our village every few days. Each family would share its meal with one Maoist. That was all we did. It was almost a custom. But one day, a landlord's private army descended upon us. They said we were Maoist sympathisers and needed to be punished. The village was burnt to the ground. Most of the families fled to other parts. A few of us ran into the forests to join the Maoists full-time. My family and I were among them. That was a few months before Mahua and Kranti joined us.'

'Okay. And how old was Kranti?'

'About eleven, maybe twelve. Irritating, in the way younger brothers can be. But Mahua absolutely doted on him. He was all that was left of her family, after all. He was a little brat, talking all the time, and a very enthusiastic member of the Bal Sangathan—our children's wing. The only time he shut up was when he had a gun in his hands. Even at that age, he was a crack shot,' says Saroj.

'So where are they now?' I ask.

Saroj's eyes mist over. 'Mahua is dead,' she says. 'So is Kranti.'

'What happened to them?'

Saroj sighs. 'I still remember that day. I woke up early one morning to a huge ruckus in the camp. Santoshji had taken over just a few months ago—the previous head died in the same battle that took Mahua's parents. He was shouting at the top of his lungs that he'd caught Mahua with a mobile phone, trying to get in touch with the police. So she attacked him with a knife. He had to kill her in self-defence, he said.'

'Do you believe that?'

'Well, I know Mahua had her doubts about the movement. She was never very ideologically committed. Once or twice, she'd told me that the way our leadership was living was very different from the ideals her father had taught her. I told her not to say such things aloud, and especially not to anyone other than me. But I would never have believed her to be a traitor. It was a nasty shock.'

'And Kranti?' I prompt.

'When he saw his sister lying dead, he went absolutely mad. He screamed that he would kill Santoshji and threw a stone at him, hitting him on the forehead. A bunch of our fighters ran to catch him. He ran away. They followed him deep into the forest. The last time he was seen, he was running down a steep slope that led to a river. He couldn't swim at all. Then there was a loud splash. By the time our people reached the river, there was no sign of him. He probably fell into the river and his body was washed away,' Saroj wipes her tears.

'Hmm, and where is Santoshji now?' I ask.

'He disappeared a couple of years ago,' she replies. 'He had developed arthritis and was struggling to cope with life in the forest. One night, he addressed us very emotionally around a campfire and thanked us for our loyalty and support. He also said he would be leaving to continue the movement from another location, and that Sooraj would be taking over. The next morning, he was gone. None of us knows exactly where he went.'

The baby shifts restlessly and Dr Shakuntala hurriedly pats her. 'Vikram, I'm going to have to ask you to stop now. This conversation has gone on for way too long. You really need to let Saroj get some rest.'

'Sure, sure, I'm so sorry,' I say soothingly. 'Just one final question. Do you remember exactly when all this happened? How many years ago?'

Dr Shakuntala looks at me warningly but Saroj quickly says, 'It's okay.' She frowns as she tries to jog her memory. This would have happened about fifteen years ago. I don't recall the exact date, but I do remember that the river was in spate, so it was probably sometime during the monsoon.'

'Thank you, Saroj,' I say gratefully. 'You've been most helpful.'

Dr Shakuntala's husband steps in just then. 'I've got a nice little improvised incubator ready for the baby, if you want to put her in there,' he says. 'By the way, does she have a name yet?'

We all look at Saroj. She smiles. 'Earlier, I'd thought of some revolutionary-sounding names. But now, I'm thinking I might call her Salfi.'

'That's a pretty name,' says Dr Shakuntala. She picks up the child and offers her to me to hold. 'SP Vikram Pratap Singh, meet baby Salfi.'

I recoil hastily. 'Er ... no thanks. I don't think I should. I might drop her or hurt her ....'

She bursts out laughing. 'All you tough guys just wet your pants at the thought of holding a baby. Really, they're a lot more durable than you'd think. Especially this one. She's a real toughie.' She smiles fondly at the infant.

'Well, she'll certainly have a great story to tell about her birth,' I say. 'And with a name like Salfi, she's bound to be asked about it a lot.'

I walk out and find Gayaram waiting outside. He looks a little nervous.

'All okay, Gayaramji?'

'Sir, we need to leave this place as soon as possible. Who knows when the Maoists will take it into their heads to attack us?' he says.

'You have a point,' I say. 'Do we have a safe house in town where we can keep her and the child?'

'There's the police guest house. We can keep her there for a few days. I think we'll eventually need to move her to Raipur or somewhere else far away, though,' he offers.

I nod. 'You're right. For now, tell the men to be on high alert. We'll call in some reinforcements as well. We'll leave here as soon as the doctor tells us it's safe to move Saroj and the baby. I'll see if we can get Sudhakar medically evacuated by chopper. And once we get back to Ambuja, I want to have a good, long look at some old files.'

CHAPTER TWENTY-TWO

'Sir, if you could tell us exactly what you're looking for, perhaps we could help,' says Keshav.

'I don't know for sure myself,' I admit. 'I'm hoping I'll spot it when I see it.'

Keshav looks completely baffled by that. I laugh ruefully. 'I know that sounds weird,' I say. 'Anyway, please don't disturb me for the rest of the day unless it's really urgent.'

I pick up another file from the pile in front of me and sneeze as the dust tickles my nose. Keshav hastily steps forward, pulling out his handkerchief. 'Arrey, laane se pehle theek se dusting toh kar dete,' he mutters, vigorously slapping the files with the cloth.

'It's okay, Keshav, thanks,' I wave him away and gingerly open the file—it looks like it might fall apart at any moment.

Keshav salutes and leaves the room. I begin looking through, jotting down notes every once in a while.

Gayaram knocks and peeps in. I look up and frown.

'I said not to disturb me unless it's urgent,' I say.

He clears his throat. 'Sir, chaar baj rahe hain. Aapne lunch bhi nahin kiya. Kuch chai-biskut lenge?'

I look at my watch, startled. It's actually 4 p.m. I'd been so engrossed, I hadn't realised the whole morning and afternoon had flown by. My stomach rumbles loudly, registering its protest. Suddenly, I feel ravenous.

'I think I'd better have some sandwiches,' I say.

'Right, sir. Main abhi bhijwata hoon,' he says, starting to withdraw.

'Gayaramji, wait a minute, please,' I say. He stops and looks at me inquiringly. 'Remember you once told me you used to write notes that you eventually planned to turn into a book or a movie?'

'That was just a pipe dream, sir,' he says. 'Why are you teasing me about it?'

'But you did write notes?' I persist.

He nods ruefully. 'Yes, I did.'

'Do you have stuff from, say, fifteen years ago?' I ask, fingers crossed under my desk.

He thinks about it, then nods. 'I think so, yes. Why, sir?'

'Because there are a whole lot of gaps in the official files that I'm not able to fill. And I'm hoping your notes might help. Can you go and get them?'

'It might take me a while to find them, sir,' he says. 'They're probably buried in a trunk under multiple layers of clothing.'

'Please find them and come back here,' I say. 'And I don't care if it takes till midnight. I'll be waiting.'

He comes to attention. 'Then I'd better get going right away, sir,' he says, and makes a rapid exit.

He's back in a couple of hours, carrying a cloth bag with a couple of big diaries packed inside. 'I found them,' he says proudly. 'There were quite a few diaries, but luckily I'd indexed them by date. I think these will cover the period you were asking about.'

'Wonderful work, Gayaramji,' I say enthusiastically. 'Please take a seat, this is going to take some time. To begin with, please tell me, do you remember someone called Bhadru?'

'Naam jaana pehchaana hai, sir. Let me see,' says Gayaram, opening up one of the diaries and leafing through it. Suddenly, he stops. 'Oh yes, Bhadru ... he's mentioned right here. He was a senior Maoist commander who surrendered and was given a full pardon. I think we even offered to induct him as a special police officer, but he flatly refused. He said he would never work against his former comrades. At least, that's what I heard.'

'What else do you have on him?' I ask.

Gayaram reads through the pages rapidly. 'After a few months of living peacefully, he began organising demonstrations. There was some road that was due to be constructed that would pass through his village and the villagers didn't want to give up their land. It seems they were unhappy with the acquisition rates that were being offered.'

Gayaram looks up at me, his eyes bright with excitement. 'You know, sir, I met Bhadru a couple of times in the course of work. What a personality he had! Very charismatic, and he could really inspire a crowd. Who knows, if he hadn't died when he did, he might have become an MP, or something bigger. He certainly commanded a lot of public support.'

'So he had an untimely death?' I ask.

Gayaram nods. 'Yes, his wife too. It was a terrible tragedy. The head of the zonal committee then was unwell and needed surgery. He was staying at Bhadru's place and they were talking to some doctors to go there and perform it. Before that could happen, we raided the place. There was a shootout and quite a few Maoists were killed—the zonal committee head among them. Bhadru came out, yelling at everyone to stop. He said he'd get the commander to surrender. But just then, a bullet hit him in the crossfire and he died. His wife screamed and came out running. She got hit and died as well.'

I stroke my chin, digesting this. 'And how exactly did we get to know that the Maoist commander was staying at Bhadru's place?' I ask.

Gayaram scratches his head and refers to his diary. 'Tip-off, sir.'

'Who gave the tip-off, Gayaramji?' I ask.

He shakes his head. 'I don't know, sir. It came from someone in the Maoist camp directly to the SP sahab. Remember Kailash Shuklaji, the one who died recently? It came to him.'

'And Santoshji became the zonal committee head after this encounter?'

Gayaram thinks about it, then nods. 'I suppose so. If Bhadru had stayed on with the Maoists, he might have become the successor. Santoshji was next in line, so he took over.'

'Well, that particular encounter seems to have worked out very well for Santoshji,' I say. 'Moving on, there was another big incident a couple of months later.'

Gayaram cocks his head to one side. 'You'll have to remind me, sir,' he says.

'The sitting MLA and a contractor were killed in a Maoist attack,' I say.

'Oh, yes,' says Gayaram. 'I remember that attack very clearly. I was part of the security team. I have it noted here in detail.'

'Tell me whatever you can, please,' I say.

Gayaram shivers involuntarily. 'Sorry sir, achaanak raungte khade ho gaye. So yes, we were heading for the ground-breaking ceremony for the new road. After Bhadru's death, the protests had faded away and the project was set to begin. There were a couple of escort vehicles in front. Shukla sahab was in his vehicle behind them, followed by the vehicle in which the MLA was seated, along with the contractor. They were followed by a couple of police trucks, then the DM sahab, with a couple of his colleagues, and some more trucks behind them.'

'Wasn't Mr Shravan Kumar Mathur the DM those days?' I ask.

'Ho sakta hai, sir. I haven't got it here,' says Gayaram, a trifle irritated at having his story interrupted.

'Sorry, please continue,' I say.

Gayaram nods. 'We were a short distance away from the site when SP sahab's car suddenly stopped. The entire convoy came to a halt. He jumped out of his vehicle, yelling that he had seen some movement in the forest. Suddenly, there were a couple of loud blasts. All of us dove for cover. As luck would have it, one of the blasts took place exactly where the MLA's vehicle was standing. I still remember how it was thrown into the air like a ball and turned over before crashing back. Then the Maoists began firing at us and tossing grenades. We fired back as best we could, but it wasn't much of a fight.'

'All four people in the MLA's vehicle died that day,' I say, reading out from a page I'd bookmarked in the case file. 'He, the driver, the bodyguard and the contractor.'

Gayaram shivers again. 'All the corpses were so badly mangled, it was hard to identify them.'

'Hmm. A rather unfortunate coincidence, wouldn't you say? The vehicle being at the exact spot where the blast took place?' I muse.

'Jiska time jab likha hai, woh tabhi jaata hai, sir,' says Gayaram philosophically.

'A couple of other people were killed in the firing, and quite a few people were wounded,' I reflect.

'Yes. SP sahab was among them,' says Gayaram.

'A flesh wound on the left arm as he led a counter-attack into the forest,' I read from the case file. 'Well, I'm sure that would have been painful, but it's not exactly life-threatening.'

'Sorry, sir?' says Gayaram.

'Kuch nahin, Gayaramji. I'm just thinking aloud. Ignore me. Well, thank you very much. This has been most informative. Mujhe lagta hai, aapka naam Google Gayaram rakh dena chahiye,' I say.

He flushes with pleasure. 'I'm glad I could help, sir.'

After he leaves the room, I pick up the phone and call Shravan Kumar Mathur. He answers after a couple of rings. 'Yes?' he says curtly.

'Sir, I had a couple of questions regarding the Devika Doria case. Are you free to talk?'

'I can give you five minutes right now. More than that, we'll have to talk later,' he says.

'Five minutes is good for now,' I say hastily. 'A few years ago, an MLA and a contractor were killed in a Maoist attack while on their way to the inauguration of a road project. Do you remember this?'

'Oh yes, I remember clearly. It's not every day that you're in a life-and-death situation. I was part of that convoy. The most terrifying experience of my life. Later, I was told the whole encounter lasted barely ten minutes, but to me it seemed to stretch on forever.'

'Yes, time can work in funny ways in combat situations,' I say. 'So, sir, a question. The road project went ahead anyway?'

'Well, work stopped for a few months. But it was a prestige issue for the government. So we invited a fresh round of bids. There was only one bidder this time.'

'Let me guess,' I say. 'Purshottam Sethi?'

'Well, yes. And he quoted quite a steep rate too, if I recall correctly. Fair enough, I suppose, after what had happened to the last guy. That project was really the making of Sethi, in some ways. Before that, he used to be a small-time contractor. After that, there was no looking back for him.'

I'm silent for a couple of moments, absorbing this information.

'Vikram, are you still there?' asks Mathur, interrupting my reverie.

'Yes, sir. Thank you, this is very helpful,' I say.

'Have you made any progress in finding out who killed Devika and Sethi?' he asks.

'I'm getting there, sir,' I reply. 'I think I'm a lot closer today than I was a couple of days ago.'

'Good to hear that. Well, if I can be of any further help, don't hesitate to ask,' he says, and hangs up.

'I certainly will,' I mutter under my breath and dial another number. This one belongs to Sanjeev Phatankar, a batchmate from the National Police Academy with an MBA in finance, who's an absolute wizard with numbers. Phatankar is happiest when peering at a spreadsheet, and I often tease him that apart from answering in class, the only human he ever spoke to during his time at the Academy was me.

'What's up, Fatty?' I say when he picks up. The nickname is an ironic pun on his surname—he's about 5 feet 10 inches and his weight hasn't crossed 65 kg in all the years that I've known him.

'All good,' he responds. 'Kya zaroorat padh gayi meri?'

'Arrey yaar, can't I just call because I'm thinking of you?' I ask.

'Of course, you can. And the only time you ever remember me is when you're stuck in an investigation and need some help. So, forget the PC and get right to the point. What do you want from me?' He's as charming as always.

'I need someone's finances looked at thoroughly. Particularly if there was any extra money coming in from the Purshottam Sethi group of companies,' I say.

'Okay. And who's this person?' he asks.

I take a deep breath. 'Kailash Shukla,' I say.

'The retired cop? The one who died recently? Abbey, what sort of booby trap are you setting for me?' he says, his voice rising.

'Yaar, Sethi was killed recently. And for your information, Shukla didn't die, he was murdered. I'm convinced the two cases are connected. My theory is that Shukla was on Sethi's payroll, but I have no concrete evidence. Tu thoda pataa kar na. Merey liye itna toh kar sakta hai,' I shamelessly wheedle.

'Hello, I'll need to look through all his bank accounts and financial records. And how do you propose I go about snooping through them unofficially?' he snaps.

'If that's your problem, then I'll speak to the DGP and ask him to assign you to the investigation. This is top priority. I'm sure he won't say no,' I coax.

'Yeah, all right. If Chandru says it's okay, I'll do it,' he grunts.

'Thanks, Fatty, you're a sweetheart,' I say, hanging up and dialling Chandrakar. After I explain the situation to him, he agrees to let Phatankar help with the investigation.

A couple of hours later, the phone rings. It's Phatankar.

'Kuch milaa kyaa?' I ask.

'It takes a while to go through a lifetime of accounts,' he says sourly. 'I've only just scratched the surface. But I found something interesting. Thought you might like to know.'

'Spill it already!' My impatience is clearly getting the better of me.

'Patience, patience,' he says. 'Okay, so Shukla has this son who works in the United States.'

'Yes, I know. What about him?' I ask.

'Well, Shukla was the guarantor of a student loan the boy had taken to study at an Ivy League college. Apparently, he was set to offer his house as collateral for the loan. But before the bank could disburse it, they returned the amount, explaining they wouldn't be needing it after all; the boy had landed a pretty luxurious scholarship from some foundation. Full cost of living and studying taken care of, and a tidy amount left over for pocket money. I wondered who this generous benefactor might be, so I dug around. Turns out this foundation has only ever made two generous donations, one of them to Shukla's son. And while the ownership pattern was very, very hazy and muddled, if you dig deep enough, you find the money eventually leads back to Purshottam Sethi,' Phatankar signs off with a flourish, his voice smug.

'Fatty, you're a genius,' I state in awe.

'I know that, though you seem to keep forgetting it,' he crows.

'By the way, you mentioned that there were two donations. What was the other one?'

'Nothing related to Shukla, from what I could figure out. It was to some NGO called Lakshmi Devi Trust that runs a women's shelter home in Thane. This donation was a lot more recent—just a couple of years ago or so.'

'Hmm. Oh well, keep digging into Shukla's accounts and see what you can find,' I say.

'Jo hukum, merey aaka.' I can picture him bowing sardonically. 'And may I ask what you'll be doing, meanwhile?'

I'm about to answer when my phone rings. I peer at the screen. It's Chandrakar.

'Gotta go, Chandru's calling,' I say hastily. 'Thanks, Fatty. I owe you yet again.'

'Sir,' I say, accepting Chandrakar's call.

'Vikram, can you start for Raipur at once?' he asks, a note of excitement in his voice.

'Certainly sir, but may I ask what this is about?'

'There's somebody I want you to meet,' he responds. 'I think you'll find what he has to say very, very interesting.'

CHAPTER TWENTY-THREE

'ACP Shreyas Shinde, Mumbai Police, sir,' the stranger introduces himself. He's of average height, and wiry, with a crew cut and upturned moustache.

'Shinde had sought permission to visit Ambuja in the course of an investigation he's conducting,' explains Chandrakar. We're all sitting in his office. 'When I heard about the case, I thought it was very important for you to be briefed as well.' He gestures to Shinde. 'Please proceed.'

Shinde clears his throat, and begins. 'A few days ago, we got a call about a gruesome murder at a women's shelter home in Thane.'

'Excuse me?' I sit up in my seat. 'A women's shelter in Thane? Is it run by an NGO called, er ....' I try to remember the name Phatankar had told me. It's sitting there, right at the tip of my tongue, and then it suddenly pops into my head. 'Lakshmi Devi Trust?'

Shinde and Chandrakar look startled. 'Yes, it is! How did you know that?' asks Shinde.

'The name came up while I was probing Kailash Shukla's murder,' I say. 'I'll explain later. Please continue.'

'Well, the person who ran the home, one Rakesh Kumar, had been stabbed to death pretty viciously. There were multiple wounds on his chest and stomach. But the women staying there weren't too upset about it. When we began investigating, we soon found out why,' says Shinde. He pauses for a moment. When he resumes, there is anger in his voice.

'That place was a horror story. The women were being forced into prostitution. Cars would be sent to pick them up late in the evening and they'd return only the next morning. Apparently, Mr Kumar himself used to molest some of them from time to time, even though his ill-health didn't permit him to go all the way. He also liked getting two or three of them together and would make videos while forcing them to perform unnatural acts for the camera. Anybody who resisted would be beaten black and blue. A real sick bastard,' says Shinde.

'I can see why people would want to kill him,' I say. 'Do you think some of the women in the shelter did it?'

'Well, that would have been the natural thing to suspect,' Shinde replies. 'But there was one thing that didn't add up. He was killed in his office. And the killer used his blood to write two words on the wall ....'

'Lal Salaam,' I finish.

Shinde's eyes widen in surprise. 'How on earth did you know that, sir? Could you please tell me what is going on?'

'We've had a series of murders where that phrase has been used,' I explain. 'I'm not sure what the exact connection between them is, but one of the victims, Purshottam Sethi, had funnelled money to the other two victims—Kailash Shukla and Rakesh Kumar.'

'Except that his real name wasn't Rakesh Kumar,' says Chandrakar, smiling like a cat that has got the cream.

Shinde nods. 'When we tried to find out more about him, we drew a blank. There were absolutely no records of his life before he popped into the system a couple of years ago. It was almost as though he'd been a phantom all his life. We did all the forensics and biometrics, and finally, one solitary match popped up, from a fingerprint taken many years ago before he escaped and fled into the forests of Ambuja.'

'Santoshji,' I whisper.

Chandrakar smiles. 'Bang on! From what we've been able to figure out, when life in the forest became too hard for him, he assumed a new identity and relocated to Thane. To the outside world, he was a respected, mild-mannered social worker. Nobody had any idea that he was actually a dreaded Maoist who was now running this horrendous racket.'

'Did he stay in touch with any of his old colleagues?' I ask, my pulse starting to race in excitement.

'He used to make occasional calls to people in Ambuja. In particular, he used to call a landline number—it turned out to be Mr Purshottam Sethi's office,' says Shinde.

'There was one other number in his phonebook, which you might find interesting,' says Chandrakar. 'Prakash Padmanabh. It seems you were right about him all along, Vikram. We shouldn't have doubted you.'

'Did Santoshji call Padmanabh a lot?' I ask.

Shinde shakes his head. 'Maybe twice in two years.'

I frown. 'That won't be enough to nail Padmanabh in a court of law. Any halfway decent lawyer will argue that Padmanabh may not have known Santoshji's real identity. He would have assumed he was a simple social worker, and there's no crime in being associated with one.'

Chandrakar and Shinde exchange glances. Chandrakar nods reluctantly. 'You're right. I guess you've learnt the hard way how the system operates. So, what do you want to do now?'

I smile. 'Now? I think it's high time I paid a visit to Mr Purshottam Sethi's office and find out what he was up to all these years.'

'SP sahab, this is an unexpected pleasure,' says Prashant as I step into Sethi's living room. His smile fades as he looks at me. 'Is everything okay?'

'That's exactly what I'm here to find out,' I say. 'I'd gone to your office and was told that you're pretty much running things now that Mr Sethi has passed away. And also that you hardly come to office any more. You're mostly operating out of here.'

'That's not true. Sethi sahab died so abruptly and in such a shocking manner that we didn't have any successor in place. Mrs Sethi has taken over the company, but as you can imagine, she's still in deep shock. And she hasn't really worked before this, so she's still finding her way. I'm helping her out as much as I can.'

'I see. Where is she now?' I ask.

'Doing puja. She spends most of the day in prayers,' he explains.

'And when she emerges, I bet she signs whatever papers you give her?'

'Well, yes. I've worked closely with Sethi sahab all these years, so I probably understand the way the company works better than anyone else. I'm trying to keep things going as he would have wanted.'

'I'm sure you are. You keep the account books here?'

'Well, yes. Sethi sahab always kept them at home too, never in the office. He liked to look at them last thing, before going to bed,' says Prashant.

'And where's Anjali in all this? Isn't she a shareholder too?' I ask.

A sorrowful expression appears on Prashant's face. 'She's not well. She hasn't been herself since the day her father died.'

'What does that mean?' I ask. 'I want to see her.'

'I don't think that's a good idea,' he hedges.

'Watch yourself, Prashant.' I'm done with pleasantries. 'I'm not here for your opinion. I want to see Anjali. Where is she?'

He doesn't answer, but his eyes flicker past me, towards one of the closed rooms. One of the bodyguards who had accompanied Anjali when she was staying with Devika is standing guard outside. He's a huge hulk with a shaved head.

'Patrick. That's your name, isn't it?' I ask.

He nods, not saying anything.

'Is Anjali in there, Patrick?' I ask.

He hesitates and looks at Prashant.

'I'm talking to you. I suggest you look at me, not at him,' I snarl. 'I'll ask one more time. Is Anjali in there?'

'SP sahab, she's not in a state to receive visitors. I don't understand why you're behaving in such a strange manner. But whatever your questions, I'm sure I can address them. Please, why don't you sit down and we'll talk over a nice cup of tea?' Prashant speaks in a soothing tone, trying to mollify me.

It doesn't work. By now, I am thoroughly suspicious. I point a finger at Patrick. 'I'm not going anywhere till I've opened that door and seen Anjali. For your own good, I strongly suggest you get the hell out of my way.'

He hesitates, still unsure about what to do. I walk straight at him and ram him in the chest with my shoulder. It feels like hitting a boulder. I feel a burst of pain shoot all the way up my arm. But I have the gratification of seeing Patrick totter on his feet. I step past him, resisting the urge to rub my aching shoulder. The door is bolted. I shove it open.

The room is dark and unlit. I blink a couple of times, trying to adjust to the sudden gloom. Dimly, I make out a shape huddled on the floor next to the bed.

'Anjali?' I say.

She tenses at the sound of her name, but doesn't respond. I step closer. She looks up at the sound of my footsteps. I get a good look at her and reel back in shock.

Anjali's hair is filthy and tangled. There is a vacant, glazed look in her eyes. Her clothes are crumpled. My mind flashes back to the time we spent together in Devika's house, to the invariably well-put-together woman whose graciousness and gentle humour were as obvious as her beauty. The person sitting before me is a sad and empty shell.

A wave of sadness washes over me as I stare at this wreck of a human being. And then the guilt hits me. I should have checked on her at least once. She was always kind to me. The least I could have done is find out how she was doing.

'Why the hell is she locked in here in this condition? She needs to see a doctor urgently,' I say.

Prashant has walked up to the door. 'We can't let her be seen like this in public. Khaandaan ki bahut badnaami hogi.'

I stare at him, barely believing what I'm hearing. 'How long has she been like this?'

'Since her father's murder. Her mind seems to have just snapped,' says Prashant.

'She needs to see a good psychiatrist right away. You had no business doing this to her,' I say. 'Call her mother. Tell her to get her ready. I'm taking her out of here.'

Prashant shakes his head. 'She turns violent if anybody goes near her,' he says, his voice rising.

Anjali whimpers suddenly. I look at her. My eyes are better adjusted to the dim room, and I make out a dark, ugly bruise on her cheek. She is looking at Patrick with abject fear.

I look at the bruise. I look at Anjali's eyes. And then, very slowly, I look at Patrick. Murderous rage floods through me. I take a step towards Patrick. He hastily steps back, raising his hands in a spontaneous defensive gesture. I take one more step towards him, and then I suddenly stop.

There are scratch marks on his wrists. They've healed to a large extent and are quite faint now. But they're unmistakable.

'How did you get those scratches?' I ask. My voice is deathly soft.

He looks at me, startled. 'Er ... I don't know. I think a cat scratched me,' he says.

'Oh really?' I ask. 'Was the cat named Devika Doria by any chance?'

Anjali whimpers again at the sound of Devika's name. Patrick clamps his mouth shut, but his expression is a dead giveaway.

'You're going to come with me to the police station, Patrick,' I say. 'I'm going to make you submit a DNA sample. I'm going to compare it with the samples our forensics team found under Devika's fingernails. And if they match, you can consider yourself a dead man.'

Panic floods his face. 'I didn't kill her. I only kidnapped her. I was following orders. She wasn't supposed to die,' he babbles.

'Shut up, you stupid oaf,' snaps Prashant, cutting him off mid-sentence. 'Don't say anything.'

'Actually, Patrick, I think you should tell me everything,' I say. 'It may be your only chance to save your worthless hide. And as for you, Prashant, you can come along with us to the station. And bring your account books. I have a friend who'd love to take a good look at them.'

CHAPTER TWENTY-FOUR

'We made a duplicate set of keys to Devika's house while Anjali was staying with her. Sethi sahab insisted that we do it, in case we ever needed to enter the house late at night while the two of them were sleeping. He also instructed us to plant bugs in the house so that we could monitor what was going on at all times. He was quite paranoid about her,' says Patrick.

We are sitting in the police station. Despite Prashant's instructions, Patrick is more than happy to sing. He has completely bought my bluff about the forensics sample.

'Why didn't we find the bugs in the house when we searched it?' I ask.

'We removed them after we kidnapped her. We knew there was bound to be a search of the house,' he says.

'Was one of them behind a chest in the drawing room?' I ask.

He looks at me, startled. 'Yes, it was. But how did you know? We'd removed it.'

'You weren't so careful about how you put back the chest,' I say. 'Anyway, it's a minor point. Go on.'

'We heard her talking to Anjali about how she'd got a story that would shake the foundations of Ambuja. Then, later in the evening, Sethi sahab got a call from some old acquaintance who used to be a police officer. He told him someone had informed him that Devika had got her hands on an explosive story dating back several years.

Sethi sahab was very worried about what the story might be. So he decided to get Devika abducted and questioned.'

'And you were the one who did it?'

He nods. 'Me and the other bodyguard. We waited till it was quite late and we were sure that Devika would be asleep. Then we went in with the duplicate key. I put a chloroform-soaked cloth to Devika's nose. She struggled to free herself, but was eventually knocked out cold. Then we quickly cleared out the bugs before leaving in our van.'

I nod slowly as I digest this information. Our efforts at finding clues would have focused mainly on the area near the entrance and the living room. If at all anyone had searched her bedroom, it would have been cursorily. No wonder we didn't find anything.

'What happened after that?'

'There is an old warehouse outside town. We took her there and locked her in. Sethi sahab came to meet us there, along with Prashant. I think Sethi sahab wanted to be there while we questioned her about the story she was working on. We planned to put a cloth above her head so that she wouldn't see his face. But she recovered faster than we expected. As we opened the door, she was already standing there with a rod she'd found. She hit my partner on the head with it and tried to run. Prashant hit her hard on her face. She fell and hit the side of her head on a metal bench near the door. She fell unconscious immediately,' says Patrick in a rush. It's almost as if the words have been bottled up and he's glad to finally have them spill out.

'So it was Prashant who killed her,' I say softly. The words come out in barely a whisper.

'It was an accident. We were just trying to stop her from escaping,' gabbles Patrick. 'Sethi sahab was furious. He kept saying, "What have you done?" We tried to revive her, but it was too late. Finally, Prashant called someone, and they came and took her away. I don't know who it was.'

'I think I can guess. But let me talk to Prashant anyway,' I say.

'Please, SP sahab. I've told you everything I know. I never would have hurt Devika madam intentionally. She was always very good to us,' pleads Patrick.

'And what do you think would have happened to her once Sethi found out what she knew? Do you think he would have just let her go back to finish writing her story? Don't give me this nonsense about not wanting to hurt her, you worthless piece of shit,' I say. I turn to the others in the room. 'Get him out of my sight before I change my mind about making him a witness.'

As Patrick is led away, I sit down and breathe deeply, composing myself. Gayaram gently knocks on the door.

'Sir, Phatankar sahab called. He was trying to reach you on your mobile but you weren't answering. I told him you'd probably put it on silent because you were questioning a suspect.'

I nod. 'I'll call him back right away. Thanks, Gayaramji.'

I pull out my phone and look at it. Sure enough, there are a couple of missed calls from Phatankar. I'd taken photos of the pages of the account books and sent them to him as soon I got my hands on them. It hasn't taken him long to get back.

'Haan, Fatty, bol,' I say, as soon as he answers.

'That's quite a spider's web you've found over there,' he says. 'Not that you would have been able to figure it out.'

'Tabhi toh main tere paas aaya hoon, yaar. Now stop crowing and tell me what you've found,' I grumble.

'Wow, in a good mood today, aren't we?' he exclaims. 'Okay, here goes. First of all, there's a whole lot of money laundering going on. I'll give you one example. That charity school that Sethi was funding? Well, they're paying some four times the actual cost of construction for it. So, let's say something should cost ten rupees. Well, they're paying forty rupees. Now, either Sethi didn't realise he was being overcharged, in which case he must have been a truly lousy businessman, or he was deliberately taking black money and turning it white.'

'Okay, very interesting. So, who is overpaying? They must be part of the laundering scheme too,' I say.

Phatankar whistles softly. 'Waah, even a thick skull such as yours can sometimes put two and two together.' Then he says crisply, 'I need some more time to look into this thoroughly, though it might not be a bad idea for you to call on the owners for some questioning. I'll send you a list.'

'Will do,' I say. 'Anything else?'

'Yup. One more interesting thing. They do a lot of CSR—generous contributions to many NGOs, most prominently one headed by a guy called Rajan Sahai. But they were careful not to have a direct link. They created fronts that paid out the money. A bit like that scholarship to Shukla's son,' he explains.

'Rajan Sahai, huh?' I mutter. 'Very interesting.'

'Sorry, you said something?' he asks.

'Nothing. Thanks a lot, Fatty.'

I'm expecting a wisecrack from him but his tone suddenly changes. 'Tu theek hai na, Vikram? You sound quite subdued.'

Wow, I must sound pretty terrible if he feels compelled to ask! It takes me a moment to recover. 'Yeah, I'm fine. Thanks, Fatty. You're a treasure,' I finally say.

He clears his throat uncomfortably. 'Of course I am. You take care of yourself. Till such time as Silicon Valley manages to come up with AI that can have intelligent conversation, I'm stuck with you. So, I suppose I'll have to humour all your requests.'

'Wait a minute. Are you actually admitting I am intelligent?' I ask.

'Umm, let's say your questions have grown less dumb over the years,' he concedes magnanimously. 'Okay, bye, I've got lots to do.'

After he hangs up, I close my eyes, going over everything I've just learnt. After some time, I look up to find Gayaram and Lokesh peering at me curiously.

'I'm ready now,' I say. 'Bring in Prashant.'

'Sir, main kuch boloon,' says Gayaram hesitantly.

'Haan, kahiye na Gayaramji,' I say.

'Sir, woh jo aapne Rudra ke saath galti ki thi, usko mat dohrana. Agar maarna peetna hai, toh witnesses ke saamne mat karna,' says Gayaram.

Despite my grim mood, I burst out laughing. 'Okay, Gayaramji, thanks for the advice. I will make sure I have no witnesses,' I say. 'Now bring him in please.'

Prashant is ushered in and made to sit down. I steeple my fingers and let him wait a bit before starting.

'How old are you, Prashant?'

'Excuse me?' He's surprised. 'How is that relevant?'

'It's a simple enough question. You can answer it, surely,' I say.

'Yes. Well, I'll be thirty-five in a couple of months,' he says.

'Oh, I'd have thought you'd be thirty at most. You're in good shape for your age.'

'Thanks, I guess,' he says.

'You never married?' I ask.

'Never found the time. Sethi sahab kept me too busy,' he says.

'Well, he isn't around any longer, so perhaps you'll have a little more time now,' I say. 'Don't you have any other family? Parents, siblings?'

'I'm an only child. My parents died years ago,' he says, shortly.

'So the Sethis were sort of family to you, I suppose,' I say. 'How long have you been working with them?'

'Fourteen years or so. I joined Sethi sahab a few months after I completed my graduation,' he says.

'And what were you doing in the months after you graduated?' I ask.

He shrugs. 'Oh, the usual. Applied for dozens of jobs, with no luck. Travelled a little. I was thinking of enrolling for a PG when I got the interview call from Mr Sethi. Luckily, it worked out.'

'That would have been a short while after he got that road project, wouldn't it?' I ask. 'The one that transformed his fortunes?'

'Yes, that's right,' he says.

'Okay. I've just found out that Mr Sethi's office used to get calls from a social worker—turns out he was actually the dreaded Maoist commander Santoshji, but living under an assumed identity. Weren't all such calls routed through you?'

'As you yourself said, he was living under an assumed identity. How was I to know Rakesh Kumar was actually Santoshji? I would receive his calls and if he said it was urgent, I would put him through. In any case, his calls weren't all that frequent,' says Prashant.

'Interesting.' I fall silent, but continue to look at him.

After a minute or so, he shifts uncomfortably. 'I fail to see what's so interesting,' he says peevishly.

'Well, for one thing, I never told you Santoshji's assumed name was Rakesh Kumar,' I say.

Prashant's mouth opens, but no words come out. He stares at me. I can almost see him trying to find an explanation for his faux pas.

'Don't bother to think of a convincing lie, Prashant,' I say. 'Instead, let me tell you a little story. Years ago, there was a small-time contractor with huge ambitions. He struck a deal with the Maoists and a corrupt policeman. The cop passed on inside information to the Maoists and got this contractor's rival killed in an ambush. He even ensured he got a minor wound so that he himself wouldn't come under suspicion. The contractor got the project he wanted and made a tidy profit.

'But this was just the start. The contractor quickly realised that he could use the Maoists to knock off inconvenient rivals or sabotage their projects. Over the next few years, all his competition vanished, he became wealthier and wealthier, till he was the biggest businessman in the area.

'But what was in it for the Maoists? Well, their local leader was probably taking his own kickbacks from the businessman. But it was also very convenient for them to have a guy like that as an ally. They could use him to fund overground activists under the garb of CSR. Or to pay off corrupt officials. He could help them launder their dirty money. Hell, he could even pump in enough money to ensure that his brother-in-law became an influential politician who would do exactly as he was told.

'Of course, that was asking a lot from one person, someone who wasn't the most scrupulous of individuals to begin with. So they decided to install their own man to keep an eye on him. A young recruit, fresh out of college. For the world, he was Purshottam Sethi's PA. But actually, he was a Maoist who worked closely with Sethi to subvert and corrupt the system that he loathed. So dedicated to the cause that he never married or started a family. An educated, mild man, but one capable of killing a person with a single blow. A man who can call the Maoists to do his dirty work for him whenever he needs to. A person whose records show a gap of a few months between the time he graduated and the time he got a job. Was that when he went into the forest to undergo guerrilla training, I wonder?'

CHAPTER TWENTY-FIVE

'Well? What do you make of the story so far?'

Prashant watches me for a bit before he answers. 'It's fascinating,' he says, then smiles, shrugging. 'Too bad you'll never be able to prove any of it.'

'Oh, I suppose if I dig long and deep enough, I might even be able to find enough evidence to back it up. But honestly, I don't want to invest that much time and effort,' I say. 'This is just to make sure you know that I know.'

'And what good will that do?'

'For starters, you won't die wondering why I killed you,' I say, bringing out my revolver.

'Wait, what?' he says, his composure cracking for the first time.

'I am not doing anything, Prashant. It's you. You will try to escape, and I will most reluctantly shoot you dead,' I say.

'You can't,' he says.

'No, Prashant. I shouldn't do this, but that doesn't mean I can't. You killed Devika, and you deserve to die for that, but I suppose you can always claim manslaughter and get away with a few years in prison. And that's assuming Patrick sticks to his story and doesn't turn hostile. I'm pretty sure you would have been smart enough not to leave any sign of your handiwork on Sethi's crooked dealings, so you can always pin the blame on him alone. The evidence against you would be circumstantial at best. So you may even get to walk scot-free. I'm sorry, but I definitely can't allow that,' I say. Even I'm surprised by how logical and calm I sound.

'I didn't mean to kill Devika. It all happened so fast. I was just trying to stop her from escaping,' he blurts desperately.

'I'm sure that will be a great comfort to her. Be sure to tell her in the afterlife. But wait, how will you do that? You are headed straight for hell,' I say.

'Don't kill me. There's still lots of stuff you don't know. I can tell you everything,' he says.

I shake my head. 'I doubt that very much,' I say.

'Sethi ordered the hit on his son-in-law,' he says frantically.

I pause at this new turn in the conversation. 'Dhruva? Was that because he'd figured out what his father-in-law was up to?' I ask finally.

'He hadn't completely cracked it, but he had his suspicions. He didn't realise just how deeply Sethi was involved, though. He thought Sethi was just paying the Maoists protection money. He confronted him the night before he went on that final trip. Sethi pleaded with him not to tell Anjali, saying it would break her heart, and promised he'd sever all ties with the Maoists. Dhruva believed him and said he'd talk to him again after he got back. He never did,' says Prashant.

A memory flashes into my mind. 'They wrote "traitor" on his chest, didn't they? So it wasn't about him being a traitor to his people.'

Prashant shakes his head. 'No, that was Sethi's idea. He took the confrontation with Dhruva very badly. Regarded it almost as a personal betrayal. Sethi was genuinely fond of Dhruva, though I'd told him from the start to keep Dhruva away from the business. He was too bright and too idealistic. It was only a matter of time before he figured things out. Sethi hoped to bring Dhruva around, but after that conversation, he realised it would never happen.'

'Is Anjali involved in any of this?' I ask.

He shakes his head. 'She's completely clueless. A genuinely good person. She worshipped her father, had absolutely no idea about his true colours. How a bastard like Sethi is related to someone like Anjali is beyond me.'

'And yet, you treated her like an animal.'

'I was trying to protect her. I didn't like seeing her like that either, but I didn't know what else I could do,' he says.

'Well, this is very interesting, but it's all in the past. Not much use to me now. I'm sorry, Prashant, but I see no point in leaving you alive.'

'Wait, wait!' He is desperate now. 'The laundering network we've created is a total labyrinth. But I can help you cut through it. Finally, all the money goes to one holding company. I can lead you straight to it.'

'Keep talking.'

'I want a guarantee first that I won't be harmed. I want to be taken to a safe location and I want to be handed over to some other senior police officer,' he says. 'I'll only share the information after that happens.'

'Don't push your luck, Prashant,' I growl. 'Do you think I'm a total moron? The moment you're out of my hands, you'll start singing a different tune and I'll be left with nothing.'

'But what's to stop you from taking down everything I say and then killing me anyway?' he asks.

'True,' I admit. 'Looks like we have a stand-off. Ah well, I suppose I'll just have to be patient and wait a few extra months for the puzzle to be solved.' I point the revolver at him again.

'Wait, let me think of a solution,' he says. Then his face brightens. 'Okay, call another officer, somebody you trust. I'll write down everything I know and give you the paper in his presence. Once you've read it and are satisfied, you can hand me over to him. Does that make sense?'

I think about it. He looks at me anxiously, not daring to blink or breathe. Finally, I nod. Relief floods his face. I walk to the door and open it. Gayaram and Lokesh hastily step back.

'How long did you have your ears pressed to the door?' I ask.

They exchange sheepish glances. 'For a while, sir,' Gayaram admits.

I indicate Prashant with a tilt of my head. 'Take him away, and take good care of him. I don't want any untoward incidents.'

Gayaram waits till Prashant is safely out of earshot, then beams at me. 'Waah sir, kya khela aapne. Even I was almost convinced you were ready to kill him. He fell headlong for your trick.'

I smile tightly. Gayaram doesn't need to know how deep the temptation was, how I was literally a hair's breadth from pulling the trigger.... I shake my head, breaking the chain of thought.

'So, which officer will you hand him over to?' he asks.

'I know just the right person,' I say, thinking of Phatankar. 'He'll soak in information like a sponge.'

'Chaliye, achchi baat hai,' says Gayaram. 'But I have to say that this idea of Prashant's, of putting it down in writing as a safeguard, is quite interesting.'

'Putting it down in writing,' I echo.

'Kya hua, sir?' asks Gayaram.

'We've established the link between Sethi, Shukla and the Maoists. We know how and why Devika was killed. But we still don't know who killed Sethi and Shukla,' I say slowly.

'Does it matter, sir?' says Gayaram flippantly. 'He's doing our job for us.'

'That's not the point, Gayaramji,' I snap. 'It's our job, not some unknown vigilante's who thinks he can take the law into his own hands.'

Gayaram doesn't look convinced, but wisely keeps his mouth shut. I resume the chain of thought that he had interrupted. 'It all started because Devika found something while going through the stuff in her father's room. Maybe it was something he wrote, something that had been lying around for years.'

'Sure, sir. It's possible,' agrees Gayaram.

'I'm going back to Devika's house to look through her father's room. I don't think anyone ever did a really thorough search of that side of the house.'

A little later, I drive to Devika's house, Gayaram and Lokesh in tow. It's only been a few days since I last came here, but already the house seems to have shrunk, as though the vitality has been sapped out of it with the departure of its occupants.

As I wait for them to open up the house, a host of memories besiege me. I stand at the entrance for a long time. Unbidden, a memory comes to me. Devika stepping into the living room, having just emerged from a bath, towelling her hair vigorously, then tossing it back casually. She smelled of soap, shampoo, moisturiser and healthy, damp youthful skin. It was a heady fragrance, more alluring than the most expensive perfume ... Devika laughing, debating some point in an argument, ganging up on me with Anjali ....

'Sir, sir?' It's Gayaram, waiting at the entrance.

'Let's get some lights on.' I snap back to reality.

'Of course,' says Gayaram. Somehow, he manages to make even those two words sound sympathetic.

We walk into Devika's father's room. It's sparsely furnished, with a bed, a study table and a cupboard. 'Not even a laptop or an iPad. I guess Madho Doria still believed in pen and paper. Well, shouldn't take us very long to do a thorough search,' I observe.

'What exactly are we looking for, sir?' asks Lokesh.

'I don't know, to be honest. Maybe a piece of paper, a journal, or even a photograph? Just see if you can find anything he may have written,' I say.

A couple of hours later, Lokesh sighs and puts down a letter he's been reading. 'Well, he certainly wrote beautiful letters to his wife, but I don't think any of this stuff is what we're looking for.'

'I guess not,' I agree, discouraged. 'It was a long shot, anyway.' And then I freeze. 'Long shot, long shot ....' I whisper.

'Having another Colonel Vinod moment, sir?' asks Gayaram, referring to the iconic investigator of the popular Jasoosi Duniya detective novels.

'I need to talk to Saroj right away,' I say, shaking my head. I have no idea what the man is talking about. 'Where did you say she is now?'

'She's been moved to Raipur, sir. She's being kept at an undisclosed location,' says Gayaram.

I call Chandrakar's staff officer and tell him that I need to talk to Saroj. He doesn't waste any time asking why. 'Please give me two minutes. She'll call you back,' is all he says.

My phone rings almost right away. It's an undisclosed number. I answer the call.

'How are you?' I ask Saroj.

'About as good as a new mother with a permanently cranky baby and a comatose husband can be,' she says, sounding tired and irritable.

'I'm sorry to hear that,' I say. 'Hasn't Sudhakar's surgery been organised yet?'

'No, it'll have to be in Delhi or Mumbai. They're still trying to figure it out. Can you please put in a word and try to speed things up a bit? Nothing seems to be moving here.'

'I'll definitely speak to my seniors,' I say, making a note to do so. 'Look, I'm sorry to trouble you, but I have a question. You told me your friend's brother had drowned in the river and died?'

'Kranti? Yes, he fell into the river while running away from his pursuers,' she says.

'Now tell me something, and this is important, okay? Was Kranti's body ever found?' I ask.

There's a long silence at her end. It stretches on and on.

'Saroj? Are you still there?' I ask finally.

'No, his body never surfaced. We thought it might have been washed many kilometres away. I kept my ears peeled for any news of his body having been found. But it never was,' she says, softly. Then, with a burst of enthusiasm, she asks, 'But why are you suddenly asking about him? Do you have any news of him?'

'Not really. Just a thought that struck me,' I say. 'Thanks. You take care.'

'Yeh Kranti kaun hai, sir?' asks Gayaram.

'A young boy who was an extremely good shot. He disappeared from the Maoist camp many years ago and was presumed to have drowned. But his body was never found.'

'And after all these years, he resurfaced from the river and started killing people. Doesn't that sound a little far-fetched?' asks Gayaram sceptically.

I pace up and down, trying to get rid of the restless energy building up inside me. 'True, but what if he somehow survived that day. Could it be him?' I punch the headboard of the bed in frustration. It takes me a second to realise that it sounds different.

'What was that?' I say, punching it again. Yes, there's that hollow sound again.

'There's a compartment of some sort in there,' I say. I run my hands over the surface. Almost exactly in the centre, horizontally and vertically, it feels slightly uneven. I press down firmly. There's a click, then the surface recedes and a strip pops out. I whip out my mobile, switch on the light and shine it into the compartment, my excitement rising.

It's empty.

I feel like a bucket of cold water has been poured on me. I sink to my haunches, defeated. 'What's the point of having something like that if you don't put anything in it?' I mutter angrily.

'Maybe there was something, sir,' says Lokesh. He too has got his mobile light on and is running it up and down the empty compartment, examining every corner.

'What do you mean?' I ask.

'Gaur se dekhiye. There was a spider's web there, which has been disturbed. Bits and pieces of it are still lying around,' he observes.

I get back on my feet. 'This means that someone got here before we did. And whatever was in there, he took it away. Could it be you, Kranti?'

CHAPTER TWENTY-SIX

The office of Acme International is in a small, dingy basement in a dilapidated commercial complex in north Delhi. Even though it's late afternoon, the office is empty but for an elderly peon who's playing solitaire on an ancient desktop. He hurriedly shuts the window as we enter.

'Are we at the right location? This place hardly looks like the office of a company that is sitting on crores of cash,' says Lokesh dubiously.

'Well, according to what Prashant told Phatankar, this is the centre of the web. The money is circulated through numerous transactions, but it finally flows into the accounts of this company,' I say.

'But it doesn't look like it,' says Lokesh, still sounding sceptical.

'Well, only one way to find out,' I say. Turning to the peon, I say, 'We've come to meet Mr Vinay Arora.'

'Haanji, main hi hoon. Kahiye?' he says politely.

I do a double take. 'Are there any other Vinay Aroras in this office?' I ask.

He shakes his head. 'Nahin ji. Bas main hi baithta hoon.'

I look at the sheet of paper in front of me. 'According to the company's records, Vinay Arora is the managing director. There are some other names mentioned as directors.'

'Let me take a look,' he says, pulling out a pair of spectacles from his pocket. He peers at the paper and looks up, puzzled. 'One of the people mentioned here is a driver who does odd jobs for the company. Another is the tea boy. I don't recognise any of the other names.'

'How many people work here?' I ask.

'Just the three of us,' he says.

'So, who owns the company?' I ask. 'Who pays your salary?'

'Bhanu Ma'am. She comes to the office only on days when there's work.'

'Doesn't that strike you as odd?' I ask Lokesh. 'An office where the owner only comes once in a while?'

The peon pipes up. 'She has her own problems, sahab. She is usually busy taking care of her husband. Actually, I think he's the real owner, because once or twice I've heard her call him and ask for instructions.'

'Why doesn't he come himself?'

'Apparently he has some major health issues and can't move around too much. I only saw him once, when they stopped by for five minutes. I'd taken some files to the parking lot and passed them on. Madamji worries about him a lot. Once or twice, I've heard her scolding him on the phone. "You forgot your medicines again? Why are you so careless, Prakash?"'

My ears perk up. 'Excuse me, did you say Prakash?'

'Yes,' he repeats. 'That was the name I heard.'

I pull out my phone and search for photos of Prakash Padmanabh. Several fill the screen. There's one with his wife standing next to him as well. I zoom in and show it to Vinay Arora. 'Is this him?'

He peers short-sightedly at the phone and then nods vigorously. 'Yes, he's the one. It's strange, the other man was also just as startled when he heard the name and made me look at pictures to identify him.'

'Other man? What other man?' I ask.

'He came just yesterday, asking these same questions,' says Arora.

'What did he look like?' I ask urgently.

'I didn't get a good look at him, sir,' says Arora. 'My eyes are a little weak and he was standing in the darkest corner of the room. But nothing extraordinary. Normal height and weight.'

Gayaram, Lokesh and I exchange glances. 'Do you think it could be Kranti, sir?' asks Gayaram.

'It's entirely possible,' I say. 'If it is, then Padmanabh's life could be in danger. We should go and warn him right away. In fact, we should put a thick security ring around him.'

'Such a thick ring that it's as good as taking him into custody?' asks Lokesh, a twinkle in his eye.

'What are you saying, Lokesh? The thought never even crossed my mind,' I say, struggling to keep a straight face. 'Let's go meet Mr Prakash Padmanabh and his wife.'

'Are you sure about this, sir? Those guys got us good the last time ....' says Gayaram.

'What was that phrase you used the other day? "Paralysis through analysis"? That's what'll happen if we keep wondering and doubting ourselves.' I gesture at Arora. 'Take him along.'

'Sahab, main chhota sa aadmi hoon. Mujhe isme kyon ghaseet rahe ho?' asks Arora plaintively, his hands folded.

'Don't worry, we're taking you in for your own safety. You're going to be our star witness,' I tell him. 'Besides, I don't want you calling them up and warning them the moment we step out of here.'

A couple of hours later, I experience a strong sense of déjà vu as I once again stand at the doorstep of Padmanabh's home. Briefly, I recall how the last encounter had gone. So much has happened in such a short span of time since I was last here ....

'Sir?' Gayaram says gently.

I snap back into the present and realise I've been standing at the doorstep for a while, my finger hovering in the air.

'There's still time to change your mind, sir,' he says. 'You don't have to stick your neck out to protect this man. Let him get what he deserves.'

'He deserves to be tried and punished by the law, not by a vigilante, Gayaramji,' I say. 'Let's do this.'

I step forward and ring the doorbell.

There is no response.

After the build-up, this feels like a complete anti-climax. I ring the doorbell again, longer and harder this time. Still no response.

I look around, at a loss. Then I hear a muffled sound from inside.

'Hello?' I yell. 'Is anyone there?'

We hear it again, as though someone is trying to yell through a gag. I take a couple of steps back, then charge and deliver a flying kick to the door.

It bursts open and I go tumbling into the living room. I look up from the floor and freeze. Bhanumati is on the floor, a gag around her mouth, hands bound behind her back. Her eyes are wide with terror. Prakash Padmanabh is sprawled senseless. There is a third person present in the room, a man wearing a balaclava mask. He is halfway through spray-painting the living-room wall. The words 'Lal Sal' are visible. I must have interrupted him before he could finish.

Abruptly, the man tosses the spray paint bottle straight at my head. I bat it away in a reflex action. In that brief moment, he whips out a revolver and points it at Padmanabh's head.

'Stop,' I yell. 'Don't do it, Kranti.'

He freezes for a moment. Then he begins to laugh, but there is no humour in his eyes, the only part of his face that I can see. They are dark and piercing. Somehow, they look familiar.

'So, you figured out who I am,' he says.

I nod. 'You led me on quite a chase. Looks like I got here just in time.'

'Not if your men keep pointing their weapons at me. It's making me very nervous, and I might just twitch and pull the trigger. Will you please ask them to put down their guns and back off?' he says.

'If I do that, will you talk to me?'

He nods. 'But only to you. You'll get up and shut the door and drape all the windows so that no sniper can take me out, then we'll have a chat. Do we have a deal?'

'Done,' I say immediately. I point at Bhanumati. 'Let her go out. You weren't going to kill her anyway.'

He cocks his head to one side. 'How are you so sure about that?'

'Because if you were planning to kill both of them, you wouldn't have kept your mask on. Neither would have been around to identify you, so it wouldn't have mattered even if they did see your face. The only person you're here to kill is Padmanabh,' I venture.

He grunts grudgingly. 'All right. You can send her out. But keep the gag on till she's safely out of the house, and make sure she doesn't scream the neighbourhood down.' He scowls at Bhanumati. 'If I hear a word out of you, I'll put a bullet in his head right away. Are we clear?'

She gives him a poisonous glare, but nods.

I look around. Every person who has accompanied me has a weapon out, pointing at Kranti. With my hands, I gesture that they should lower their guns. 'All of you, step out. Gayaramji, please untie the lady and escort her out of the house.'

'Sir, I won't leave you alone,' says Gayaram.

'Don't worry. I'll be fine. Kranti has very specific targets and I don't think I'm on that list. Isn't that right, Kranti?'

'Well, you're not on the list as of now. That could change if you try something stupid,' he says acerbically.

'Don't worry, I won't,' I reassure him.

Everybody backs away slowly. Gayaram unties Bhanumati and leads her out. As he passes me, he says, 'Sir, be careful.' There is real concern in his voice.

'Don't worry. Just make sure the house is surrounded so that no one can get out,' I say. Then I shut the door. I try bolting it, but the latch is busted.

'Just prop a chair against it,' says Kranti. I oblige, then draw the curtains so that no one can look into the living room.

'You can take off the mask, Kranti. It's only the two of us now,' I say.

CHAPTER TWENTY-SEVEN

He thinks about it, then shrugs. 'Fine, have it your way. But turn your back on me. I don't want you making any sudden moves while I'm removing the mask.'

I comply, waiting till he says, 'You can turn around now.'

I do so and come face-to-face with Kranti. We stare at each other for a long, silent moment, and then I smile.

'What's so funny?' he asks.

'I always wondered how people never realised that Clark Kent is Superman,' I say. 'But it's true, even minor changes can completely transform a person. More than the physical appearance, it's the posture and body language, I guess.'

'Superman, huh? I should be flattered, I guess,' he says.

'Of course, Superman doesn't go around killing helpless people in cold blood,' I say, my voice hardening. 'Why are you doing this?'

'Helpless? Him?' says Kranti, pointing at Padmanabh, who's lying prone on the ground. 'He's not helpless. My sister was. She was a helpless young girl and this animal raped and killed her, along with four of his friends.'

'In this condition? He hardly looks capable of doing any such thing,' I say.

'This was fifteen years ago, you fool. He wasn't always like this, you know,' snaps Kranti.

'And you've known this for fifteen years?' I ask. 'What were you doing all this while?'

'Actually, I've only known for a few days,' he says. 'Oh, I knew that my sister had been framed and killed, but I never knew the exact details of what happened that night. I only found out recently.'

'And how exactly did you find out? Was it something to do with Devika Doria's father? The secret compartment in his bed?'

He blinks in surprise, then laughs. 'Oh, you found that. Good for you. Too bad I cleaned it out before you got there.'

'Yes, I have a whole lot of questions for you,' I say. 'How did you know about that compartment? How did you get to it when the house was being guarded by the police? But wait. First tell me what happened that night your sister was killed. And how is Devika's father connected to all this?'

'Madho Doria. That was his name. We should stop referring to him just as Devika's father. He had his own life, his own personality, you know,' says Kranti.

'Fine. Madho Doria. I know that he visited a Maoist camp for some days and struck up a friendship with you,' I say.

'Not just a camp. The camp. The Maoist headquarters deep in the forest. I can still see it in my head. What a sight it was! A city of tents in a clearing in the forest. You reached the clearing through interwoven trails. Each of the trails was marked by ropes, which had colourful buntings on them,' he says, a faraway look in his eyes.

'You really loved it there, didn't you?' I ask softly. He's starting to reminisce, and I want to keep him talking as long as possible. It will help strike a rapport with him, and I might even be able to catch him off guard. But for now, I want this conversation to continue. So I try my best to look attentive and totally focused on his story.

'I thought I had arrived in fairyland,' he acknowledges. 'I was the poor orphan of a popular former commander who had died tragically, so I pretty much had the run of the place. I'd spend most of the day going from one tent to another. Each tent was like a department, you know. There was a tailor's tent, a medical tent, even a computer tent with battered old laptops and ancient printers that ran off a tractor battery.

'I had friends in every tent. All of them used to chat with me, maybe offer me a sweet or fruit or whatever little goodie they might have. The only tent that was strictly off-limits was the one at the centre of the camp, the "meeting room" of the leadership.

'But my favourite place was the kitchen. It was right next to a stream, so there was a continuous supply of running water. The walls were made up of sacks of dal and rice piled high on top of each other. For stoves, we'd dug some trenches in the ground. When we needed to cook, we'd toss in leaves and branches that the younger kids in the camp would bring, and light roaring fires. Then we'd simply place aluminium vats over the fires and cook.

'By the time they finished feeding everyone and cleaned up, it would be time to prepare the next meal, so the kitchen pretty much worked throughout the day. I could go in any time and be sure of getting something to eat. That was very important for a growing young boy,' he laughs.

'Must have been a lot more interesting than school?' I prompt.

'Well, they did have these classes where they taught Maoist ideology and history to kids and tribals,' he says. 'But they practised what they preached about equality and simple living—at least the cadres did. Everybody took turns cooking and digging toilet pits. Everyone had the same basic equipment—one uniform, one set of clothes, a blanket, a bed sheet, a plastic sheet, a rucksack and a bar of soap. If you needed shampoo, you used the black silt from the riverbank. The forest gave you whatever else you needed. If you think about it, you can live very comfortably on that much.'

'Very idyllic,' I mutter.

'It was, actually,' he says. 'Oh yes, I was a completely committed little revolutionary. Cheerfully ran errands all day long, participated in all the street plays and cultural activities that they organised. Even after that, there was quite a bit of free time for the youngsters. We didn't have mobile phones or tablets to while away the hours, you see. A lot of kids would hang out at the river, splashing in the water and playing. I couldn't—I'd almost drowned as a small child and had a phobia about deep water. So I started hanging around the firing range.

'Pretty soon, I discovered I was a natural. They wouldn't give me a weapon of my own, I was still considered too young. But I could shoot better than anyone in the camp, including the so-called marksmen.

'That was where Madho Doria first met me, at the firing range. He'd come to interview Santoshji and he'd heard that my sister and I were staying in the camp. He knew my father from before; he'd interviewed him when he was leading the protests against the road. So he asked to meet us. When he saw me with the rifle, he was shocked. I was just a little bit taller than the gun. He was even more shocked when he saw the target sheet with all my bullets neatly grouped together.'

'And he took a liking to you?' I interrupt.

'Yes, over a funny thing. There were two plastic bottles peeping out of his rucksack. I asked him what they were for. He said one was for drinking water and one was for when he had to relieve himself. So I took a plastic pouch and snipped off a corner and told him, "You use this pouch and give me one plastic bottle. I can put it to better use." He laughed uproariously at that. After that, we chatted every now and then. He asked me if I didn't want to live in a town, go back to school. I told him, very truthfully, that I was having the time of my life in the forest.

'He was a strange man in some ways. He had the option of sleeping in a tent, but he preferred to lie on the ground under a tree, staring up at the sky. Once, I asked him why he didn't go inside the tent and he said, "People pay thousands to stay in a five-star room, why give up the chance to sleep for free in a thousand-star chamber?"

'He didn't talk all that much, but he really listened. Whether he was speaking to a child or a top leader, he made you feel you were the most important person in the world to him. He was an adult, but in just a few days, he became my best friend in the camp.

'One day, he told me his work was done and he would be returning home. He asked if I wanted to come back with him. He said he'd try to get me some scholarships and make sure I completed my education. But I said I liked it in the forest. After a long chat, he ruffled my hair and said he would devote a long part of his article to me. Then he went off.

'I didn't really know what happened that night for many years. I only found out when I discovered his journal. Apparently, he was restless and fidgety, and he couldn't fall asleep. He knew he'd be leaving the next day, perhaps never see any of us again, and that was making him emotional. He kept tossing and turning. Finally, in frustration, he decided to take a walk. When he had first come to the camp, he wasn't allowed to go anywhere alone. But by now, his minders trusted him completely. They were sleeping peacefully, so he left them like that and went for a stroll.

'It was a pleasant evening and he walked for a long while, immersed in his thoughts. At some distance from the camp, there was an old, abandoned structure. Perhaps it had once been a temple, but it had long since fallen into disuse. Hardly anybody went there anymore. But that night, he saw a faint glow of light coming from there.

'Curious, he walked towards it to explore. As he got closer, he heard voices that seemed familiar. There was a broken window. He peered in through it. To his shock, he saw Santoshji sitting there, along with Kailash Shukla, Purshottam Sethi, Rajan Sahai and a fourth man whom he didn't recognise then. They had a bottle open and were passing it around, swigging freely from it.

'He hurriedly backed away from the window. There was an alcove in the wall—perhaps a statue had once stood there. He flattened himself against it and began listening to what the men were saying.

'Sethi was outlining a plan to Santoshji. There were a few major projects coming up for bidding. Sethi told Santoshji that he was facing competition from an aggressive new contractor who had just expanded to the area.

'"Aap ek baar help kar do. Phir project hamara ho jaayega aur profits ka hissa aapka," Sethi told Santoshji. Shukla then piped up, "Arrey, humko bhool mat jaana. Kaho to ek joint operation kar dein? Iss saale ko bhi thok denge, jaise pichhle contractor ko udaaya tha. Aur usse pehle uss hero Bhadru ko."

'There was a gasp at this. The men fell silent and looked at each other. "Somebody's here," one of them said. They all looked around. Madho pressed firmly against the wall, terrified that he might be discovered.

'Suddenly, a young girl screamed, but her voice was abruptly cut off. "Got her," said the stranger triumphantly. "She was hiding behind a raised pedestal platform in the other room, listening to us all this while."

'"What do you know? It's Bhadru's little girl. No wonder she got a nasty shock when she heard us," said Santoshji.

'Madho didn't dare step out from his hiding place, but he understood that Mahua had been caught eavesdropping on the men. He never did find out why Mahua was there in the first place, though over the years he came up with many theories.

'Perhaps she had come for an assignation—the junior cadres were strictly forbidden to have romantic relationships, but teen hormones will do what they will. But there was no else there apart from her. Perhaps the boy never turned up, or he ran away, rather than hiding inside the building, at the sight of strangers.

'Perhaps, like Madho himself, she had stepped out for a walk, was puzzled at the sight of outsiders coming to meet the Maoist leader, and tried to discover what was going on. Perhaps she had decided to run away, but saw strangers arriving on the route she was planning to take and decided to take shelter in the building. Or maybe she liked to pray and had come to the abandoned temple to do so, since prayer and religion were banned in the camp.

'Whatever the reason, she was discovered by these dangerous, unscrupulous individuals. "We can't let her go now. She knows too much," Santoshji said.

'"I suppose so. But it's a shame to waste a tasty young morsel like this," said the stranger. "Shukla, hold her down. I'll cover her mouth so that she can't scream. Sahai, you stand guard outside and make sure no one disturbs us."

'"Why do I have to miss all the fun?" Sahai protested.

'"Arrey, tumhaara bhi number aa jayega. Don't worry, we'll take turns," hissed the stranger. "Now stop wasting time."

'Sahai came out and looked around casually. Madho shrank back further into the shadows. As long as he remained where he was hiding, he would not be visible.

'Muffled cries and grunts became audible from within the structure. Madho stood there, tormented by conflicting thoughts. If he tried to stop the men, he would be overpowered and killed. If he tried to run and get help, he would be spotted and probably shot down.

'At one stage, he decided to make a break for it anyway. To hell with the consequences, he thought, I can't let this go on. But he had a daughter and a wife. "If I die here, what will become of them?" The thought paralysed him and rooted him to the spot.

'Then another thought occurred to him. "When they finish and come out, I'm going to be spotted anyway. What do I do then?" As he realised the danger he was in, sweat burst out on his forehead and his heart began racing furiously.

'Just then, he heard the stranger's voice calling out. "Oye Sahai, come and take your turn. Make it fast." The others laughed raucously.

'Sahai looked around cursorily once more and then went in. Nobody emerged to replace him, perhaps because they felt it would be all over in a few minutes anyway. Madho thought fast. "There's a grove about two hundred metres away, off the main path. If I sprint now, perhaps I can make it before somebody else comes out. In any case, what choice do I have?"

'He said a quick prayer and raced for the grove as though his life depended on it—which, in fact, it did. As he reached the sanctuary of the trees, he felt a wave of overwhelming relief wash over him. A second later, it was replaced by a sense of utter shame at his cowardice and failure to help the young girl. He sank to his knees, praying for forgiveness.

'He'd been there for barely a few minutes when the men emerged. The first rays of the rising sun were just starting to peep through the foliage. The men were laughing and chatting, as though they'd achieved some major feat. The sight of their smug faces sent a wave of nausea through Madho. He clapped a hand over his mouth, afraid that he might retch and give himself away.

'"Sethi, you carry several mobiles, don't you? Take out the one you use the least. Transfer or delete all the important stuff from it. Then leave it with me. I'll go back to camp and say I caught the little bitch trying to give away our position to the police. When I confronted her, she attacked me. I was forced to kill her," Madho heard Santoshji say.

'"What do I do now?" thought Madho, his brain working frantically. "Santoshji will get back to camp before I do. It will be my word against his. Nobody will believe me, and Santoshji might just have me executed on the spot. Best I keep my mouth shut about what I heard and saw. Oh my God, people there will be waking up right about now and won't find me. They'll wonder where I am. I need to make up some story. Wait, there's another path from this grove that goes to the river. I'll go straight there, and then head back to camp from there. In case somebody asks me, I'll say I woke up early to go to the river."'

CHAPTER TWENTY-EIGHT

'So, Madho went straight to the river from the grove?' I say, the pieces of the puzzle starting to fall into place. 'Which is why he was already at the river when you went racing there?'

'Yeah, a stroke of good luck for me,' says Kranti. 'He just wanted to get away for a bit from everyone. But once there, he was overcome with grief and self-loathing. He sat there and wept, losing track of time. Suddenly, he heard a commotion in the distance and looked up—just in time to see me slip and fall into the river.'

'I fell right into the water, then came up gasping for air. I went under again. The river was in spate and I couldn't really swim. That's when I realised with complete clarity that I was going to die. I even remember thinking that it was a good thing. I'd be reunited with my sister and parents. Then, suddenly, I was pulled out of the water, spluttering and choking.

'There was a bend in the river at the point where he pulled me out, and there were boulders blocking the view, so he was able to carry me away without anybody noticing. We went deep into the dense forest. "I need to find a place to hide you," he kept saying. "I can't be gone for long."

'Just then, we saw a small cave. He ran in there with me. It was pitch dark. He put me on the ground, took out his flashlight and shone it on the walls. At one place, erosion had formed a small, natural ledge.

'"Can you fit in there?" he asked. It was a tight squeeze, but I was quite small and skinny for my age. I crawled in. He quickly picked up some branches that were lying around and covered me with them.

'"Stay here," he said. "No matter how hungry or thirsty or tired you get, don't leave this place. Your life depends on it. I'll come back for you. Whatever it takes, I'll come back. I promise." Then he was gone.

'I'm not sure how long I was in there. The first couple of hours were the worst. In the distance, I could hear yelling and shouting and people looking for me. I was cramped, cold and terrified. I was still wearing my wet clothes. In retrospect, that was a mistake. But if I'd taken them off and left them somewhere, they could have given me away.

'Suddenly, I started shivering. Maybe it was the damp clothes. Maybe it was the delayed shock, now that I was no longer running for my life and the adrenalin rush had worn off. Whatever it was, I'd never felt so cold. I hugged myself to keep my teeth from chattering. It was no use. I shivered so much, my muscles went into spasm. Every inch of me was in agony.

'After some time, the shivering stopped. Then I felt my body temperature begin to rise. I was radiating so much heat, I felt like an oven. I realised then that I was coming down with a high fever and it was very probable that I might die. For a moment, I was seriously tempted. It would be so easy to just give up, lie back and let death come for me.

'But one thought held me back. I knew my sister was innocent. There was no way she could have done what she was accused of. And the man who had framed and killed her was still out there.

'Lying there, in that dark, confined space, I made myself a promise. If I survived, I would consider it a rebirth. And I would dedicate my second life to avenging my sister. As I made that resolution, I felt a great peace settle over me. I lay back and fell asleep.

'I was unconscious for most of the time after that. Even when I woke up, I was mostly delirious. I had strange, fevered dreams and visions. At one stage, I found myself lying in my mother's lap. She wept as she gently stroked my brow. Maybe it was a dream, or my tormented mind playing cruel tricks on me, but it felt completely real.

'A few hours later, I saw her again. She was standing at the end of a tunnel looking at me wistfully. The tunnel was dark, but I could make out a bright, clear light behind her. Then my father walked up to her and put an arm around her shoulder. "We have to go," he said.

'"My little baby," she said, a pleading note in her voice.

'"It's not time yet," my father said. They both looked at me, love shining in their eyes. Then they turned and walked away from me, into the light.

'I wanted to shout out to them. "Don't leave me here, alone. Take me with you," I longed to tell them. But my mouth was dry and my throat was sore. I tried saying the words but only a meaningless croak came out. I broke down and wept then, utterly exhausted, I fell back into deep slumber.

'Madho Doria came back for me a long time after that. He had returned to the Maoist camp after hiding me in the cave. Luckily, in all the excitement about my escape, no one paid much attention to the fact that he had not been in the camp all this while. Only one person, the man assigned to be his minder, asked him where he had been. Madho told him he had gone for a walk by the river and returned when he heard the commotion in the camp. The minder told him he'd missed all the excitement.

'But then, when it was time for Madho to return home, Santoshji had started having second thoughts about letting him go. He said that if Madho wrote about the fate that had befallen the young children of a famous commander like Bhadru, it would reflect badly on the movement.

'Madho begged and pleaded with Santoshji. He said he had always been fair in his coverage of the Maoists. He also promised that he would not write a word about either Mahua or Kranti in his piece about his stay in the camp, nor would he ever talk about what had happened to them.

'It was touch and go for a while, but Santoshji finally relented and let Madho leave. Madho thanked him profusely and took his leave. He was escorted back to the drop point by his handler and a couple of others. They had been very careful to not let him figure out the trail when they brought him in, but were more casual on the way out. Madho and his minder had spent a lot of time together. On the way back, Madho casually planted the idea that if Mahua had been trying to contact the police, then perhaps the location of the camp was not secure and they should move out from there.

'He waited a couple of days, hoping his ploy had worked, and then went back into the forest. It was highly risky, and he didn't have to. But he had made a promise. Besides, his cowardice that night, and his inability to save Mahua, had seared his conscience. He was determined to save her brother as a sort of penitence.

'Luckily for him, the Maoists had heeded his subtle advice to move camp, though they might have done so anyway, given that they tended to move frequently. He found the camp deserted. After making sure there were no stragglers, he crossed the river and made his way to where he had left me.'

'That's quite a story,' I say, as Kranti finishes his tale. 'So where did you go after that?'

'Madho had an elder sister who died a few years ago. She lived in Bhopal and taught at a college there. He didn't want me staying in Ambuja, where somebody might recognise me, so he took me to her. She was a widow and didn't have any children. She took me in. Madho would send her money to help pay for my upkeep, though I had very limited needs.

'I studied. I lived the life of a small-town boy. But I never forgot the vow I had taken in the cave that day. I enrolled in the NCC, I kept up my shooting. I did a lot of extra-curricular reading and research. I always knew that I would return to Ambuja one day, and when I did, I wanted to be ready,' says Kranti. 'But I never told anyone about my plans, not even Madho or Devika.'

'How did you come to know Devika?'

'Madho's family would come to visit during our school vacations,' he says. 'She and I spent a lot of time together. In fact, she once told me that her father maintained a journal. Every once in a long while, after a couple of drinks, he would write in it and put it away. Once, she asked him what he was writing. He said it was stuff he had seen or done that he could never share with the world, but he wrote it anyway to ease his pain. She asked him if she could read it, and he told her, "Maybe after I'm dead."'

'When the killings had just begun, I thought you might have got to her,' I say.

'Did you see "Lal Salaam" written anywhere in the vicinity of the crime scene? I wrote it every time I killed one of the men who had raped and murdered my sister. I was punishing only them. In any case, I couldn't possibly have killed Devika,' he says.

There's something about the way his voice softens when he talks about her. I stare at him, and then it strikes me. 'You loved her.'

He glares at me, then nods. 'She was the only woman I ever loved, the only one who ever understood me. The only time I ever felt truly alive was when I was around her.'

'Did she know?'

He shakes his head. 'The first time I confessed my feelings to her was the last conversation we ever had. It came as a shock to her. She said she'd always thought of me as a sort of brother. She loved me, but she didn't have romantic feelings for me. Oh no, those were reserved for you.'

I gape at him. 'She actually said that?'

'Pretty much confessed it. I was quite upset with her rejection and asked her if it was because you two were spending so much time together. Word gets around in small towns, you know. She said her feelings for you had nothing to do with her emotions for me. She could never have thought of me romantically even if you hadn't come along. But she did tell me that she loved you and planned to tell you when the two of you met next.'

I shut my eyes briefly as grief rushes through me. Grief for the all-too-little time that Devika and I had shared, for what might have been if she had only lived.

I open my eyes and find Kranti staring at me, assessing my reaction to his words. 'You must really hate me,' I say.

'I did for a while,' he admits. 'When she first told me, I wanted to chop your head off. But now that I've had some time to think about it, I realise it isn't your fault that Devika didn't love me. She never would have. Now, I just wish I could have her back again, as my friend and confidant. I wish I hadn't parted from her so bitterly. I wish I'd insisted that she move out of her place and go somewhere safe the moment she started talking about finding her father's journal.'

'She told you about that?' I ask.

He nods. 'I'd gone to her place to confront her about the rumours that were flying around about the two of you. In the course of the conversation, I confessed my feelings to her. After she told me it wasn't possible, she tried to change the subject by saying, "Remember that journal of Baba's that I used to talk to you about?

I found it in a cavity inside his bed's headboard!" I should have heard the full story. But I was so upset, I lashed out at her by saying, "Don't bring up your father right now. He was a far better person than you." At that point, she broke down, "No, he wasn't. He was a coward."

'I was quite startled to hear that, so I asked her what the hell she was talking about,' Kranti says, his eyes starting to glisten. 'That's when she told me that her father saw my sister being raped and killed. He could have tried to stop it, but didn't. All these years, Devika and I had built him up in our minds as this heroic angel who took a poor orphan under his wing. And then it turned out that he hadn't done me any favours at all. He was simply trying to ease his guilt for not having the guts to do anything while an innocent young girl was brutalised and killed by a bunch of savage beasts.'

'If he had, he would have died as well, and so would you,' I point out.

'Very pragmatically spoken. Tell me something honestly, SP sahab, if you had been in that situation, would you have just stood and watched?' he asks me fiercely.

'No, I wouldn't have,' I answer truthfully. 'I couldn't have.'

'Exactly,' he says. 'Nor would I. Nor would Devika. We would have preferred to die rather than live with that sort of guilt. We thought Madho Doria was that sort of man too. It was heart-breaking to have our illusions shattered. I was so angry, if he'd still been alive, I might just have killed him myself.'

'Devika must have been shattered,' I say.

'I think for the first few hours after she found out, she was quite numb. But when she began speaking to me, the full impact of her father's cowardice hit her and she broke down,' he says. 'At one stage, she said, "I can't bear this. I have to tell Vikram everything." She tried to call you, but her call went to your voicemail. She started to speak, but then I hastily cut her call. By then, I'd already decided that I was going to hunt down each of my sister's killers. I didn't want the police blundering around, getting in my way.

'Of course, I didn't tell her that. I told her that she should first get the story published, and only then let the law take its own course. Once she agreed, I left her place and started planning my revenge.'

'And after she died, you went back and retrieved the journal?' I ask.

'Yes. I replayed our last conversation in agonising detail, and I recalled her telling me about the journal,' he says. 'So I went searching and found it. Devika had told me the story only briefly. I read it all over again in excruciating detail in the journal. It was only after reading it that I realised my parents' death was not a tragic coincidence but a deliberate, cold-blooded murder.

'There was another thing I found out from the journal. Madho had written about the man who'd caught Mahua listening to them and then raped her with his friends. He'd caught only fleeting glimpses of him, but the voice made a deep impression on him, especially because he said all those terrible things so matter-of-factly.

'Years later, he heard the same voice while covering a talk by a renowned academician. And that's when he realised that the man who led my sister's gang-rape and murder was none other than this bastard right here. Well, I'll be taking care of him soon enough. After that, there will only be Rajan Sahai left to go. He is on a foreign tour right now, but he'll have to return one day. And I'll be waiting.'

'No, Kranti,' I say. 'Your killing days are over. You're going to hand over the gun to me, and we're going to walk out of here peacefully.'

He laughs out loud. 'Haven't you heard a word of what I just said? You must be totally mad if you think I'm going to just let him go after everything he's done.'

'I understand what you're going through ....' I begin.

'No, you don't,' he snaps. 'You're a great one to talk, SP sahab. Apne marey huve dost ka ek video toh aapse dekha nahin gaya. You went berserk and were ready to kill a stranger. And now you want me to forget about what was done to my entire family?'

'No, these men deserve to be punished,' I say. 'But that's not your job. Leave it to the police and the courts.'

'The police? Which has people like Kailash Shukla? The courts? You brought Prakash Padmanabh to court a few months back, didn't you? How did that work out?' he sneers. 'You won't get any better results this time. There's nothing conclusive to link Santoshji with Padmanabh. Nor with Acme International. I've looked through all the records. On paper, the boss of that firm is that peon. It's only his word that Padmanabh's wife used to come there and give orders, there is absolutely no documentary evidence to support it. Even if, by some miracle, you convince a judge to treat her as a suspect, the trail ends with her. Padmanabh goes scot-free, like he did last time.'

'Criminals make mistakes. We'll find something if we dig deep enough and hard enough,' I insist.

He shakes his head. 'These people are masters at gaming the system, SP sahab. Besides, you can't possibly arrest him right now, simply based on what's written in a fifteen-year-old journal. Any lawyer will argue that it could be a fake document. And if I let him go now, he and his comrades will know that I exist. I'll never again get an opportunity like this, to bring him to justice. It's the only way to make him pay for his sins.'

'I can't let you do that,' I say.

'Why? Are you worried that the blame will fall on the police? That you failed in your duty? Don't worry, I'll give you a flesh wound or something. You can cook up some story about how you tried to stop me but were wounded in one-on-one combat. You can even say that in the course of our negotiations, you discovered that there's an internal feud that has caused fissures among the Naxals and all these killings are a result of that. The Naxals will get blamed, they'll become suspicious of each other, I'll get my revenge, and the police will come out of this smelling like roses. It's the perfect solution, if you ask me.'

'And how do you propose to walk out of here? The place is surrounded by cops.'

He smiles. 'With you as my hostage, of course. We walk out together, with me holding a gun to your head. I will threaten them that if someone tries to follow us, I'll blow your brains out. I have a getaway vehicle safely parked about five hundred metres from here. Once we get there, I'll knock you out cold. It might hurt a bit, but we need to give you a convincing injury. You can even claim you tried to grapple with me again before I knocked you out. If you make your story heroic enough, you might even get a medal.'

I shake my head. 'That's something someone like Kailash Shukla would do. I'm no Kailash Shukla.'

'No, you're not,' he agrees. 'You're a well-meaning but ultimately ineffectual officer, caught in a spider's web. You blunder around thinking you're making progress, but all you do is get ensnared deeper and deeper. Oh, you may make the odd arrest, and you may even get the occasional conviction, but those are just the small fry who are too unimportant for the system to protect. You'll never get the really dangerous criminals like Prakash Padmanabh. My way is the only way of bringing them to justice.'

His words sting, but I try to ignore them. 'That's a great speech, but it doesn't change anything. You'll have to kill me first,' I say, my voice rising.

'Or you'll have to kill me,' he retorts, his voice rising too. 'That's the only way you can stop me. Are you ready to do that? Will you shoot me dead, even though you know in your heart that I am right?

To protect this man, who has committed the most heinous crimes? It's your call, SP sahab. Choose wisely.'

Slowly, deliberately, he points the gun at Padmanabh, who has just started to stir and moan. I tense, my mind in a whirl. If I have to act, I have to do it now. Somewhere, deep inside, his words have struck a chord with me. Can I really bring myself to shoot him?

He looks at me, a mocking smile in his eyes. 'I'm shooting on the count of three,' he says. 'Make up your mind. One, two ....'

EPILOGUE

Fifteen years ago

The boy grabbed the bottle of water that Madho offered him and emptied it in two deep gulps. He choked and sputtered, some of the water coming back out through his nose and mouth.

'Aaraam se, aaraam se,' said Madho, gently patting the boy's back to help him breathe. 'Don't worry, there's lots more water for you.'

'I'm hungry,' mumbled the boy, his voice hoarse.

'I've got a couple of bananas,' said Madho. 'Have these for now. Hopefully, in a while, we'll be able to get you some proper food.'

He handed the bananas to Kranti. The boy snatched them and gobbled down the first banana, barely pausing to chew it. The fever had burned what little fat he'd had, and his eyes looked huge in his sunken face. His hair was a dishevelled, dusty mop. He barely appeared human.

Madho remembered the smiling, chattering boy he'd met just a few days ago, and his heart broke for the wreck in front of him. No one should have to go through what he has, especially at such a young age, he thought sorrowfully.

Kranti took a little longer over the second banana. After he was done, he leaned back with a sigh.

'Feeling better?' Madho asked.

'A little,' responded Kranti. He spoke slowly and carefully, as though he was getting familiar with talking again after having been quiet for so long.

'I'll take you far away from here,' promised Madho. 'Away from all the terrible things that happened here. It's all in the past now. I'll help you to build a new life, Kranti.'

The boy rose to his feet. There was a spark in his eyes. 'That's not my name. All of us who came to the camp had to take new names. This name was given to me by the men who brought me here. When I leave, I'll leave the name behind too,' he mumbled.

'So what's your real name?' asked Madho, rising to his feet and extending his hand to the boy.

The boy took Madho's hand and hauled himself up. His legs trembled as he stood, but he forced himself to remain on his feet. He looked Madho in the eye. When his voice came out this time, it was firm and clear.

'My father named me Bhoomi,' he said.

ACKNOWLEDGEMENTS

They say it takes a village...

For me, my village, my home and I were defined by my Dadu, my maternal grandfather, who gave me a pencil to put to paper at the age of seven or eight and asked me to bring alive the story of a clock. Intent on honing my writing skills, he told me to imagine what the life of a clock might entail, imagine as time passes how many people it affects and what the clock must think of it. In the sands of time today, I look for those moments of pure discovery and joy. His name is Nirmal Chandra Bagchi and he taught me to write, to think, to be fearless. My Didu, Usha, my maternal grandmother, stood patiently by, watching the daily creative drama unfold. To them I owe a debt that can never be paid.

All it took was a casual conversation with Anuj Bahri, in a bookstore, for me to start looking towards writing for a creative release. I kept telling him how I didn't have the discipline to get through a story, he kept telling me that if the story was interesting, I would turn to it every day, and so I did. Thank you, Anuj, for helping me find my way and for being in a constant state of exasperation (intended, I am sure, to goad me into meeting deadlines).

Now, if one ever needs a godmother, Sharvani Pandit is the best an individual can be blessed with. No, she is not the kind to whip up a golden carriage. She's the one who will be there when the carriage turns into a pumpkin. Ever patient, indulgent, she barely lets you know the treasure trove of work she has had the privilege of dedicating to the creative churn of our country. Vani, to you, 'thank you' would not suffice. The debt is heavy and I bear it with pride.

I imagine Karthika V.K., my editor, to have been an amazing class monitor while she was in school. Diligent, disciplined, precise in her observations, there are many facets to her quiet personality which I discovered as my work progressed. That she had such faith in me was in itself a huge blessing. Karthika, you debated and deliberated on every sentence of this book. For being kind, open-minded, democratic and forgiving of all the deadlines I missed, thank you.

This story has been raging in my head for over a decade. I still remember the 9 o'clock TV debate I went to where one of the panellists was nonchalant about the death of our jawans, coming close to saying it was their duty to die—after all, we were at war. I remember the seething rage I felt, wondering what of those who loved them, what if they were watching the debate. The rage never ebbed. Inspired by it, I wrote reams and reams, only to realise I had to write a fictional account, which on paper looked like justice. There have been exceptional officers who have given a lifetime of service to the country, especially in confronting the challenges in the red corridor. Some have retired, some are still in service, and they all have their stories about investigations, people they could never catch, and the frustration they experienced (which, at times, took such a turn that they gave up on themselves and on the system)—it is to them that I owe the greatest debt in the pursuit of this story. For the sake of their privacy, they shall remain nameless. However, as a tribute to them, I say, 'Thank you, SK, AS, RS, SL.'

I have had the greatest privilege of being in public life for two decades; first as an actor and, for over a decade now, as a politician in office. The only constants in my ever changing world have been my audience, my people, my family. To them I say, thank you for your company, your blessings, your thoughtfulness. Thank you for surviving my adventures.